TRUE GREY

TRUE GREY

A Dulcie Schwartz feline mystery

Clea Simon

This first world edition published 2012
in Great Britain and in the USA by
SEVERN HOUSE PUBLISHERS LTD of
9–15 High Street, Sutton, Surrey, England, SM1 1DF.

British Library Cataloguing in Publication Data

Simon, Clea.
  The grey.
  1. Schwartz, Dulcie (Fictitious character)–Fiction.
  2. Detective and mystery stories.
  I. Title
  813.6-dc2.

ISBN-13: 978-0-727-8215-8 (cased)

All Severn House titles are printed on acid-free paper.

Severn House Publishers support The Forest Stewardship Council [FSC],
the leading international forest certification organisation. All our titles that
are printed on Greenpeace-approved FSC-certified paper carry the FSC logo.

Typeset by Palimpsest Book Production Ltd.,
Falkirk, Stirlingshire, Scotland.
Printed and bound in Great Britain by
MPG Books Ltd., Bodmin, Cornwall.

For Jon

ACKNOWLEDGEMENTS

Many thanks to my wonderful first readers: Jon Garelick, Karen Schlosberg, Lisa Susser, Brett Milano, and Naomi Yang. You saved me from numerous inconsistencies and conservatorial no-nos. All errors remaining are mine, not yours. My agent Colleen Mohyde is a constant source of encouragement, as are the wonderfully supportive Sophie Garelick, Frank Garelick, Lisa Jones, and writing buddies Caroline Leavitt and Vicki Constantine Croke. Editor Rachel Simpson Hutchens and her staff are a writer's dream. Purrs out, people. May your days be filled with love.

ONE

B *lood. So much blood. She had not realized that the human corpus could contain so much. But the precious ichor glistened jewel-like no longer. Much like her terror, like the screams frozen in her throat, life's elixir had begun to solidify and darken, staining the red-gold hair a dull brown, its very essence transform'd before her eyes, which too began to dim . . .*

It was like a nightmare. Like *the* nightmare. The room, the bookshelves. The marble statue, dripping blood. Only, instead of her reading of the horror – and then having it appear, laid out in all its dreadful gore – she had stumbled upon it, with no warning. No warning she could have interpreted, that is.

Before her lay Dulcie's worst dream, her vision of predawn terror – down to the cast-iron bootjack, one boot still stuck between its outstretched jaws. Down to the book splayed out on the floor, the title on the front – *Lives of the Saints* – a rebuke to everything she knew. This was it: the nightmare made flesh. The scene she had been forced to view every night this week, until she'd woken up gasping and drenched in sweat.

Only this was worse than her nightmare, because there was no waking from the vision before her. No playful kitten to cuddle until the horror faded, and no purr to lull her back to a more peaceful sleep. No, this was not a phantom of the dark. The time was one in the afternoon. Broad daylight. And the carnage before her was real.

'What? What?' Dulcie stood there gasping. Unable to get enough air. Unable to think, especially as the stars began to circle and close in, the darkness taking out her field of vision. Unable to leave . . .

'*Dulcie, step back.*'

The unexpected voice, so soft and so calm, startled her into a hiccup. 'Mr Grey?'

'*Dulcie, please step back.*' It was, without a doubt, the voice of her late, great cat. Unless, of course, she was hallucinating. *'Trust me, Dulcie. Please.'*

And so she did, in the process closing her mouth and ending the cycle of hyperventilation that had nearly caused her to pass out. And as she drew back into the doorway, she realized, not everything was exactly as she had dreamt it. There were, in fact, several crucial differences.

The boot stuck in the boot-jack was a high-end cowboy style, with the kind of patterned leather that had begun its life on some large reptile's back, rather than the formal rust and sable two-tone proper to a hunt outfit. The marble bust on the floor, its ear broken off and its pointy nose covered in blood, was not of a Roman senator, but of the great horror writer Edgar Allen Poe. The matted hair, still glossy despite the clotted gore, was black rather than rich auburn. And the body that lay sprawled across the rug was not some horrible but anonymous apparition, the manifestation of angers and anxieties freed only to emerge at night. It belonged to the woman Dulcie had come to meet. The woman who, less than forty-eight hours before, she had publicly sworn to kill.

With her wits finally returning, Dulcie took a further step back and one more again. Catching herself as she reached for the knob, she froze for a moment. Close the door? Leave it open? The heavy wooden door had been ajar when she'd arrived, the afternoon light casting its shadow down the hall. The visiting scholar's suite was isolated for privacy; the only other door off the hall opened on to the junior common room. The odds of anyone coming by were slim. Though someone – Dulcie realized with a chill – had certainly been here before her.

Unless . . . She looked at the Poe and up at the shelf. Could a freak accident, a stray vibration, have sent the heavy bit of statuary tumbling down?

'Dulcie . . .' It was Mr Grey again, the edge of a growl in his tone.

'It's possible,' she murmured to the dust motes. 'I mean, if she were standing in just the right place. And I know *I* didn't do it . . .'

Her eyes came down to the body again, to the gore fast turning dark on the rug, dulling the blue-black sheen in the raven's-wing hair. 'I couldn't have—' She choked. The room started to spin again, the stale air thick and cloying.

'*Dulcie!*' A sharp pain like raking claws along her back startled her upright, pulling her eyes away from the floor, the woman . . . *that*. At the same time, she heard voices, a flight or more down the stairs. Several voices, raised in alarm, and the clatter of feet as people rushed up to the suite.

'*Dulcie!*' The voice was still soft, but now it carried an undeniable urgency. A sense of command. '*Dulcie, run!*'

And so she did.

TWO

'**O**h, my,' a small, soft voice said. 'Oh, my.'

Only two days earlier, Dulcie had been happy. Hard at work three stories below ground in a windowless room that let in none of the glorious late-summer sun, she had gladly given up the warm September afternoon and its accompanying breeze for the pile of burnt-looking papers before her. As the low hum of the air-conditioning system kicked in, keeping the ambient temperature and humidity about right for a salad bar, she should have been utterly blissful. Would have been, in fact, were it not for the fussing of the little clerk standing beside her.

'Oh, my,' she heard again. 'Oh, my.' Coming from anyone else, the muted cry – almost a whimper – could have been the sound of agony, or even despair. Dulcie knew Thomas Griddlehaus, however. As quiet as he generally was, the slight, balding man was not naturally calm and could as easily be stressing out about a misplaced box of paper clips as a family tragedy. He was, like all librarians, a bit of a zealot.

In a good way, of course, Dulcie reminded herself. As the chief clerk of the famed Mildon Collection, Thomas Griddlehaus had a greater knowledge of rare books and documents than anyone Dulcie had ever met, an intimacy he had been more than willing to share with her, a mere graduate student. But as fussy as a cat, with a lot less fur, he could be a tad annoying.

He had, however, helped her authenticate the printed page that now lay to her left. One of only a few that had survived a fire – and the subsequent water damage – in Thomas Paine's original library, it had no cover and no title page. But coming, as it did, from the great statesman's library, Dulcie had no doubt that it was from a mysterious horror novel the American statesman had praised in his letters. A novel, she was sure, that had been written by the author of *The Ravages of Umbria.*

Doing her best to tune out the bespectacled clerk, she read the printed page again: '*The essential ichor besmirched his raven locks. All life, all essence, lay there, turned now to cooling mass, his heart forever still'd. Her own raced like a stallion into the dark and windswept night. A night as black as sable, as black as the lifeless head that now lay stain'd, upon the library carpet.*'

From the print, Dulcie turned to the handwritten page before her, maneuvering an oversized magnifying glass above it. A mere scrap of paper, stained and ragged inside its protective polypropylene wrapper, this page contrasted sharply with the sterile surroundings of the rare book collection. It was, however, the reason she was here today, her rationale for sacrificing the last gasp of summer. A sacrifice that would be worth it, if only she could concentrate.

'*Blood. So much blood. She had not realized that the human corpus could contain so much. But the precious ichor glistened jewel-like no longer.*' It read so much like the printed version, Dulcie could barely contain her excitement. Could this be a first, rough draft of that story? '*Much like her terror, like the screams frozen in her throat, life's elixir had begun to solidify and darken . . .*'

'Oh, my,' Dulcie heard again. Out of the corner of her eye, she saw the little man wringing his delicate, white hands, and tried not to be distracted. She didn't think she'd been doing anything wrong. The librarian had already replaced the first batch of papers she had requested – the special collection's policy restricted users to five of the fragile fragments at a time – and she was being very careful, only touching the edge of the clear film with her gloved hands. It was only recently that he had granted her the right to remove the pages from their cushioned, non-acid storage box herself, and as she turned back to her reading, she wondered if stacking even five high was too much for a treasure like this. With its crumbling edges and dark blotches, it looked like the filter from last week's coffee. What it could prove to be, however, was immeasurably more invigorating.

'*Much like her terror, like the screams frozen in her throat, life's elixir had begun to solidify and darken . . .*' She read again, doing her best to ignore a faint creak, as Griddlehaus shifted from one lace-up oxford to the other.

It wasn't that she was unsympathetic. The unassuming little clerk – Griddle*maus*, she sometimes thought of him – might be twenty years her senior, but she counted him as a colleague. He had already been incredibly helpful over the past year as she expanded her work on her thesis: from an analysis of *The Ravages of Umbria* to a more comprehensive study of the novel's author. In addition to judging her adequately trained to handle documents, he had granted her the right to keep a private file folder in the library, an honor usually reserved for postgrads. Plus, his help navigating the collection's huge inventory of uncataloged, unidentified remnants had resulted last month in her first major academic paper: *Political Vision and Proto-Feminist Theory in the Early Gothic Novel*. Just today, they'd started on a new stack of boxes, identified simply as 'PHILA, 1805–10', and the uncharted treasures within. If only he would give her the quiet she needed to study them.

'*Much like her terror,*' she read, for the third time, '*like the screams frozen in her throat, life's elixir had begun to solidify and darken, staining the red-gold hair a dull brown, its very essence transform'd before her eyes, which too began to dim . . .*'

Something was different. Dulcie closed her tired eyes. It had taken her more than an hour to decipher the ornate and faded script this far, carefully maneuvering the mounted lens over the brittle surface, and now she doubted what she had read. It seemed so familiar, so dreamlike. But, yes, she saw when she looked again: this was what the handwritten page said. It sparked a memory, and Dulcie grabbed the soft pencil, the only writing implement allowed in the Mildon, and scribbled out the passage. It had changed from what had made it, ultimately, to the printed page. But not, she hoped, in any essential way.

Another creak, and something that sounded suspiciously like

a sigh, but Dulcie tuned them out. This, in front of her, was what mattered. Could it be? The actual handwritten draft of that second novel?

Despite the doubts of her thesis adviser, Dulcie had come to believe that the book existed, that this second novel, even better than *The Ravages*, not only had been written but could be found. Some of her peers, and Dulcie had learned to shoulder their scorn, didn't even consider *The Ravages* to be a great novel. Dulcie knew otherwise, however, and unlike these naysayers, she hadn't been willing to dismiss the unnamed Gothic author's subsequent silence as the result of critical disappointment or something even more dire, be it ill health or family responsibilities.

No, Dulcie had known that 'her' author, as she privately thought of her, had kept writing. Through her careful textual analysis, Dulcie had already traced her literary footprints – following a trail of daring political essays as the author moved from London to the fledgling United States in the first years of the nineteenth century. Even her thesis adviser had conceded that Dulcie had made an important discovery. But to find another novel? That was the ultimate prize for a scholar: a lost work. And it just might be within her reach.

For comparison's sake, Dulcie reached for her Mildon folder, checking what she already knew to be true. Yes, that same passion showed up in the author's political writings. Dulcie reread one bit of an 1803 essay:

> *A woman, some say, has no place in the world, lest she be daughter or widow or wife. The first we all are, tho' the family ties may chafe as we gain majority. The next oc-curs by chance, and guarantees not freedom from those onerous ties of family, not of blood, perchance not e'en of choice. The last, though, is most to be pitied. Those who submit to such disequal bonds may be bless'd by af-fections and by the gift of a child. Too often, those bonds cripple us, tearing all natural joys from our hearts, our babes from our arms, and our affections from all that we would hold dear. No, 'tis better for a woman to stand alone, for to be friendless is to know that which is true for our Sex. 'Tis better far than the False Hope of Love.*

'The False Hope of Love.' Dulcie nodded. That would have made a dandy title, perfect for the dramatic romance of a book like *The Ravages*. But the few hints that Dulcie had found of the lost second work suggested something darker. Last spring, at this very table, she had read a letter from Paine's library, suggesting that such a novel existed – a great work, but one that played on horror, rather than love. And this one piece of paper, so brown and blotted inside its protective cover, just might be the beginning of it.

'*Those red-gold locks, besmirch'd by life's gore, she now aggrieve*—' No, that was wrong. Dulcie squinted. Addressed? Yes. She read on: '*—addressed. The Si*—'

Sign? Sight? A dark patch, mold or water, obscured the next word. Carefully, her hands sweating inside the archivist's white gloves, she adjusted the magnifying glass to examine the page more closely, bringing it down as far as she dared. One errant move and the thick lens could crash down on the polypropylene envelope and the brittle page inside, just as she was about to—

'Oh, my goodness.' She'd almost forgotten about Griddlehaus; reading could do that to her. He was right behind her now, his soft voice impossible to ignore.

'Yes?' She heard the exasperation in her voice and tried to smile, to soften it. But as she turned around, willing at last to acknowledge the little man, she saw that Griddlehaus wasn't even looking at her. Instead, he was staring at the paper in his hand. Despite his usual care for all things documentary, its edges were already wrinkled and damp. 'Oh, my.'

'Thomas – Mr Griddlehaus, what is it?' Dulcie kicked herself. He really was upset, and she craned around to see what kind of bill or notice he held. 'Why don't you tell me? It can't be that bad now, can it?'

He blinked up at her then, his eyes large and soft behind his oversized glasses. Holding out the paper to her in one trembling hand, he looked like he might cry.

'Mr Griddlehaus?' She took the paper from him. But if she was expecting a warning notice – perhaps about a beetle infestation or some change in filing procedures – she was in for a shock. 'Wait – is this . . .?'

He nodded, his eyes filling with tears, and waved her on to read more.

She looked back at the paper. It was an official interlibrary request issued by the office of the dean of research. According to its typed instructions, a visiting scholar, one Melinda Sloane Harquist, had been granted permission at the highest level to look through the Mildon collection. Miss Sloane Harquist, a personalized note from the dean himself added, was particularly interested in literary fragments from the late eighteenth and early nineteenth century, especially those written by unnamed female Gothic novelists.

The scholar, the note continued, was to be given all access and help possible in her search for a previously undiscovered work. She was, it concluded, the author of the soon-to-be-published blockbuster, *Anonymous Unveiled: The Real-Life Heroine Behind The Ravages of Umbria.*

THREE

'How could I not know about this? How could I never have *heard* of her?' As the warm day had progressed into an equally sultry night, Dulcie had moved beyond her initial shock. Sitting at the People's Republik with her friends, her joy in the day's work – in that single page – was forgotten, and she was progressing well into anger. 'I mean, she's been in none of the journals. And what kind of name is Sloane Harquist anyway?'

Chris, her boyfriend, reached over and took the mug from her hand. Dulcie really only drank beer to be social, and the way she was gesticulating now was likely to spread her untouched brew among her companions.

'Well, maybe this woman hasn't published before.' Chris took an exploratory taste of Dulcie's beer and grimaced. Despite the pub's noisy air conditioning, some of the day's humidity had followed them in, and Dulcie had let her brew get warm. 'Maybe she's been saving it all up?'

'Ha.' Trista Dunlop, Dulcie's best buddy in the department, scoffed at the idea. 'She's been hiding out, waiting to spring this on us.'

Dulcie glanced up. Trista had actually finished her thesis and her postdoc research had nothing to do with the Goths; the 'us' was pure friendship. 'Thanks, Tris. I'm just . . .' She reached for the beer and took a sip without noticing its temperature. 'I'm just confused.'

'This doesn't mean your thesis isn't going to be good. *As* good,' Chris corrected himself. Beside him, Jerry – Trista's boyfriend – nodded vigorously. Computer science students, they'd both had to adjust to the relatively arcane and convoluted nature of their sweethearts' field. 'Or better,' he tried again.

Dulcie didn't even answer, and Trista stopped any further well-meaning remarks with a look. A bleached blonde with multiple piercings, Trista could stare down the best of them, and even six-foot-two Chris blanched.

'Another pitcher?' Jerry asked, standing.

'Why don't I come with you?' Chris nearly knocked his chair over in his haste.

Left alone – as alone as they could be in the crowded pub – Dulcie let out a sigh and shook her head one more time. 'Trista, I . . .' But words would not suffice.

'I know, kid. It's awful.' Trista slid over to take Chris's seat, the better to talk over the jukebox. 'I bet she doesn't have half of what you have, though.'

'Doesn't matter,' said Dulcie, her dispirited tone at odds with the lively music. 'I've already shown my hand with my paper. Anyone who reads that will know I'm on the trail of a missing work. Only the only thing I've found since those political essays is that fragment today. And I haven't even started the work of verifying.'

Trista nodded. She knew the drudgery that followed the thrill of discovery. 'You've started though, right? You're not giving up?'

'I've plugged it in.' One advantage of having mathematically minded beaus was the customized software Chris and Jerry had worked up for the friends: Type in a phrase and it searched for similar wordings in any online library. The resulting metrics didn't do all the work, but they did provide a short cut. 'But that's just a start, Tris. You know that. And she's going to publish. First.' There was no response to that, and the friends sat in companionable silence as ZZ Top filled the room.

'Chris doesn't get it,' Dulcie said finally. 'He wants to help, really. But he doesn't understand.'

Trista nodded. 'If only we could keep her out of the Mildon.' She seemed to be thinking out loud. 'Do you think that clerk, Griddlehaus, would help you?'

'I don't know.' Dulcie had to admit, she'd thought about it. 'He's pretty law abiding. Especially after, you know, what happened last spring.' The scandal that had brought down the Mildon's director had come close to ruining the collection's reputation. 'He's been specifically instructed to give her access – and to help her.' Dulcie almost choked on the word. 'The letter came with a personal note from that new associate dean, what's his name – Roger Haitner?'

'Robert Haitner? That whey-faced prig?' Trista's specialty – Victorian literature – tended to creep into her slang. 'He's been trouble ever since he was appointed. You know, that little bugbear and his rug were behind the elimination of Luther's position.'

'I didn't.' Rather pale herself, as well as diminutive in height, Dulcie winced a bit at Trista's insults. It was true that the dean's hair, suspiciously dark and thick, appeared fake, part of what seemed to be an attempt to look – and act – younger than his age. The rest, however, was news. Dulcie had heard that the documents restoration department had lost some of its funding. She'd come back from summer vacation to find Griddlehaus as upset as she'd ever seen him, but she hadn't known the cause. 'You'd think, if he wants this woman here, he'd have been more careful about cutting jobs and alienating people.'

'Maybe it's something special about her.' Trista started to smile, a tight, mean smile. Even Dulcie had heard about the dean's reputation as a Lothario. Everyone had. 'But maybe there's something we can do about it on the other end. We may be stuck with him, but we can trip her up a little. Let her know she's not welcome in Cambridge.'

'No.' Dulcie shook her head again, sadly. 'I don't know what's going on – I mean, with the dean and all. I do know she's got pull. That letter was like an all-access pass. And even if she didn't, I can't stand in her way. I mean, it's not her fault that I've been slow.' Trista's brow furrowed, rousing Dulcie. 'Maybe I can talk to her.' She affected a cheer she didn't really feel. 'See what she's looking for. Maybe I can find some part of the *Ravages* she isn't interested in. Some little fact she doesn't care about.'

'Dulcie, are you serious?' Trista looked up and accepted a fresh mug from Jerry. Chris sat one chair over, his feeling of helplessness showing on his face. 'You want to make peace with this, this—'

'I don't *want* to, Tris.' The anger was surfacing again. 'I don't *want* to talk to her or try to get along with her. I don't want to have anything to do with this . . . this Sloane Harquist person. But I think I have to. I think it's the only way to get through this, the only way to see if I may still have something to say in my own thesis.'

In an uncharacteristic move, she picked up her own mug and took a long pull of beer. Choking a little, she wiped her mouth, her lips set in a new determination. 'Truth is, if I had my way, I could murder her.'

FOUR

'Maybe you really should talk to her?' Chris sounded so tentative that Dulcie was seized by guilt. 'You know, a little scholar-to-scholar confab?'

'Have I sounded that fierce?' Dulcie looked up at her boyfriend. They had left the pub early, Dulcie's mood not getting any better in the crowded bar. Now they sat on his old sofa, Dulcie holding Esmé, their cat, in her lap. She'd been focusing on Esmé, letting the young feline bat at her outstretched finger with one white mitten. Now she studied Chris's pale, thin face and wondered out loud. 'Have I become an ogre?'

To his credit, the slim computer geek smiled at the idea. 'Hardly.' As he pushed his bangs back, though, he revealed worried eyes. 'But I've never seen you so angry, Dulce. You can be a little scary when you get that worked up.'

Dulcie felt herself flush. She was taller than Thomas Griddlehaus, but in the grand scheme of things, she'd be considered petite. A little round, perhaps, but hardly threatening.

Just then, Esmé pounced, biting the finger she held between

her paws. 'Ow, Esmé!' Dulcie pulled back, and caught the sharp look the green feline eyes gave her. Size, they said, had nothing to do with ferocity. 'Sorry,' she said, leaning over to rest her head on her boyfriend's chest.

'I don't blame you.' He wrapped his arms around her, drawing her closer. The movement should have disturbed the cat, but the little animal only readjusted. 'I mean, you have reason.'

'Tell me about it.' She sniffed, the tears that had been threatening since that afternoon coming dangerously close to the surface. 'I just felt so . . . blindsided.'

'And you had no idea?' he'd asked – they all had. It was inconceivable. 'Martin Thorpe really owes you one,' he said.

She shook her head. Her thesis adviser wasn't omniscient. 'He reads the same journals I do,' she said sadly. 'He gets the same notices of publications and of meetings. It's just—'

'Inconceivable.' Chris finished her sentence.

Dulcie felt her eyes closing. It had been an exhausting day, and she'd been so upset she had drunk more than she'd intended. She didn't even like beer, really. The pub was simply social, the grad students' 'other place' away from home or work. And on their budgets, anything beside the on-tap special was prohibitively expensive. She was going to have a headache in the morning, she realized, starting to drift off. As long as she didn't have the dream again: all that blood darkening the red hair. Or was it black? Somehow she couldn't be sure . . .

Teeth woke her. Esmé's teeth, sharp and quick. 'What the . . .?'

'What happened?' Chris, she realized, had fallen asleep on the couch beside her.

'This cat. She keeps biting me.' Dulcie looked down. Esmé stared back, unblinking. 'What is it, Esmé?'

'You think she's trying to tell you something?' Chris yawned and would have stood, only the little cat reached out one white paw. 'Oh, she's so cute.'

'Cute for a tyrant,' Dulcie muttered. 'She's got you wrapped around her paw. What is it, Esmé? You know you could tell me directly, if you wanted.'

She could have, Dulcie knew. Although she and Chris barely discussed it, they both had heard the voice of the young cat, speaking in quite articulate English. Usually, however, that feline voice wasn't directed to them, but to Mr Grey – Dulcie's late great cat whose presence lingered in spectral form, as a kind of feline guardian over all their lives.

'Maybe she just doesn't want us to go to bed.' Dulcie sighed. 'You know, cats are largely nocturnal.'

'Well, I'll play with her tomorrow.' Chris stood and stretched. 'Now, though, I've got to get some shut-eye. I'm not used to these daytime shifts.'

Dulcie smiled up at her boyfriend. He'd worked overnights at the computer lab almost as long as they'd been together. Over the summer, he'd taken time off, and these last few weeks on the same schedule had been heavenly. 'Darlene covering again?' The new girl had jumped at the higher-paying shifts.

Chris nodded. 'I don't think she'll mind getting back to daylight hours, though.' Although she had yet to meet Chris's new colleague, he had already told Dulcie about the younger girl's relatively new romance with the Dardley House senior tutor. 'We know how rough it can be.'

She nodded, but kept her thoughts to herself. With the term revving up again, he had to do the practical thing. They both did. That meant, for her, taking as many sections as the department would give her – and as many as Thorpe would approve. For Chris, it meant the overnights. Soon, Dulcie knew, he'd be at the lab at this hour, guiding hapless undergrads. Then the only one she'd have to talk to would be Esmé.

'Wait a minute, Chris.' He turned on his way to the bathroom. 'What did you mean, I should talk to her?'

'Just following up on something you said to Trista.' He yawned again. 'Maybe find out if there's some area she hasn't written about. Maybe there's something she isn't interested in, but that you are.'

'Find some niche that I could call my own.' Dulcie looked back at the cat. Esmé seemed to be regarding her. 'Write a thesis out of the leftover scraps.'

'It doesn't have to be like that.' Her boyfriend's voice was clear, but Dulcie was suddenly aware of another presence. Although she could clearly see her current pet on her lap, she felt the undeniable prick of feline claws on her forearms, making the hair on them stand up. 'It could be, well, collaborative.' Chris was still speaking.

'Maybe there is something she missed . . .' The claws could be a warning – but they could also be an alert, telling her not to miss her opportunity. 'Something I know that she doesn't.'

'Exactly.' Chris sounded relieved. 'That's my girl, Dulcie. I can't see you giving up.'

'Not when I have such a great support network.' Dulcie lifted the corporeal cat to the floor and stood to follow her boyfriend. That slight pinprick was gone, leaving only the memory – and a question. 'Come on, Esmé,' she said to the cat, who responded by bounding ahead of her into the bedroom. 'Mr Grey?' She looked around the empty living room. Nothing. She turned the light off and waited, still nothing.

Chris came out of the bathroom. 'Are you coming to bed?'

'Yeah, in a minute.' She passed by him and reached for her toothbrush. 'I was wondering though.' Her toothbrush had suddenly become the most fascinating object in the world, and she stared at it hard. Maybe then he wouldn't see the tears gathering in her eyes. 'What about Mr Grey, Chris? *He* had to have known that something was wrong. Didn't he? And if so, then why didn't he let me know?'

FIVE

B *lood, she hadn't expected so much blood. The dark'ning ichor lay pool'd around the body, its flow now halted by the ebbing of the very essence of the creature's Being. Blood, so much blood. She felt her own carmine pulse racing in her Veins. Could it be the same vital fluid as now lay cooling at her feet? In truth, she had not expected such a Human trait in one she considered a Wraith, a Spectre. A creature both foul and Unclean. Then again, she knew that the evil creature, the thing that now lay cold and still before her, had feasted upon her very Essence, a Vampire of the Soul. Only the Creature's curls showed brightness now, red and gold. The blood had cooled. Blood . . . There was so much blood.*

Dulcie woke with a start, her heartbeat throbbing like the neighbor's house music. She'd had the dream again, the horrible dream. In it, she had first seen the text, the description of terror, penned in a feminine hand, archaic and yet elegant. And then the words had faded, showing the carnage that she had started to read about. In the dream, she was the writer – and felt the chill of horror in her own self. Only this time, it was different. Worse. She wasn't only viewing a gory scene. She was involved, somehow. Deeply involved with the body that lay cooling on the library floor.

Breathing deeply to still her racing heart, Dulcie made herself go over it again. Only by deciphering its shadowed meaning, she was sure, would she be free of the horror that woke her, night after night.

Beside her, Chris stirred, and she slipped out of bed. He worked so hard, she didn't want to wake him. The first time she'd had the nightmare, three nights ago, he had woken her. She had opened her eyes to see his worried face. He'd been shaking her gently. Urging her to wake, to throw off whatever bad dream she was in. She'd been making strangled sounds, he'd told her, as if she'd been trying to scream – to wake herself.

Dulcie reached for her robe and shrugged into it. At least she'd progressed to waking herself up. And any progress was good. With that in mind, she made her way to the kitchen, where she'd left her laptop, to find Esmé sitting on the keyboard, batting at the mousepad. Distracted by the news, she must have left it open, and the movement of the cat had caused the screen to become active, glowing bright behind her like the moon outside.

'Esmé, no.' Dulcie reached for the cat, who had pounced on the computer's touch pad. 'There's no real mouse there – no!' As she lifted the rotund feline off the machine, Esmé squirmed and bit – and Dulcie dropped her. The little tuxedo responded by jumping back up on to the table, but Dulcie was too fast for her and closed the laptop. Esmé yowled with disappointment.

By the time Dulcie had washed her hand – the bite had barely scraped her skin – Esmé had calmed down and assumed a perch on the window sill instead. Silhouetted against the light of a full moon, the little cat looked quite regal. Her black fur glowed, catching the light. Almost, Dulcie thought, like . . .

'Mr Grey?' She kept her voice soft. It was too much to hope for. But when she felt a warm pressure against her shins, she knew she was right. Scooping Esmé into her arms, she went to join the spectral feline by the window, and for a moment the three stood there, looking out at the still city night. Dulcie felt her pulse slow to normal in the feline presence. Even Esmé seemed preternaturally calm.

'*You are troubled, little one.*' Mr Grey didn't speak out loud, but Dulcie knew his voice. Quiet and deep, it filled her with warmth. '*Tell me.*'

'Mr Grey.' She paused. What she had wanted to ask him about was his silence. Why hadn't he warned her? But he was here now, and she didn't dare risk chasing him away.

'It's the nightmare, Mr Grey,' she said instead. In truth, it had unsettled her, and in his company, with her other cat in her arms, Dulcie would dare to revisit it. 'On other nights, I've seen her writing. That's why I've thought she's my author. Or maybe, well –' there was no point in being coy around her all-seeing friend – 'me. But she has dark hair, not like mine.' The image of the dead man's hair – red and gold – came unbidden. Dulcie's curls were touched with red, but not like that. 'I guess what I read today is influencing my dream,' she continued.

'She's been writing some kind of horror scene. Something truly frightening. I mean, more so than anything in *The Ravages*.' Gothic novels were filled with cheap thrills – ghouls and ghosts, and all sorts of human evil as well – but Dulcie's favorite had focused more on the relationships between the characters. Particularly on the heroine, Hermetria, and her unfaithful attendant, Demetria.

'At first, when Griddlehaus handed me that box and I found that page, I was thrilled. If that page really is her manuscript, maybe I can be the one to tie the book to her. To link her to another novel.' She looked over at her pet. For all that he seemed to understand everything about her, she really couldn't tell what he comprehended about her thesis. Did Mr Grey know about the hundreds of pages that the library held? The boxes of papers she had yet to go through? Maybe he knew, maybe he even knew where – or if – the rest of that strange horror story could be found. Cats, she knew, always seemed all-knowing. Sometimes, though, they just wanted to nap.

'Ow!' Esmé had grabbed her finger and nipped it again. 'Esmé, please.'

'*Go on, little one.*' For a moment, Dulcie wasn't sure which of them he was addressing, but when Esmé quieted down again, she continued.

'I just always thought I had an edge, you know? I thought maybe I was dreaming of her writing that book – the missing book. Maybe it's just such a scary work that the fear has been coming through. But tonight was different. Tonight, she wasn't writing about a murder. She was witnessing it, as if she . . .'

She fell silent, unable to go on, the chill of the terror returning. Esmé, in her arms, twisted to look up at her, and Dulcie found herself staring into the young cat's deep green eyes. The round little cat was warm and solid, a comforting presence. Reality, even if that reality got fur in her keyboard and left bite marks on her palm. Still, it was Mr Grey's voice that found her.

'*You feel a connection. Something beyond what others would experience.*'

She nodded. A lot of graduate students said they lived and breathed their subjects. In Dulcie's case, the connection went even deeper – into her dreams.

'*A bond that reaches beyond time. Beyond, even, life itself.*'

She nodded again. Everything he was saying was also true of her relationship with her cats.

'*Such a bond has its dangers, little one. Life has a flow, a forward pitch. For those who do not honor that flow—*'

'There you are.' Chris stepped into the kitchen, rubbing his hand over his face. 'Did you have that nightmare again?'

'Yeah.' She turned to face him. Mr Grey had disappeared; she sensed his leaving just as she'd sensed his presence. And she still hadn't asked him why he had failed to warn her. Still, her boyfriend offered comfort of another kind. Esmé squirmed to be let down, and bounded over to rub against his shins.

'Hey, little girl. You on duty tonight?' He reached down to pet her, and she stood up to shove her head into his hand.

'She was helping me make sense of it.' Dulcie came over for her own hug. 'Esmé and Mr Grey.'

'Huh.' He put the kettle on, and Dulcie reached for the mugs.

At this hour, only cocoa would do. 'Did you come to any conclusions?'

'He was talking about connections, about how I'm linked to the woman in the dream.' Like a dream, Mr Grey's words were fading. 'There was something else, though. Something about the flow of life – about letting life progress.'

'Makes sense to me.' Chris sat and Esmé jumped into his lap and began to knead. 'And you are. Moving on, that is.'

'Well, the dream is changing.' Dulcie didn't want to think about the other possible interpretation of Mr Grey's words. That he was telling her she had to let go of the past. Of him. That maybe he hadn't come to warn her for some bigger reason. 'Only, not for the better. Instead of writing a bloody scene, now I have her in it.'

'You're not seeing her . . .' He paused, looking for the right word. 'Her *end*, are you?' Concern had overcome the fatigue in his pale and tired face, and Dulcie rushed to comfort him.

'No, nothing like that.' It was funny, though. They both knew that the author of *The Ravages*, the subject of Dulcie's thesis, lived two hundred years before. Therefore, it made sense that she had *died* two hundred years before, too. 'It's a man, and it doesn't look like her. In fact, this time he looked more like me. Or, really, like Lucy always tells me I was supposed to look like, with the flame-red hair and everything.' Chris nodded. He had heard Dulcie's mother's rants.

'Maybe I'm dreaming that now because of what I read today,' Dulcie continued. 'I mean, if the page in the Mildon is what I think it is, she first wrote the victim as a redhead, then changed it to black hair. Which is funny, because the image of blood drying is much more striking if you put it on light hair.

'What's also different is that it's becoming less like a story, and more like it's happening as I see it. Maybe that's just because she's writing it and it's so vivid.'

'Well, that's good.' He stroked the cat absently. Esmé, Dulcie noticed, did not react with a bite. 'Isn't it?'

The kettle whistled, and Dulcie got up to make the cocoa. 'I guess so.' She brought the mugs to the table. Esmé reached to bat at the spoon. 'It's just that from the way she's looking at the scene, I think she was involved somehow. And I think, maybe, Mr Grey is trying to warn me.'

She looked up at her boyfriend. For a moment, even Esmé held still. 'I think my author might have been a murderer.'

SIX

The phone woke Dulcie. The phone – and Esmé bounding across her stomach as if the little cat had planned to answer it herself.

'Hello?' Phone in hand, Dulcie reached for the clock. After nine – they'd gone back to bed around four. Chris must have let her sleep in, and after a moment of panic, she remembered it was Friday. She had no morning sections today.

'Dulcie! You haven't gone yet, blessed be!'

'Lucy?' Dulcie sat up. To deal with her mother, she needed to be a little more awake.

'Of course, it's wrong to intervene, but in a situation like this, with Mars in a grand trine—'

'Lucy, would you hang on a minute?' Lucy – Dulcie hardly ever called her mother 'Mom' – always talked a mile a minute. Her tendency to assume that whoever was listening had been party to whatever thoughts had come before didn't make it easy to catch up. Shaking off the grogginess of her troubled sleep, Dulcie took a drink of water – and a deep breath – and prepared to engage her sole parent once more. 'OK, I'm here now,' she said slowly and deliberately, in a futile attempt to set the tone. 'So tell me, where am I supposedly going? And what is the situation?'

Dulcie had chosen her questions with care. Even half asleep, she remembered that the grand trine had something to do with an astrological alignment. And she was under no illusion that Lucy's hesitation about intervening had anything to do with her adult daughter's privacy. If Lucy felt she could boss the planets around, her own daughter's free will wasn't worth taking into account. Better to get at what her mother wanted – or was afraid of – so she could calm her down, and get on with her day.

'Because of the eclipse, of course!'

'Of course.' Dulcie and Chris had visited over the summer
and one of her mother's parting gifts had been a lunar calendar.
Her mother had been very excited about the September eclipse.
For the life of her, Dulcie couldn't remember why such a natural
occurrence warranted an early-morning phone call. 'Mom, did
you sleep last night?' It wasn't yet six thirty West Coast time,
and while that might not be early for some, Dulcie knew her
mother was far more a Daughter of Luna than of Sol.

'We had a circle, Dulcie. The sky was luminous.' Well, it would
be out in the woods. Dulcie realized belatedly that she shouldn't
have let her mother go off on a tangent and decided she had time
to get dressed as Lucy rambled. Sure enough, even as she'd pulled
a shirt over her head, she could still hear her mother's breathless
enthusiasm. '. . . enmeshed in the sacred oak!'

And something else – the beep of call waiting.

'Lucy!' She reached for the phone. 'Would you hold on a
second?' Without waiting for an answer, Dulcie clicked through
– to nothing. Well, whoever it was would leave a message. 'Sorry,
I had another call.'

'I'm not surprised. Your planets rarely come together like this.
It must be more than two hundred years since they last . . .'
Dulcie let her mother go on, the coincidence of the timing
distracting her. It had to be coincidence, didn't it? 'Which is why
I don't want you to repeat that error.'

The unusual silence that followed prompted Dulcie to realize
that some response was required. 'Repeat?' Before her coffee, it
was the best she could do.

'Haven't you been listening?' Luckily, Lucy didn't wait for
an answer. 'You have to be careful, Dulcinea, especially in the
next few days. An eclipse doesn't just cover up a source of power,
it unleashes all sorts of echoes and shadows – time past and
present. It opens passageways between the worlds. We cannot
foretell all the implications. Oh, that's the breakfast chime. I've
got to run, Dulcie. I'm blessing the chai today.'

With a final invocation to the goddess, Lucy hung up, leaving
Dulcie to wonder how shadows ever were leashed, and whether
anyone, even Lucy, could foretell an implication.

'Lucy?' Chris got up to pour Dulcie's coffee as she entered
the kitchen, still pondering. He had already fed Esmé, she noticed

with gratitude. The little cat barely looked up from her corner nook, so busy was she with what looked like fresh Fancy Feast.

'Yeah. There's a lunar eclipse tomorrow.'

'Ah.' He handed her the mug. He had some first-hand experience of Lucy, and Dulcie was warmed once again by his nonchalance. 'And it has some kind of special message for you?'

'Oh, damn. Hang on.' The missed call! She hit the numbers for voicemail, and snuck a sip while her new password – ESME – went through. When she heard the voice on the other line, she knew she'd need the rest of the pot.

'Ms Schwartz?' It was Martin Thorpe, the department's interim head and her thesis adviser. 'Something has come up. Something rather urgent and – ah – timely. We need to meet as soon as possible. Please call me as soon as you get this.'

'Well, that's interesting.' She doctored her coffee with more milk, the easier to drink quickly. Chris looked at her, waiting. 'Lucy called to tell me that the eclipse is drawing forth shadows, or something like that. Anyway, there are dark forces at work, and I'm not to go to "the meeting", whatever that means. But Thorpe must have found out about the other *Ravages* scholar. Because he's just as insistent. He wants to meet.'

'I don't think you have much choice, Dulce.' Chris had the decency to look concerned.

'No, I don't,' Dulcie agreed. 'And I don't think Lucy has any particular insight into Thorpe or the whole Sloane Harquist situation. I just, well, I guess I was hoping that I'd wake up and it all would have gone away. And getting a warning doesn't make it any better.' Especially because of the strange timing. 'My mother even said something about this not having happened for two hundred years.'

'Dulce, I know Lucy loves you, but I wouldn't give too much credence to anything she says.'

'You're right.' She bent to kiss her boyfriend. 'Let me call old Thorpe back and then go face that particular dragon.'

'May the stars align!' Chris had the inflection down perfectly. 'Blessed be.'

'Blessed be yourself.' Dulcie found herself smiling, despite everything that awaited. Neither of them noticed that Esmé had stopped eating as Dulcie spoke. And that the little cat's back was now arched in horror – her fur rising, as if size alone could ward off an attack.

SEVEN

'I knew you should have been writing more quickly. Should have been sending papers out for review, for publication last semester. Last year, even. I blame myself, really.'

From the way Martin Thorpe was fretting, Dulcie almost believed him. Her adviser made another circuit of the small, worn rug, muttering about journals and opportunities missed. Dulcie had never seen him so upset. 'I shouldn't have let you lollygag so. Lost essays, a lost novel . . .' He shook his head, which even in the bad office light was visibly glazed with sweat, and mopped it with a handkerchief. 'Wildgoose chases.'

'Only they're not.' After twenty minutes of Thorpe's nervous pacing, Dulcie was getting dizzy. It was worth interrupting him, if only to make him hold still for a moment. 'Wild geese, that is.'

Thorpe stopped short, right on the carpet's fringe, and stared at her. Dulcie swallowed. The balding scholar might be tightly wound, but he was her adviser – and the interim head of the department to boot. And, despite his words, Dulcie knew that if one of his tutees failed to produce a publishable thesis, he wasn't going to shoulder any of the blame. No, he would place responsibility for this debacle squarely on her.

'I did identify some previously lost writings, and I got one good paper out of them already.' As Dulcie spoke, she gained a little of her confidence back. 'I think I'll have more soon, too.'

He looked up, beady eyes quizzical behind his glasses, and Dulcie faltered. She hadn't had a moment to check her laptop, to see if Chris's software had uncovered any similarities between that one passage she'd copied down and any of her author's known writings. She couldn't now. Thorpe didn't know about the program, and this wasn't the time to introduce it. He already thought she was lacking as a scholar. 'I mean, if I weren't on the trail – if there wasn't a lost manuscript – well, then why would this Sloane

Harquist person want to go into the Mildon? I figure she must have found something referring to additional work.'

Without revealing her secret, it was the best argument she could make for herself – and for her thesis. And so she sat back, blinking, and waited for her sweaty adviser to pronounce her fate.

'It's not that simple.' He was prevaricating also, she recognized the signs. At least he had stopped pacing, freeing her to breathe almost easily. 'I did sign off on your current semester.'

Dulcie looked up at that. She knew her adviser had approved her continuing work, but she'd thought that was automatic. After all, in addition to last month's paper, she had produced rough drafts of several chapters. There was more going on here than she'd originally thought.

'I started writing last spring.' Five years wasn't that long for a doctoral thesis. Not in the humanities. 'It's just that when I found those letters and then the page from the book, I thought it more important to start searching . . .'

'Yes, yes.' He waved her to silence. 'New material. A potential breakthrough.'

'So—' She stopped herself. This was not the time to ask Thorpe why he was so worried. Clearly, there was something else going on. Something political, she suspected. Something about that new dean.

She did have another question for Thorpe, though. One that her adviser might be able to answer. 'Assuming this visiting scholar is on the track of the lost book . . .' She hated to even voice the question out loud. However, she had to know. 'Do we know if she found any of it?'

'Maybe she found a complete copy.' Thorpe shrugged, making him look a bit like a damp vulture. 'Maybe she is simply seeking confirmation.'

Dulcie sank back in her chair. That was a possibility she had not even had a nightmare about. 'You don't know?' she managed to squeak out.

He shook his shiny head, staring down at the open folder on his desk with an air of concentration that made her curious about its contents. She leaned forward, but all she could see was the university letterhead.

'This is all very hush-hush,' Thorpe continued, pulling the paper toward him. 'Dean Haitner himself signed off on everything. She has, I have to say, unprecedented access and support. I gather he sees her as a potential addition to the faculty. He's already talking about establishing his legacy with scholars like her.' He looked up at her and blinked. His eyes seemed to soften. 'I'm sorry, Ms Schwartz. These things happen, you know. It is why I've been pushing you.'

'I know,' she said. 'I guess I should just go talk with her once she arrives. Find out if there are any oddments –' she was proud of herself for not using the word *scraps* – 'that I can focus on.'

'That's the spirit.' Thorpe slapped the folder closed. 'Only, one thing.' He looked up again. 'As a member of the department, you will be invited both to her talk on Sunday and to the master's reception that will follow. I will make a point of introducing you, if you would like, and you may be able to arrange a private conversation after, if she can spare the time. However, please do not disturb her before her presentation, Ms Schwartz. As a visiting scholar under the aegis of the associate dean for research in the humanities, Ms Sloane Harquist is to be considered a VIP, and she has specifically asked to be left alone to conduct her research.

'Oh, and one other thing: all other work at the Mildon is to be suspended during her visit.'

EIGHT

D ropping her books on her desk wasn't polite. Neither was it as loud – as horribly cataclysmic – as Dulcie hoped.

'Dulcie?' Her office mate, Lloyd, looked up from his reading. 'Bad morning?'

'Bad day. Bad week.' Ignoring the student papers that had cushioned the books' landing, she flopped into the chair and put her feet up. 'Bad five years. And that electronic gate thing upstairs? That's bad, too.'

'Well, it *will* be a good thing.' Lloyd looked like he wanted to say more. Dulcie knew what it was: the new security system, at the entrance to the basement offices, had been installed in part because Dulcie had been attacked down here. 'The card reader isn't fully calibrated yet.'

'I had to swipe mine three times,' Dulcie said. 'I felt like a criminal myself.'

She knew she was sulking – and that her office mate had problems of his own. Right now, however, she needed some sympathy. And so when he started to disagree, elaborating on the installation at the top of the stairs, she cut him off. As she caught him up on what had happened, he finally responded as she'd hoped: with a gratifying display of sympathy and, in her defense, righteous anger.

'Can they even do that? I mean, close the Mildon?'

She nodded. 'It seems someone has special permission from a special friend.'

'That's crap, Dulcie. I'm sorry.' Lloyd sat back in his chair, shaking his head and rubbing his chin. For a moment, Dulcie had a vision of him in twenty years, a tenured professor, weighing a dialectical argument while stroking an as-yet-nonexistent beard. 'Any idea who the friend is?'

'That new dean of research, Haitner.' She shook her head. 'Seems he wants to make his mark by bringing in his own scholars. Loyal to him.'

'Thorpe.' Lloyd spat out the word with a bitterness only another grad student could give it. 'If he were half the adviser he's supposed to be, he'd be fighting for you. He'd at least get you into a conference room with this Miranda person.'

'Melinda – and thanks.' Dulcie went over it all in her head. 'I'm not even allowed to contact her. I guess that doesn't matter. Sunday is only two days from now, and I don't even know where she's staying.'

'Wait, I might.' Lloyd pulled open a desk drawer and began rummaging through it. 'You know Rafe Hutchins? Senior tutor at Dardley House?'

Dulcie nodded. Rafe was a few years older, an American by discipline if not birth. He'd designed the English 10 syllabus that all the section leaders still used.

Lloyd registered her assent and kept talking. 'We were supposed to go to that Peruvian film-fest tonight – he was telling Raleigh about it.' He still flushed a bit as he mentioned his glamorous girlfriend. 'But now he has to host some kind of bigwig this weekend. Has to make sure the guest suite is all cleaned up.'

'Could be her.' Dulcie thought about it. 'She's not a dignitary, but she is a visiting scholar. Would you be willing to give him a call?'

'That's why I was looking for this.' Lloyd held up a small leather address book. 'I've got his cell number here.'

While Lloyd made his call, Dulcie tried to get to work. It was early in the semester for most student papers, but English 10 kicked in early, and since she was teaching two sections this fall that meant a double load of three-pagers.

'Hey, Rafe. I'm calling to ask a favor for a friend.'

Dulcie winced, wishing that Lloyd was a bit more discreet. Better he should lead up to her request than start with it.

'And that's this weekend? Before the tea?'

Dulcie turned away. If she couldn't see her office mate, it should be easier not to listen. Besides, she'd been waiting all day for a moment to herself. Pulling the laptop from her bag, she watched it boot up. Chris's program should have finished running by now. If it had found anything . . . No, she was getting ahead of herself.

The little machine whirred and glowed, and she bit her lip, waiting. As the screen assembled its usual desktop visuals, she thanked Lucy's various deities for the foresight that had led her to type in the fragment from the Mildon. Even if the program tied that text in with something her author had written, she'd still have work to do. Before she presented her evidence to Thorpe, she'd have to look up the correlating passages. She would, she admitted, pretend she had found the connection the old-fashioned way – by reading – but it wasn't like that would be false. The program simply gave her a leg up. And with the Mildon closed to her for the foreseeable future, the work of verification would be a good use of her time.

Finally, the program appeared, a smiling Cheshire cat face – courtesy of Chris – greeting her. She clicked for her results, and got, instead, a familiar prompt: *Insert text?* The cursor blinked in anticipation. *Insert text?*

This made no sense. She had typed in that fragment, the bit about the 'life's elixir staining the red-gold hair.' *Insert text?* She scrolled down further. There was a blank, where the copy should have been. Where the copy *had* been, she was certain. But now all she saw was white space, down to the bottom of the form. *Insert text?*

She hit 'Search', typing in 'life's elixir' and 'red-gold'. Nothing.

This wasn't possible. Chris had designed the program for her. It was easy to use, and he had taught her to save. She clicked on 'History'. There she could see several passages from 'The False Hope of Love' essay, bits she had used in her paper. And, yes, one newer file – only identified by a string of numbers.

'Here's hoping,' she muttered to herself, maneuvering the mouse. She clicked.

Corrupted file, the screen said. *Insert text?*

The cursor blinked, and Dulcie fought the urge to curse. Lloyd was still on the phone, and their shared office was small, too small for one woman to have a meltdown without disturbing her colleague. Taking a deep breath, she closed her eyes for a moment. Something had gone wrong; it wasn't the end of the world. She'd ask Chris about it tonight. In the meantime, she'd simply enter it again. She should have time to locate it again this afternoon. The Mildon wouldn't be closed yet.

'They're *not* using the cream sherry? That's crazy.' Lloyd's voice reminded her of just why she couldn't research at her leisure. She had to admit, it stung.

Dulcie found herself staring into space, both trying to and trying not to listen. Melinda Sloane Harquist was getting the royal treatment, while she was laboring – trying to labor, anyway – in a basement. Even with her desk lamp on, the office felt gloomy. Partly, that was the dearth of natural light; partly it was the dust that never quite got cleaned away. The office wasn't entirely windowless, but the slanting rays from the one deep-set casement window – high above their shared, smaller bookcase – only highlighted the swirling dust.

'No wonder my computer is messed up; this place is filthy,' she said to herself. 'Probably why the card reader doesn't work, too.' Lloyd looked up, and she waved him away. 'Instead of working, I'm staring at dust,' she murmured more quietly. 'Dust and . . . whiskers?'

There, on her desk, sticking out from beneath a pile of student essays, she saw it: the thick white whisker of a cat. 'That's funny.' She moved the papers aside carefully, so as not to send the filament flying. 'Must have come in on my coat. Or . . .'

She paused and looked up. Lloyd was still talking, but she no longer cared to eavesdrop. Instead, she carefully excavated the paper that the whisker had lighted upon. It was a sheet from a yellow legal pad, the kind Dulcie used for rough notes.

With a frantic intake of breath, Dulcie spread the sheet out before her. But, no, it wasn't the rough copy of that excerpt. Without even deciphering her cramped scrawl, Dulcie could see that she'd written with black ink, not the pencil allowed in the Mildon.

She reached for the edge of the paper, the better to start crumpling it up. At the very least, it would make a satisfying projectile. One that Esmé would love to chase. Or . . . she paused. That whisker . . .

'Mr Grey?' She was whispering now, leaning over the long, lined sheet as if talking directly to it. 'Are you here?'

Nothing. Nothing beyond Lloyd's voice, that is, which now seemed to be agreeing to something or other.

'It was probably one of Esmé's,' Dulcie realized, with a sinking feeling, and turned her attention back to the page. There was nothing of import here, just some old notes from the previous semester. Her handwriting really was atrocious. Not at all like . . .

She stopped, frozen. That was it. What she had found in the Mildon was a handwritten draft, perhaps the first version of the book. And if the Mildon had the first draft in its collection, that gave Dulcie, as a resident scholar, an edge. No matter what else this Melinda Sloane Harquist may have found at Ellery University or wherever, she wouldn't have the original manuscript. Even if she had more of the complete book, in its final printed form, she'd have a harder time proving that the author of *The Ravages* had written it without the handwritten manuscript. Of course, during her stay here, it was possible she might stumble upon the same page that Dulcie had. But Dulcie had another advantage: she'd

been familiar with that handwriting. She'd seen it often enough in
her dreams. If only she could get back in and keep looking . . .

The gruff sound of Lloyd clearing his throat broke into
her thoughts, and she looked up, annoyed, momentarily forgetting
the reason he had been on the phone.

'Dulcie?' Lloyd was looking at her with a questioning gaze,
and she realized he'd probably been speaking to her.

'I'm sorry.' She brushed the curls back from her face. 'I got
caught up in an idea.'

He nodded absently. 'Well, that's good, I guess. And I have
some good news, too. For starters, Rafe confirmed it *is* Melinda
who's coming to stay in the guest suite. And as far as getting in
to talk with her, he'll do what he can. She's giving this talk on
Sunday – you probably know about that – and then she's supposed
to go to the monthly master's tea later that day, too. So you could
meet her there, if you wanted to deal with a house's worth of
undergrads. But he told me there's also going to be some kind
of private welcoming reception for her tomorrow, Saturday. Seems
she or – no, the dean – has ordered that they get a proper drinks
cart from the student bartenders. The master's sherry isn't good
enough for our visiting scholar.' He paused. Under ordinary
circumstances, they'd both be thrilled by this little bit of gossip.

'Too good for Harvey's Bristol Cream?' As distracted as she
was, Dulcie managed a smile.

'Top shelf all the way, I gather.' Her balding office mate leaned
in. 'I wonder what the deal is? No offense, Dulcie.'

'None taken.' Lloyd had learned from Dulcie about the prejudice
against the Gothics. 'And I don't know. I mean, a new work would
be important to *me*, but it's not like we're going to find out she
really wrote Shakespeare's sonnets.'

Lloyd looked interested for a moment. Then – as his quick
mind calculated the dates – he came back to the moment.

'However, I may be able to help you. Rafe says he can't get
you in to the drinks party. That guest list is set. But he thinks you
might be able to talk to her first. Turns out, he was asked to have
her suite ready by two. The party is at five. She can't take three
hours to get ready for a party, can she?'

Dulcie held her tongue. Ever since leaving the commune – what

Lucy called an arts colony – she had learned that most of her gender was capable of doing just that and more. But if gorgeous Raleigh hadn't initiated Lloyd into the finer points of mainstream American primping, then Dulcie liked her the better for it.

'So, will he introduce me?' Now that meeting the mysterious scholar was a real possibility, Dulcie felt a little twinge of nerves.

The look on Lloyd's face – a grimace of discomfort as he shook his head – didn't help. 'There's the catch, Dulce.'

Dulcie held her breath. She'd have to sneak in. Dress as a bartender. *Be* a bartender. But Lloyd kept talking. 'You see, there's a little bit of weirdness you should know about.'

'More than I'm already dealing with?' Lloyd nodded. 'Shoot,' she said.

'Turns out this Melinda Sloane Harquist is not a complete stranger to the university. Or to Dardley House.'

'Oh?' Dulcie couldn't read Lloyd's face.

'Melinda Sloane Harquist – better known as plain old Mellie Harquist – did a term as an exchange student, back when she was an undergrad at Ellery.' He was watching her, so Dulcie thought back.

'The name sounds vaguely familiar.' She remembered a lot of dark, curly hair, and a lot of fuss at mixers.

'They called her "Mellie Heartless" then,' Lloyd offered.

'Oh, yeah.' Dulcie remembered now. 'Every guy was crazy for her. She was the It Girl of Comp Lit.' At the time, Dulcie had been suffering from an unrequited crush on a junior who rowed crew – one of the many who had fallen for Mellie. In retrospect, the pain was gone – but not the sense of awe.

'That was her, but I bet you don't remember who finally won dear Mellie's favors?' Dulcie shook her head and waited. 'Rafe Hutchins, then the boy wonder of the lit department. They were the hot couple for, oh, about a summer. Then she went back up to New Hampshire, and broke poor Rafe's heart.'

Dulcie felt relief wash over her – so her rower hadn't gotten his heart's desire either! This was followed immediately by guilt. 'Poor guy. So the "Sloane" in her name? She must be married.'

'No, it's an old family name. Maybe her mother's maiden name, or something.' He paused, Dulcie's situation clearly in mind. 'She was always looking for her roots or something, Rafe said.'

Dulcie nodded that she understood. At least she'd had the commune. 'And after all that, he has to host her?'

Lloyd nodded. 'It's not that bad. It's been a while. He's got a new girlfriend. It's just – awkward, you know?'

She did. 'And calling on old intimacies to sneak in a visitor would probably be uncool.'

'To sneak in a potential *rival*.' Lloyd stressed the last word in a way that made Dulcie smile.

'May the goddess hear you,' she said. 'And thanks, really, for setting this up. I'm a little afraid it's going to be more like me in Oliver Twist mode, begging for scraps.'

'You're getting your Dickens – oh, never mind.' Lloyd reined in his Victorian mindset, and turned serious once again. 'Really, Dulcie, I know she's got this book ready to come out, but there's something more going on. If her work is set in stone, then why does she need access to the Mildon now, at this late date? And if she weren't worried about competition, then why would she have it closed to anyone else – closed to you? I mean, you're the only other person who is researching this author.'

'That we know of,' Dulcie responded automatically, her mind already wandering. 'It is funny. I mean, I published about that essay. But it's not like I've found anything solid since.' She thought of the handwritten page. Of the handwriting. 'Nothing I can prove, anyway. It's really lousy timing.'

Lloyd was watching her, waiting. Despite everything, she couldn't help but smile. ''Cause I think I'm this close, Lloyd. In fact . . .' She looked down at the notes in front of her. 'If I only had one more day in the Mildon, I think then I might have something. I think I'm on the brink of something big.'

NINE

She didn't take the time to explain it to Lloyd – the whole dream thing would sound too weird – but he'd cheered her on anyway as she'd gathered her papers and left the office. She'd been so happy she'd barely noticed the tie-up at the new turnstile, as three of her colleagues kept trying to swipe their cards.

Surfacing into the balmy afternoon, she made a mental list. Lucy would have an astral reason for all the elements coming together, and for once Dulcie was almost ready to agree with her. Her edge – her recognition of the handwriting – was as insubstantial as, well, a whisker. Still, her dreams had come through for her before.

Plus, there were other positive notes: Lloyd had arranged for her to meet with this Melinda before the visiting scholar's big talk. That was key, Dulcie had thought, for two reasons. The first was tactical: if she could find out what the visiting scholar was specializing in, then maybe she could safely claim the new book as her own turf. As much as she loved *The Ravages*, the idea of a previously unknown book excited her.

Besides, it seemed possible – likely, even – that the visiting VIP already had some area of specialty within the larger scope of the author's work. Trista's general area of concentration, for example, had been Victorian fiction, but her thesis had homed in on 'Architectural Details in the Later Victorian Novel'. Lloyd, who theoretically covered the exact same period, was toiling away at 'The Mid-Victorian Epigraph: Wit Carved in Stone'. Nothing could be more different.

Knowing what this Melinda's specialty was before the big presentation would also serve as the intellectual equivalent of a leg-up. After the talk, when Thorpe came up to question her, as Dulcie knew he would, she could have her answer ready – and be prepared to defend her right to continue with her thesis. 'Oh, Melinda isn't dealing with the American years,' she could say blithely. Or, 'She's not concerned with the possibility of a lost novel.' Maybe it would even be true.

The second reason for Dulcie's renewed optimism was more personal – and, admittedly, less likely. As supportive as Trista and Lloyd tried to be, Dulcie worked alone, essentially, the outcast of Literature and Language. And although her friends in the department always trod carefully, she knew that the bias against the Gothics was still huge. The idea of meeting someone with whom she could share her passion was appealing. They would be colleagues. Who knew? They might even become friends.

Her mind had raced with the possibilities – if she wanted to, Melinda would be in a position to do her a world of good. If Melinda introduced her, or even deigned to mention her as a scholar doing something, *anything* complementary to her own work, it would help legitimize Dulcie's research. Perhaps she would invite Dulcie to that exclusive gathering before the talk. Perhaps they would publish together, farther down the postdoc road. As she strode across the Yard, Dulcie was positively optimistic.

The final piece, she told herself as she trotted up the stairs of Widener, was that manuscript page. She should have time – more than twenty minutes till closing – to find it again. And this time, she'd make sure she kept a copy until her laptop had been able to process it.

She was so busy picturing her progress – which page to pull from which box – that she was stunned to see Mr Griddlehaus standing at the front counter, shaking his head.

'I'm so sorry, Ms Schwartz,' he said. 'I thought you must have heard.' He went on to tell her that as of midday, everything having to do with Gothic novels had already been put on hold – locked away and made inaccessible to other scholars in anticipation of Sloane Harquist's visit.

'But . . . but . . .' Dulcie heard the whine of frustration in her voice. 'She's not even here yet.'

'I know, Ms Schwartz. It's out of my hands.' Griddlehaus looked stricken as he explained. University scholars were allowed to request material during the lockdown, but for all intents and purposes, all works pertaining to Dulcie's subject were off limits. 'I do feel terrible about this.' He looked so sad, Dulcie wanted to cheer him up.

'That's OK, Mr Griddlehaus,' she said, and as she spoke, she realized that the ban really didn't affect her: what she was looking for wasn't classified yet as 'Gothic'. Plus, she had another reason to be sanguine. 'I figure, if she's pulling all these books, it means she's still fishing.' She confided to the clerk. 'And I'm more interested in the uncataloged work anyway. The boxes I was just looking at.'

As soon as the words were out of her mouth, she knew something was wrong. Although they appeared to be alone in the hallway, the little man pulled her in to the rare book collection's sterile reading room. His eyes darted back and forth, the movement exaggerated by his oversized glasses, before he leaned in to whisper in her ear.

That's when her final shred of optimism was shattered. 'You can't,' he said, drawing back to look around once more. 'I'm not supposed to say anything, you know. I was told that it was a confidential request. That it was worth my job.'

Dulcie drew back in surprise. That anyone could threaten – would even want to threaten – such a competent librarian was beyond her. But before she could protest, he motioned for her to lean in again.

'But you have a right to know.' His eyes flicked back and forth across the room. 'What she requested, it's more than these titles. She called this morning and was quite insistent. Almost, well, threatening.' His voice dropped with disbelief. 'I told her that I had her list, and that I was fully prepared to hold these particular works for her. But she brushed that off. She almost *laughed*, Ms Schwartz.'

He looked into Dulcie's face. 'She had a new request, a more urgent one, she said. She wants to look in the uncataloged material as well, and on the same terms I told her, that, well, there's reams of it – much of it barely legible. She said she didn't care, and she stressed that she needed sole access. I argued with her, Ms Schwartz. I told her that this would deeply inconvenience an entire community of scholars. I almost, Ms Schwartz, said she was being unfair.'

He shook his head, either amazed at her stubbornness or his own daring. 'It did no good. She reminded me that she had the dean's backing, without reservation. She told me I had to start pulling material for her own private use from those uncataloged works, and I was to start immediately. Specifically, she said, I was to pay special attention to anything relating to Thomas Paine, especially any correspondence from the last five years of his life. And also to any recently uncovered fiction from those years. In particular, any unattributed or unclaimed fragments of fictional works of horror.'

TEN

Writing, she was writing again. Furiously, but with joy – a pleasure long denied more sweet for having returned. Once again, the words were flying, thoughts coming so fast she barely had time to dip her nib. An image of horror, so fraught with terror, she shivered as she penned the lines, her own raven curls falling forward, as if to shield her from any inquisitive soul. Pressed a little too hard and – wait! Seated at her desk, the writer cursed quietly. An unladylike sound, but not an unusual one – not to the eyes that watched her, unblinking. Green and gold, they saw her retrieve the razor, hone once more a pen long overdue to be replaced. Watched as she paused – that image, with its ravenous, foul face, so familiar and yet so feared – and started, with a cry. The razor, the nib – some movement had provoked her outburst, and yet she bit down on her pain. She was not alone, not any more. She could not risk a sound, instead letting her lips pale with pressure. And the eyes watched as she did, at the slow welling, of the blood that dripped, dark as ink, on the page.

Dulcie woke with a start, grateful for the respite, and gasped as she saw the green eyes watching her, unblinking.

'Esmé!' She shook her head to clear it, and the sleeping vision receded, pulling Dulcie back into the modern day. Responding to her name, the cat yawned and stretched out one white mitten. 'What are you doing here?' Dulcie asked.

It was an odd question, but the little tuxedo didn't seem to mind. Instead, she looked over toward Dulcie's desk. There, Dulcie could see, her laptop was open and glowing. The cat must have been sitting on it again.

'Is it the warmth, Esmé? Is that it?' She couldn't really blame her pet. After all, she must have left the machine open. 'Was it the light that made me dream of writing, Esmé?' The tuxedo didn't answer, and Dulcie was left with the impression that her

pet was watching her, waiting for some kind of response that she
had yet to give.

'I guess it doesn't matter, does it?' Sitting up in bed, Dulcie
gathered the cat into her arms and watched as the laptop screen
faded into sleep mode, wishing she could do the same. Esmé didn't
seem similarly inclined, however, and once she was settled in
Dulcie's lap she started her morning toilette. Human carelessness
had, presumably, messed up her impeccable black coat. 'It's the
two of us against the world.'

That wasn't fair, nor entirely honest, and Dulcie knew it. Unlike
the author in her dream, she was alone, but the day outside looked
bright and fine – and Dulcie wasn't hiding from some mysterious
watcher.

Besides, her loneliness was at least partly her own fault. Chris
had received a late-night phone call from Darlene, who had asked
him to cover for her. He had been planning on taking back the
overnight shifts – at least some of them – for weeks now, so this
shouldn't have been that big a deal. Only they'd had words earlier
in the evening, their quarrel prompted by the malfunction of
Dulcie's computer.

'I know I saved it.' Dulcie had been tired and cranky. Her
disappointment at the closure of the Mildon had blown the loss
of the excerpt into a major frustration. 'Your program is broken.
It lost my file.'

Chris had looked worried at first, and had taken her laptop.
'It's not the program,' he announced, after a few minutes of
furious typing. 'Whatever you had in here was accessed badly,
that's why it's corrupted in the memory, and then you erased it.'

'I did not.' Dulcie had been using the program for several
months now, with no problems.

'You did, Dulce.' If he'd been looking at her, instead of at the
screen, he might have held back the next words. 'I tried to idiot-
proof it, but there's only so much I can do.'

The evening had gone downhill from there, to the point where
they'd both been somewhat relieved when Darlene had called,
pleading some sort of domestic crisis.

'She is seeing someone,' Chris had said, as he disengaged the
cat from his sneaker laces. 'And it hasn't been going on that
long, so maybe they do need some extra time together.'

Biting back the more bitter of her possible retorts, Dulcie had smiled and hugged him. He might not be the most sensitive man at times, but he hadn't meant to screw up her work – or insult her. She knew that.

Sitting in her lonely bed, however, she regretted what she thought of as her generosity. Not only had the nightmare left her with a racing pulse, it had raised some questions. The kind she longed to bounce off someone.

'Why has the dream changed?' In lieu of her boyfriend, she asked the cat. 'I mean, I'm glad that I'm not seeing a murder any more, but there's still the same sense of dread, right at the end.'

Esmé continued to wash, moving on from the smooth black fur of her back to her white hind foot. And Dulcie had to admit that the cat had a point. 'I know; it's because my situation has changed, right?'

Without Chris – and without another shot at that tantalizing manuscript – Dulcie faced the day with a heavy heart. Her toilette done, Esmé did what she could, scampering around until Dulcie – running late and hurrying to the kitchen – nearly tripped over her in her distraction.

'Esmé! Can't you watch it?' Dulcie heard herself snap, and caught herself. 'I'm sorry, kitten. It's not your fault I lost the excerpt and can't get back into the Mildon. It's not your fault I'm going to be late for section. Nothing's your fault.'

Whether it was the unexpected outburst or the sudden apology, the round little cat stopped her heedless scurrying. Instead, with her head tilted ever so slightly so that the whiter side of her nose was uppermost, she examined her person.

'*What's wrong, Dulcie?*' The voice, so quiet and yet so definitely there, startled Dulcie to the point where she almost dropped her coffee.

'Esmé?' Dulcie swung around to look at the little cat. 'Was that you?'

'*Who else?*' The cat flopped, exposing a fluffy white belly.

'I thought – no, never mind.' Dulcie sat heavily in a kitchen chair. 'You never speak, and I was beginning to think . . .'

'*You thought it was* him, *huh?*' Esmé stretched her white legs above her portly tum. '*You think the old man runs everything around here, don't you?*' She flexed her pink toes and ended up rolling herself over. *'Meant to do that,'* she muttered, and Dulcie suppressed a smile. *'But, I'm right, aren't I?'*

'I don't know.' Dulcie didn't want to be disrespectful, especially after that undignified move. In truth, she hadn't given much thought to the relationship between the two feline presences in her life. 'I guess, I thought Mr Grey had seniority.'

'Huh!' The little cat extended one foot and began to wash it furiously. *'As if there were such a thing as cat tenure! No, our bonds are deeper and more subtle than you could ever know, with your concerns of legacy and birthright.'*

'Birthright?' Dulcie paused to do the math before realizing that Mr Grey had been neutered. 'No, it's not possible.'

'I said we were more subtle, as so should humans be. But wait.' The little cat stopped mid-wash and stared up at her person. *'You were about to say something about my intellect, weren't you?'*

'Not at all.' Clearly, Dulcie had lit upon a touchy subject. 'I was thinking that you speak so rarely, I was beginning to wonder if perhaps you had lost—' She stopped herself, suddenly aware of the need to tread carefully. 'That perhaps you chose not to converse with us.'

'Nuh!' With a not inconsiderable effort, the little cat swung herself around again. *'What is this "chose"? As if we didn't all have our own roles to play.'*

With that, Esmé scrambled to her feet and galloped off to the living room.

'Our own roles? Like jobs?' Dulcie was tempted to follow up, but from the sounds in the other room, Esmé was already busy with one of her toys. Maybe that was her job: catnip monitor. And Dulcie's? Well, with the Mildon off limits and her thesis hanging by a thread, she had little better to do than actually try to teach. If she hurried, she told herself as she screwed on the top of her travel mug, she'd make it to her section on time. Even the strange conversation with the cat had cost her a few minutes she could ill afford. For her Saturday section was all the way down by the river – in the library of Dardley House.

Dardley House, where Melinda Sloane Harquist would be holding court in only a few hours. The visiting scholar had her sights set on Dulcie's topic – and seemingly had no interest in sharing. For all that Esmé had been talking about connections, Dulcie couldn't see how that would work here. Maybe cats simply were superior creatures. Taking a sip from the mug, Dulcie clattered down the apartment stairs and set off.

English 10, the year-long survey course by which potential majors lived or failed, had been one of her favorite classes, she reminded herself as she darted across a one-way street with barely a glance at traffic. Like most such courses, it covered way too much – jumping from Puritan sermons to Mark Twain's satires, all before midterms. As an undergrad, Dulcie had loved the way it drew connections between these, linking entire schools of thought through philosophical arguments over time. Only now, teaching the course, did she understand that for some students, those links were a bit too much.

'The key is attitude,' Dulcie rehearsed to herself, as she waited for a light. 'Let yourself see how ideas can do the connecting.'

She tried a few takes on it, attempting to sound as encouraging as possible and startling another pedestrian as she spoke out loud. 'It's all about attitude,' she said, and realized she was beginning to sound like Esmé.

Wednesday's lecture had involved the course's first difficult leap, from those early sermons to the first-hand reports of Kentucky explorers. Some of her students – she was thinking of two in particular – were not going to make it, she feared. Well, speaking of roles, it was her responsibility to reach down and haul those two up. The fact that this section was held in one of the conference rooms of Dardley House was neither here nor there. Melinda Sloane Harquist wouldn't have arrived yet, anyway. And she would get to talk to her later. The Dardley clock rang the quarter hour. Nearly eleven. Picking up the pace as she turned on to the walkway to the house entrance Dulcie took another chug of coffee. Almost there. Which meant a few more moments to focus on the task at hand.

'Try thinking about the mindset of the writers.' It sounded good. Maybe it would work with the scared and scattered undergrads she was about to face. 'How did they view this big new country of theirs? Were they frightened? Invigorated? A little bit of both?'

Such questions invariably brought up her thesis topic. *The Ravages* was not covered in any of the big courses – Dulcie had only discovered the remaining fragments of the book in a graduate-level discussion group she'd wiggled into in her junior year – and its author was firmly identified with a British tradition. Still, she couldn't help asking herself the same questions. Her author had been here, somewhere. A newcomer to a new world, fleeing some kind of danger. What had she thought of her new world?

'I don't care.' She was steps from the open door when a woman burst out of the house's front door, voice raised nearly to a shriek. The clock chimed again, but it didn't come close to drowning her out. 'I'm sorry, Rafe, but I don't,' Dulcie heard, between peals. 'You're always on about grabbing the opportunity, about networking, about bettering yourself. You should talk!'

The owner of the voice – a young black woman – stopped on the path and turned. Arms akimbo, bent slightly at the waist, she seemed to be using a good deal of her energy to yell at the young man who had followed her out the door and was holding it open. Glancing at him, Dulcie got the impression of cheekbones and a certain grace, the kind that some men took advantage of. Maybe she had reason to be angry.

'You're a hypocrite!' With that one last cry, she spun on her heel and took off. Dulcie stepped off the path to let her pass, unsure whether to offer condolences or turn her head. As it was, she went by too quickly, and Dulcie had only a moment to see her dash a tear from her cheek as she stalked off toward the road.

Head down, Dulcie pretended to be looking for her ID as she approached the main entrance of Dardley House. The double doors were oversized, more fitting for a castle than an undergraduate house, but the dark-haired man managed to almost block them anyway as he stood there, looking slightly stunned. Dulcie got a quick impression of Heathcliff on the moors – lost, dark, and undeniably romantic.

'Excuse me,' she said, as gently as she could. In an ideal world, she'd have ducked aside for a few minutes and left the abandoned lover to collect himself. However, even if most of her section was likely to be late, she should at least try to be on time.

'What? Oh, sorry.' Heathcliff – Rafe – stepped to the side, pulling one of the heavy doors open for her. She smiled up at him. She and Chris didn't have many screaming fights, not any more, but after last night, she could certainly relate. 'Maybe you should go after her?' As soon as the words were out, she regretted them. This was a private matter, none of her business. But certainly they must have both been aware of her, scurrying through their private affairs.

'What?' He looked over at her, and she saw that his eyes were a startling green. 'Oh, Darlene? No, no, she's right.' He stepped into the foyer beside her, and let the door close, as if those words had decided something. The main entrance where they now stood was tiny, just a short passage that opened at its other end on to a courtyard and, from there, all the interior rooms of the house. Despite the presence of a security booth – Dulcie could see the student guard on duty, tow-head bent over a book behind the glass partition – the enclosed space gave their conversation an air of privacy, if not intimacy. 'I have to let her make her own decisions. I mean, I've got my own unfinished business.' He shrugged broad shoulders. 'Anyway, sorry you . . . ah . . . had to see that.'

'I've been there,' Dulcie could say, honestly. 'Relationships!' She tried to sound world weary, and realized too late that she wasn't making sense. Still, she realized, she might as well take advantage of the occasion. 'If you don't mind – are you Rafe, the senior tutor?'

'Yes?' He looked apprehensive, and she wondered just how much unfinished business the handsome young man had. And with whom. The little foyer began to feel claustrophobic.

'I'm Dulcie Schwartz, Lloyd Pruitt's office mate?' Those green eyes looked dazed, and she hurried to fill in the blanks. 'I'm here because I teach the eleven o'clock section. English 10 – 10 at eleven,' she was gibbering. 'We still use your syllabus, you know. The way you divvied it all up – matching Jonathan Edwards up with *Moby Dick* is brilliant.' He was waiting. 'Lloyd talked to you yesterday? About meeting with your visiting scholar?' She leaned in and dropped her voice. The student in the security booth appeared to be reading, but she couldn't be sure how much was public knowledge. 'Melinda Sloane Harquist?'

'Yes, yes, of course.' He ran his hand through his hair. This close, Dulcie couldn't help noticing how muscular his arms were. Yes, he could have won the heart of Mellie Heartless, at least for a time. 'She's not here yet.'

'No, no, of course not. And I have my section. It's just that, hearing your name . . .' She left it at that, and he nodded.

'She'll be staying in the suite off the junior common room, second floor of the F entryway. You go through the courtyard and it's the last entrance on the right. Do you know it?' Dulcie nodded. Dardley was organized around its six stairwells, each with its own entrance on to the courtyard. Though a top-floor hallway connected most of the entryways, labeled A through F, this set-up meant a lot of exercise for the undergrads. 'She's supposed to arrive by two, and the reception isn't until five. If you came by at three or three thirty, you'd have plenty of time to talk.'

He rattled off the schedule as if by rote, Dulcie noticed. He must memorize such things as part of the job. Dulcie had a flash of Esmé again, and looked up at him. 'That will be OK? I'll be able to get in?'

'Sure.' He shrugged, his mind still clearly elsewhere. 'Just show your university ID at the door and come in.' He nodded toward the student guard, who still hadn't looked up. 'I'll make sure the door to F won't be locked.'

Well, it wasn't exactly an introduction, but it would serve. Dulcie thanked him and received a distracted nod in return. She followed him into the courtyard, with its battered lawn and scattered picnic tables. Around her, the house curved like a brick castle, punctuated by the green entryways and – on the far left – the French doors of the dining hall. Her own class took place in B, in a ground-floor conference room, but she turned to watch him duck a Frisbee as he crossed the patchy grass over toward F. The Frisbee landed in his path, and as he reached for it, someone called.

'Coming in?' She nodded, turning toward the door the girl held open for her. This was courtesy, rather than necessity. The courtyard doors, Dulcie knew from experience, were seldom locked. That's what the main entrance, with its security post, was for. The entrance she'd just breezed right through, Dulcie realized, as the door swung shut behind her. Where nobody had even asked for her ID.

ELEVEN

'So, like, is Professor Rutledge saying that "Sinners in the Hands of an Angry God" is, like, a joke or something?'

Dulcie took a deep breath to keep from rolling her eyes. Not even the sun shining in from the courtyard could pierce Didi Givency's foggy thought process.

'What the professor is trying to do, Didi,' Dulcie spoke slowly, hoping that some of her words would get through the freshman's perfect bob, 'is to try to show the line of influence, through the use of metaphor and hyperbole.'

'Which one is metaphor again?' The shellacked freshman turned and asked her neighbor, as if Dulcie weren't sitting at the head of the table, five feet away. Of course, her neighbor was Andrew Geisner. Six-foot-two and handsome enough that most of the women in the class would take any opportunity to turn toward him. 'The "as if" one?'

Dulcie sighed. She knew that she shouldn't, and that she should hide her frustration. To his credit, Andrew looked a bit abashed at the attention, ducking those marvelous cheekbones down as if he could hide behind his surfer-blond hair. The poor girl didn't stand a chance. With so much else going on, however, Dulcie was having trouble summoning the patience to deal.

'A metaphor is a figure of speech . . .' Thalia, the sophomore across the table, took up the gauntlet, answering the question in her usual pedantic manner. Slightly too loud, definitely condescending, but right now, a life saver, Dulcie thought. She smiled and nodded for the skinny sophomore to continue. 'A description that's not literally applicable – do we all understand "literally"?'

This was going too far. Dulcie was about to interrupt her, when she realized that several of her students were staring at the bespectacled student with rapt attention. Very well, she not only had been outmanoeuvred as a scholar, now she was being shown up as a teacher. Maybe if Thalia kept rambling on, they'd actually learn something. Besides, she thought as she glanced at the clock, the section had only ten more minutes to go.

'But what about the whole "as" and "like" thing?' Didi really shouldn't talk and chew gum at the same time, Dulcie thought. How did a girl like Didi get into university?

'*Dulcie.*' She didn't need the feline reminder to make her realize just how uncharitable her thoughts had become. Maybe the girl was a chemistry whizz. Maybe that perfectly done hair sheltered the brain of a mathematician, one who had chosen to broaden her education with a literature survey course.

Maybe, the morning's interaction coming back to her, she didn't know her role. What did Esmé mean, anyway? And what was the relationship between her new pet and Mr Grey? The voices in the room faded into the background as Dulcie pondered her feline messengers. She had wondered why Mr Grey had not warned her about this Sloane Harquist person. Now she had to ask what part Esmé played in everything.

'Ms Schwartz?' She came back to life to find everyone staring at her.

'Sorry.' She ducked her head. 'Is everything clear now, Didi?'

The freshman shrugged. From the smug look on Thalia's face, she'd probably fielded several other questions from her classmates while Dulcie daydreamed. Dulcie couldn't help it. The sophomore annoyed her.

'Great. So, Thalia?' She turned toward the sophomore, trying to keep her voice level. 'Why don't you share your thoughts on the burgeoning anti-American strain in the country's first century?'

The skinny girl opened her mouth, and then closed it, and Dulcie immediately felt a pang of guilt. Here, sitting around the table in what was supposed to be a collegial gathering, she had intentionally tripped one of her students up. This week's lecture had dealt with the new republic's growing pride in itself, its sense of itself as something fresh and new. Something very different from the Old World.

As the color rose to Thalia's thick-framed glasses, Dulcie decided to bail her out. 'Our class has only touched on it, but try to recall what we read of Thomas Paine's writings. In the wake of war in Europe, the United States fell into political turmoil. France, after all, had been our ally – and England our enemy. But some of the émigré writers who came here looking for a fresh start found something very different.'

Around the table, twelve pairs of eyes were watching her, when it hit her. She couldn't talk about the discrimination that the author of *The Ravages* had faced. She couldn't discuss the persecution that led her to disguise her writing, perhaps write in hiding. She had no verified literary examples to offer them – no proof. But she was Dulcinea Schwartz, fifth-year doctoral candidate. She was not going to be daunted by an English 10 section.

'Sophie.' The ponytailed sophomore was always reliable. 'Does this spark any ideas?'

'Actually, it does.'

Dulcie smiled. Sophie was one of her best students, the kind Dulcie liked to encourage, but between her weight and a tendency toward acne, she usually hid behind her long, thick hair. Maybe the ponytail was a sign that she was becoming more sure of herself, Dulcie mused, happy for an opportunity to coax the chubby girl out of her shell.

'If you compare the political essays of the early eighteen hundreds with those from only a few years earlier . . .' Sophie was nailing it, drawing on some of the same raw material Dulcie had read. For a moment, Dulcie felt a twinge of jealousy. Once her skin cleared up, would this girl be threatening her too? Making her own name in Dulcie's area of expertise?

No, she shook her head slightly. To think like that was madness. That would be like . . . well, maybe a little bit like Mr Grey feeling defensive about Esmé. Though, to hear the young cat tell it, some tension had developed. Something like the tension that now ran up her back, raking the small hairs on her neck as if claws had been drawn over them.

Dulcie felt her color rising and turned away from the table, ever so slightly. From here, she could see the left side of the courtyard. Not far from the hour, already students were crossing – heading from their rooms to class or over to the dining hall. A tall, dark-haired man wandered into view and paused, as if enjoying the sun. Rafe? Yes, it looked like the senior tutor. He must be taking a breather from cleaning the suite. Having such

an important guest might be trying – especially when that VIP
was your own ex.

Moments later, the black girl – Darlene – appeared from
the same direction. They must have made up after all. The
girl – young woman, she corrected herself – was too far away
for Dulcie to see her face. And she was still walking quickly,
her long legs crossing the courtyard with the minimum strides
necessary. There was something different about her, though.
Maybe it was the way she was carrying herself, upright and
confident. Maybe it was the way her arms swung by her sides.
Dulcie had a strong sense that the young woman wasn't crying
any more.

If the couple had been enjoying a make-up tryst, they'd
finished just in time. Moments after Darlene had disappeared
from the courtyard, she saw another figure crossing the courtyard. Short and solid, the human version of the brick walls that
surrounded them, assistant dean Robert Haitner huffed and
puffed as he strode, head down and purposeful, toward the
dining hall. He was wearing a trench coat, way too warm for
this weather even if it hung open and loose, making Dulcie
wonder if this was his attempt at fashion. Despite his suspiciously thick, dark hair, the dean was no longer a young man.
Surely, at his age – from here, she guessed he was forty-five
or fifty – he didn't have to try so hard. Then again, maybe being
only an associate dean meant he had to try harder.

'Ms Schwartz?' She was called back to herself. Once again,
all eyes were on her.

'I'm sorry, folks.' She wasn't going to make the same mistake.
These were young scholars, her students. 'I've been caught up
in issues in my own thesis, and I guess I've been distracted.' She
paused, considering how to make amends. 'Does anyone have a
specific question for me?' As if on cue, the clock started chiming.
The hour was over. 'I'd be happy to stay later, if anyone would
like my undivided attention.'

For a moment, Sophie looked like she was about to say
something, and Dulcie smiled at the girl in what she hoped was
an encouraging manner. Then the bell chimed again, and as one
her students stood, gathering books and notebooks together.
Saturdays were hard that way, and Dulcie kicked herself for her

lapses. This was her job, what she needed to be focusing on. She was good at it.

'Was that odd or what?' She heard one of her students ask, his identity masked as they funneled into the doorway. 'I guess somebody had a hangover today.'

TWELVE

Lunch. That was probably what she needed, Dulcie decided. Lunch or a nap. But the thought that she was going to be confronting Melinda Sloane Harquist in only a few hours was turning what might be incipient hunger pangs into mild queasiness. And as for a nap, well, while Mr Grey might approve, the thought of getting home and relaxing enough to snooze seemed unlikely.

Gathering her own papers together in the quiet of the empty room, Dulcie thought about Darlene and Rafe – and about calling Chris. Her boyfriend hadn't gotten home before she left, but there was the chance that he was puttering around now. Then again, he may very well have gone to sleep in the last hour and a half. Over the past year, they'd gotten into a routine: when he worked nights, he'd call her when he awoke. Better to get back into that habit, Dulcie told herself. As much as she wanted to make sure they had made up, she should let the poor guy rest.

On any other day, she would head to the library. Even with the Mildon closed to her, she could lose herself, deep in the subterranean stacks. The quiet, the books, that was what she'd lived for. Today, however, whenever she thought of her thesis – of *The Ravages of Umbria* – all she could think of was what might have been.

'Dulcie Schwartz, you're acting like a clueless kitten,' she said to herself finally, heaving her bag on to her shoulder. And with a determination that Esmé would have been proud of, she decided to head into the Square and get some lunch.

The moment she stepped out of Dardley, Dulcie felt better. The September day had warmed into perfection, the first hint of autumn color adding a golden accent to a startlingly blue sky. As she walked, Dulcie shed the sweater she'd been wearing – a rough oatmeal-colored cardigan Lucy had knit – and spread her arms. The day was warm, almost unnaturally so. Her mother was, at the very least, well intentioned. Everything would work out.

'Dulcie! There you are.'

At the sound of her name, Dulcie looked up to see Lloyd barreling down the walkway, waving his arms. She waved back and waited until he reached her, panting.

'I've been trying to call you.' Lloyd wiped a hand over his sweaty forehead. 'I'm just glad I remembered your section.'

'Why? What's going on?' As she talked, Dulcie reached into her bag. She'd turned her phone off before the section started. As it booted up, she saw that she had four messages waiting, all from Lloyd. 'Is it Chris?' Suddenly the day seemed cold. 'Is anyone hurt?'

'No, no. Nothing like that.' Lloyd leaned over, with his hands on his thighs. Dulcie had never seen her pudgy office mate out of breath before. Then again, she'd never seen him run. 'Didn't mean to scare you.'

Dulcie exhaled, suddenly aware that she had been holding her breath, and waited while Lloyd caught his.

'It's Rafe Hutchins,' he said finally. 'There's been, well, I guess there have been some problems.'

'Rafe?' She had spoken to the senior tutor barely an hour ago. 'But I was just talking to him.'

Lloyd shook his head. 'I don't know, Dulcie. Something's come up, and he called me about fifteen minutes ago. I think it's got to do with the dean – Dean Haitner.'

'I just saw him go by, too.' Dulcie felt a twinge of remorse. Rafe had agreed to do her a favor, because of his friendship with Lloyd. Had the dean somehow found out about it and decided to punish the tutor? Dulcie didn't know the man, but she'd heard about his ego. She wouldn't want to cross him, and she certainly didn't want to be the cause of someone else getting stuck in the doghouse. 'I didn't introduce myself though.'

Lloyd stopped her before she could continue. 'It's not you. It's this Melinda. I gather she's been getting threats. Rafe said he didn't know the details. "Nobody tells me anything," is what he said. But the dean is up in arms about her safety and adamant that she not be "bothered". So, well, I know that Rafe said he'd sneak you in . . .'

'No, I understand.' Suddenly the day wasn't quite so fine. Still, she managed to force her face back into a smile. 'I appreciate you asking for me in the first place.'

'It shouldn't have been a big deal.' Lloyd looked as bothered as she felt, the color coming back into his face as his breathing settled. 'I mean, come on, you've published already. And she's just another postgrad.'

'Not quite.' The smile faded. 'She's got friends – or at least *a* friend – in the dean's office. And, well, she's got everything in the Mildon on lockdown. At least, everything I care about.'

'This isn't right.' Lloyd looked past her, toward Dardley. 'Look, I've got an idea.'

Dulcie nodded, waiting.

'We're here. Why don't we both go over there now? I'll talk to Rafe, and if you're there – well, nobody is going to see you as a threat. For starters, you're a member of the university community. You're my office mate, and we're visiting Rafe. And, well, maybe she's already arrived, in which case, popping in to say hi would be the most natural thing in the world.'

'Lloyd, you're positively devious.' Dulcie felt her high spirits returning. 'Raleigh is one lucky girl.'

'Why, thank you,' said Lloyd, linking his arm through hers as they headed back down the walkway to the red-brick house.

THIRTEEN

'We're visiting Rafe Hutchins,' Lloyd explained to the freckled student in the guard booth. 'Lloyd Pruitt and Dulcie Schwartz.'

The young man nodded and handed them the ledger to sign. Either the dean had put a bug in his ear about security or he had finished his book. After they'd slid the ledger back under

the glass divider, he'd even checked their IDs. Only then had
he buzzed open the inner door, letting Dulcie back into the
courtyard she'd left less than fifteen minutes before.

Lloyd turned toward the left, and Dulcie stopped him. 'I saw
Rafe and the dean both going up there.' She gestured toward the
farthest entrance way.

'Of course. I was thinking he'd be in his rooms, in A. But I
gather the dean is running him ragged. We'll go look for him in
the guest suite first.'

Lloyd led the way across the courtyard to the entrance marked
with a small, gold 'F'. 'So much for extra security,' he said. The
heavy green door had been propped open by a stone.

'Well, it is a nice day,' said Dulcie. 'Plus, it's not like it's an
exterior door.' She looked around. Students had begun to fill the
courtyard. Two women sprawled on the sparse grass, perhaps
hoping to extend their tans, while others emerged from the dining
hall holding lunch trays. 'They look so carefree.'

Lloyd turned toward her, concern showing on his face. 'Dulcie,
everything will work out OK. I know it will.'

She nodded, unable to respond. 'At any rate, I don't see Rafe
or Darlene out here.'

'Come on.' Lloyd pulled open the heavy door, and Dulcie
stepped inside. The way Dardley was laid out, many of its
windows, as well as its courtyard, opened on to the river, and
in this last entryway, even the stairs benefited from the natural
light. At the first landing, Dulcie paused to look out the
window. On this late summer day, the sun on the water was
dazzling, the sparkle seemingly synchronized with the sounds
of footsteps racing up the stairs above them. Behind her, out
in the courtyard, someone screamed – and the scream
collapsed into laughter. A door slammed, hard, and she found
herself squinting in pain.

'You all right?' Lloyd sounded worried, so Dulcie nodded,
feigning a heartiness she didn't feel.

'It's the glare. It got to me. I've had a headache all day,' she
lied. 'This view is incredible.'

'Wait till we get up to the second floor,' said Lloyd as they
walked on. It was funny, Dulcie thought, how he had been the
winded one, and yet now he was climbing the curling stairs with

no difficulty. Meanwhile, her lie had become truth – the pounding in her head bringing with it the most claustrophobic feeling she had ever experienced.

'Hang on a minute, Lloyd.' She stopped a few stairs up. 'I'm not sure about this.'

'Dulcie, are you sure you're OK?' Lloyd's face was drawn with concern. 'You've gone all pale.'

'I'm just not sure we should be doing this.' She stopped herself. 'That *I* should be doing this.'

'Visiting Rafe?' He stepped back down and was looking at her curiously. 'Dulcie, have you eaten today?'

'I had coffee.' She was leaning on the wall. 'It's just . . .' She gestured at the wall, at the curving stairwell that rose above her. 'This place, it's not right – I don't think I should be here right now.'

'And I don't think you're fit to go anywhere. Sit, Dulcie. Catch your breath. I'm going to get you something from the cafeteria.'

Unable to form any words, she nodded and sat, heavily. Despite the warmth of the day, the stair beneath her felt cold.

'Do you want me to call for help?' Lloyd hesitated two steps below her.

'No, no, you're probably right.' She lifted her head, trying for an optimism she didn't feel. 'Maybe you could get me some yogurt.'

'I'm getting you something with sugar. And if that doesn't help, I'm calling health services.' Lloyd stared hard at her face for a moment, then turned to trot back down. 'Back in a flash,' he called back up, and she saw the light grow and then recede again as the courtyard door closed behind him.

'Someone's going to be cursing,' she thought to herself. Lloyd must have kicked the rock out of the way in his rush to get her sustenance.

Unless somebody had come in after them. Dulcie tried to remember what she had heard, before the dizziness had descended. Her head ached; she closed her eyes. Voices . . . a young woman, her tone defiant. What had Esmé meant, anyway, talking about Mr Grey in that way? Was there a rivalry between them, something she had never known about? Was Esmé simply acting out

– perhaps because of her still-kittenish ways? Or could she have picked up something of her own issues?

'*Dulcie!*' The familiar voice pulled her upright. 'Mr Grey?'

'*Dulcie, take care*—' The sound of feet on the hard stairs above her drowned out the quiet voice. '*Your words,*' she heard, '. . . *jealousy.*'

A chill washed over her. 'I could kill her.' She'd said it. She hadn't meant it. Wasn't one of her students asking for an example of hyperbole today? No, that was metaphor. Either way, as Lucy's daughter she had grown up with the 'rule of threes'. Whatever you do – whatever you think, even whatever you wish – comes back to you, threefold. And her wish had been . . .

No, she didn't mean it. Still, grabbing the banister Dulcie pulled herself up. Her head was throbbing, almost blinding her with the pain. She wasn't going to wait for Lloyd, though. Lucy might not be right about the details, but her heart was good – and on this point, Dulcie agreed with her. She had to go make peace with the interloper, even if this Melinda didn't know that they had been at war.

'Hello?' She called up the stairs. Nothing. Those footsteps must have belonged to the resident students; this section of Dardley House was four stories high and the hallway at the top connected to the next entrance. 'Hello?'

She started up. Lloyd would find her. Besides, it was his friend who had rescinded the invitation to drop by; it would be better if he weren't involved.

'Hello?' She craned her neck, trying to look up the stairwell. 'Anybody there?'

The library, she recalled, was on the second floor to the left, where its windows would look over the courtyard and the river beyond. As an undergrad, she had loved to study there, although in truth the abundance of sunlight often made the room a little too warm for anything but a snooze. To the right, she recalled, were the various house offices. The junior common room – which, despite its name, tended to be used for senior staff meetings, was down here, too. And, at the end, the visiting scholar's suite.

Ascending to the landing, Dulcie turned to the right and found herself facing a closed door. She took a deep breath and knocked. Nothing. 'Hello,' she called into the crack between the dark oak and its frame. 'Anybody there?' She knocked again. Nothing. Then, on a whim, she tried the knob. It turned.

'Hello!' Dulcie opened the door and called down the hall. 'Hello?'

The door was unlocked for a reason. Rafe would be back in a moment. Lloyd would catch up with her. Maybe Melinda had already arrived, and was back in the suite, unpacking. With doors this thick, she probably hadn't heard Dulcie calling.

Her head pounding, Dulcie took a step into the hallway. It was dark, any natural light swallowed up by the high ceilings and wood paneling. Framed photos of men in shorts, holding oars, looked down on her, their names faded to sepia illegibility.

'Dardley Lights, 1925,' she was able to make out. 'Varsity Champions.' The faces were white and ghostly in this light, only the heavy moustaches worn by all eight of the rowers adding a touch of levity to the picture. She moved on to the next, which was labeled 1941. These men – undergrads, probably – looked lighter still, thin and pale. The world was at war then, she realized. Sports were probably not distraction enough from what they would soon be facing, out in the real world. Dulcie leaned in, hoping to read their names, and found herself looking at a shadow between two of the rowers. Grey and indistinct, blurred by movement perhaps, it drew her. Another face, about shin high. Was it a cat?

A sudden thud caught her by surprise. A door slamming – or a window closing – and she jumped back. The door on to the landing had closed, blocking out even the faint natural light and making the long hallway suddenly claustrophobic. Dulcie fought the urge to retreat – she'd come this far – and denied herself the reassurance of checking the door. Of course it wouldn't be locked; she wouldn't be locked in. These were the house facilities, in regular use by the university community.

By force of will she made herself continue on. There was a light visible at the hallway's end, the warm glow of a lamp, perhaps, tucked into a niche. Seeing it, she exhaled, suddenly aware that she had been holding her breath. 'No wonder my head hurts,' she muttered to herself. 'What with the not breathing and all.'

She licked dry lips and took another step down the hall,

toward the light. Reaching it, she saw it came from a door
that stood slightly ajar. Peeking inside, she could see the edge
of a large meeting table, the midday sun reflecting off its
polished surface. That was the light source, then, the sun
reflecting off the warm wood. Peaceful and strangely organic,
as if it were alive. For a moment, she was tempted to go into
the large, quiet room – the junior common room. Through the
open door, she could see an oil painting of a man in a powdered
wig. Lord Dardley, she assumed, for whom the house had
been named. He'd been educated here – no, he'd donated his
library, she recalled. Three hundred volumes and the equivalent
in sheep, or some such. In those days, that was enough to
make a name for yourself at the university, she thought with
a stab of bitter-sweet regret. She didn't even know if the curled
and coifed lord had been a scholar of any renown.

Her headache had faded, replaced with an overwhelming sense
of fatigue that caused her to lean against the door jamb. From
this angle, she caught a glimpse of an easy chair, its brown leather
undoubtedly warmed by the sun.

'Esmé would love to nap there,' she thought, the image cheering
her. There was something particularly tempting about the scene.
'Mr Grey would have, too.'

Maybe it was the warmth, maybe the quiet: this wing of the
building faced the river, rather than the courtyard, and this room
in particular exuded a peacefulness that seemed to calm Dulcie's
throbbing head. Maybe it was the thought of her cats. She longed
to slip into that easy chair and rest.

She hadn't earned peace, though, not yet. Even if it was just to
make up for her violent wishes, Dulcie knew she had to go meet
the visiting scholar. Even if nothing came of it, she had to try.

Resisting what felt almost like the tug of a tide, she stepped
away from the door and turned to continue down the hall.

'Dulcie,' she heard the familiar voice and turned involuntarily.
Mr Grey hardly ever made an appearance at the same time as
he spoke to her, but the old habit was so hard to break. 'Dulcie.'
The voice sounded sad.

'I know, Mr Grey.' In the hushed dark of the hallway, she
was barely whispering. He would hear her, though. Of that she was
sure. 'I got your message. I'm here to make amends.'

'*Three times,*' the voice said, and Dulcie strained to hear. It was fading – he was fading – and she experienced a sharp pang as she realized that her thoughtless words may have chased him away. '*Three times warned.*'

'What, Mr Grey?' She knew about the rule of three, but she'd only said those awful words once, hadn't she? She must have misheard. The air was so still in this hallway, even the faintest echo would have carried. 'Mr Grey?'

She turned around again. The long hallway was behind her. The meeting room, with its faint glow, stood empty, luring her away from her duty. No, the only option was to continue on to the door at the end of the hallway, which stood closed.

'Hi there!' Dulcie tried for jaunty as she knocked. Her headache was almost gone by now, but there had to be something wrong with her sinuses. There was a pressure in her head, as if the pounding had battened down something oppressive and fierce. 'Ms Harquist? Ms Sloane Harquist?'

She knocked again. Nothing. She should turn around. Lloyd must have returned by now. He was probably waiting for her at the bottom of the stairs. He might be worried. For all she knew, he could have gone off to fetch the university police. An ambulance. Rafe.

She wasn't supposed to be here. This Melinda Sloane Harquist, 'Mellie Heartless', would reveal herself soon enough. Tomorrow, Dulcie could join the rest of the department in hearing her speak, and then she could figure out what, if anything, she could salvage of her own thesis.

Enough. Dulcie leaned her throbbing head against the door, as if the cool, dark wood could act as some kind of a salve. To her surprise, it moved.

'Ms Harquist?' Dulcie stood up, but the slight pressure had been enough. The door had opened an inch, letting a sliver of light into the hallway. 'Rafe?'

With the lightest touch of her fingertips, she pushed the door and let it swing further, revealing a wall of books and a small end table, bare of anything but a lamp. 'Halloo?'

It was undoubtedly empty, just like the common room. Melinda Sloane Harquist wasn't due to arrive for an hour or two yet. Even if she was at the university, she was probably meeting with the dean. At the Mildon, getting the lay of the land. Or, simply, at lunch.

'Ms Harquist? Are you there?' Dulcie debated whether to leave a note. She didn't want to get Rafe in trouble, but since she was here . . . Fishing out her notebook, she scribbled a few quick words.

'*Welcome – I'm a fifth-year doctoral candidate, also looking at* The Ravages, *and I'd love to chat. I'll be at your talk, or maybe you can call me?*' She added her number and looked about for a way to affix it to the door. No, there were no nails protruding. This wasn't the kind of door anyone would stick a thumbtack in. Well, since the suite was unlocked, Dulcie took a step in and found herself in a book-lined chamber. She'd tuck it right under that lamp. That way, anyone entering would be sure to see it first thing.

'Hello?' There was no answer, and the room felt still. 'I know, Mr Grey,' Dulcie whispered to the quiet. What she was doing was wrong, but the temptation was just too great. After all, someone had to be here. She could see, at about waist height, that somebody had set a pile of papers on the edge of the bookshelf. Peering over, she saw typed pages, the sun reflecting off the binder clips. It looked thick; Dulcie estimated three hundred, maybe three hundred and fifty pages. Drawn by curiosity, she walked further into the room. Surely, it couldn't hurt to take a peek.

Anonymous Unveiled, she read. This was it – the manuscript of Melinda Sloane Harquist's book. Dulcie took a breath. To read this, here, in its unpublished – probably uncorrected – form was crossing a line. She should walk away. Maybe she could get permission to look at it later. Maybe Melinda would want her to review it, peer to peer.

Anonymous Unveiled . . . Mr Grey, she knew, would not approve. Lucy, however, might say the book was here for a reason. For a brief moment, her impulse struggled with her discipline, but as with the last dumpling, temptation won. Dulcie flipped open to a double-spaced page and began to read:

'*If, as seems likely, our mysterious and yet wildly wayward*

*author was involved in the scandal, then isn't it probable that
in light of her willful ways she* caused *the scandal?'*

'Wow,' Dulcie said out loud, in an unconscious echo. This
Sloane Harquist woman certainly liked her alliteration. 'I
wonder . . .' Dulcie reread the opening, when some other
words hit her: Likely? Probable? This was speculation, not
fact! Dulcie leaned forward to read more – maybe this woman
hadn't made any great new discovery – and started back as
a fly zipped right by her eye. Blue and fat, it buzzed as it
circled, almost as if it were drunk, she thought, swatting at
it without effect. Where was she?

'*The scurrilous doings, the scandal of the year, which shock-
ingly would entangle prominent members of the fledgling
government.*'

'Wow,' Dulcie said again, the single word forced out in
disbelief. Sloane Harquist not only loved her alliteration, she'd
never met a polysyllabic word she didn't like. Maybe, Dulcie
tried to be charitable, this was a rough draft. After all, something
was scrawled in the margin in an elegant, if almost illegible,
cursive: *Missing man? Paine?* Well, that made sense. Melinda
had decided to insert a reference in what seemed to be an
introductory passage. Dulcie squinted at the rest of the line.
Change? See . . . It was no use. Sloane Harquist's handwriting
was decorative, but harder to read than Dulcie's own, and so
she went back to the typed copy.

'*As we can see in the overwrought – nay, wordy – writing in
the description, "life's elixir had begun to solidify and darken".*'

Dulcie stiffened: that phrase. It was the same one she had
commented on. Biting her lip, she read on. '"*Staining the red-
gold hair a dull brown.*"'

Dulcie's heart sank, the heat – the humidity – making her
feel ill again. It might as well be summer, Dulcie thought. It
was awfully warm in the room. That lamp had been left on all
morning, probably, adding its incandescent glow to the glare
of the midday sun off the river. There was a funny smell, too.
Not just the Charles – the river had been cleaned up in recent
years. Something a little sweet, like some cold cuts had gone
off in the fridge.

That fly buzzed around her head, and Dulcie waved it away again. Then another, right by her. Heading past her, toward a seating area, where a leather sofa and two armchairs huddled beneath more bookshelves.

The flies were heading toward that oversized sofa, and Dulcie found herself turning in that direction, too. That's when she saw the bust lying on the carpet, white against the dark of the shadowed Oriental rug. It must have fallen, she thought, walking toward it. It must have been up on the bookshelf and become unbalanced. Already feeling more than a little guilty, she reached for the statue. If she could figure out where it went, she'd slip it back into place.

The bust was heavier than she had first thought, the white of the stone fooling the eye into thinking it was light, and Dulcie had to use both hands to lift it. As she hefted it, she saw that the nose was chipped and there was a smudge, like mud or paint, on its side. Resting the thing against the end table, she wiped at it and was a little surprised to see that her hand came away dark red. Paint, then. Or . . .

The buzzing grew louder, as another fly flew by, and Dulcie turned to look. The sound was furious, frantic, drowning out everything in her head. Drowning out everything except the sight before her. On the carpet, hands flung outward, eyes open but unseeing. Not seeing. Never seeing again.

Dulcie gasped, unable to breathe. The pounding in her head threatened to take over, the noise of the fly a deafening roar, as Dulcie released the statue and it crashed, once again, to the carpet with a deep, dull thud. Dulcie didn't hear it, though. Didn't register the voices below her either. The last words she'd heard echoed through her mind – *warned,* she'd heard. *Three times warned.*

Mr Grey had been trying to help her. Mr Grey – not Esmé with her petty jealousies, her strange dissent. Mr Grey. Only Dulcie hadn't listened.

FOURTEEN

'**D**ulcie!'
At last the sound of Lloyd's voice penetrated Dulcie's panic. She had heard Mr Grey, coming to her rescue, urging her to run. But she had only taken a few steps before she saw her office mate, standing in the doorway, several faces crowded behind him. One, she could see, was wearing the uniform of a university EMT.

'In here,' she gasped, gesturing for them all to come in. That's when she saw the smudge on her hand. The blood, she corrected herself. And that's when the world began to go black.

'Sit down, miss.' The EMT was by her side, and she was being maneuvered into a chair she hadn't noticed before, just behind the door. Lloyd stood, hovering. 'Please, put your head down, miss.' The EMT was talking to her. 'Can you tell me where you're bleeding?'

'I'm not.' She shook her head, confused. But the undignified position – her head between her knees – was helping. Without sitting up, she started to explain. 'Lloyd went for help because he thought I was sick. I mean, I *was* sick. I've had a hell of a headache, but this isn't—'

'Oh my God!' Another voice, male, that Dulcie didn't recognize. She tried to sit up, but the EMT had his hand on her upper back. 'Melinda! Help!'

'That's what I was trying to tell you.' Dulcie turned her head to address the EMT, but he was already clambering to his feet.

'Mellie! Darling!' Even from the back, Dulcie recognized Dean Haitner. He'd changed into a suit, probably for the reception, but his tie was already askew, his jacket rucked up. With his hands up in the air – then in his thick hair – he appeared to be dancing.

'Please, sir. Step back.' The EMT moved him aside and knelt by what Dulcie knew was a dead body. 'Sir, please.'

*　　*　　*

'Darling?' Dulcie knew she wasn't at her best, but she didn't think that 'Darling' was one of the names in the visiting scholar's long list. No, there was something else going on here, and suddenly Dulcie knew for sure why this particular guest had received special attention. 'Darling?' She turned to find Lloyd staring at her. 'So the rumors about him are true? He was going out with her?'

'Dulcie, I thought you were sick . . .' He seemed a few steps behind her. 'I thought you couldn't go up the stairs.'

'I couldn't, Lloyd. I had the worst headache you can imagine.' Sitting up, she brushed her hair out of her face – and felt the sticky wetness on her fingers.

'But you came up here. You came up here.'

'Oh my God! Oh my God!' The EMT was talking to the dean now, trying to turn him away from rug, from the sight of Melinda Sloane Harquist lying on the floor. 'Oh my God.'

'Nobody was supposed to have access.' Rafe, the tutor, was staring at Dulcie. 'I told Lloyd. There had been threats.'

'I know.' Dulcie tried to wipe the stickiness off her cheek. 'But the door was open. I thought I'd ask her—'

'The door was *open*?' Rafe was leaning in toward her. 'Or unlocked?'

'I just wanted to leave a note.' Dulcie couldn't wipe it off. The stickiness, the dark crimson stickiness was everywhere.

'Where is it?' The dean's focus had changed. 'Where is it?' His voice was growing louder.

'Where's what?' Rafe turned toward the dean in confusion.

'Her book – her thesis! The reason for all the precautions!' The dean was still gesticulating madly, sweat popping out on his brow. 'She was convinced someone was going to try to steal it.' He paused and seemed to see Dulcie for the first time. 'And you – you're covered in her blood.'

FIFTEEN

'One more time, Ms Schwartz.' The big detective gestured with his pen. 'Let's just go through it again, together. OK?'

'I've done that – we've done that – already. Twice, at least.' Dulcie was sitting in the university police office, in a small private room she'd never seen before. In front of her, with the pen, the pad, and the exasperated look, was her old friend, Detective Rogovoy. But any sense of comfort she should have gotten from the familiar face was gone – dissipated by his utter lack of reasonableness.

'I can't tell you anything more.' Dulcie tried once again. 'You've written it all down.'

Rogovoy sighed, a heavy exhalation that made his not inconsiderable bulk rise up and collapse again. For a moment, Dulcie thought he might deflate entirely, a thought that she found a little scary. Then he inhaled, and she found herself relaxing.

'Ms Schwartz?' He didn't sound any happier though. 'Dulcie?'

She nodded, a prickling feeling beginning in the back of her head. That headache – the one that had laid her low after section – was coming back again. Or, no, this felt like pinpricks, sharp claws digging into the base of her skull. A warning? She shook it off. No, this was an ordinary headache, not a message from Mr Grey. It had been a horrible day – tragic – but surely the worst part had already happened. Mr Grey had been looking out for her: that original headache had been sent by her spectral pet, an attempt to keep her from entering the suite, she was sure. That hadn't worked though, and she had blundered into a tragedy.

She rubbed the back of her neck. Tension, that's what it had to be. Tension and the stale air of this small, white room. Rogovoy had to let her leave soon. He might only be a cop, but he worked at the university. He had to know that she was a trained scholar, and that meant a trained observer – and she had already related everything that she had observed during her brief, horrible time in the visiting scholar's suite.

'I know you, Ms Schwartz.' Dulcie looked up into the detective's troll-like face with a bit of surprise. The deep-set eyes on either side of a particularly lumpy nose looked sad, and she wondered if he felt her pain. But, no, he couldn't have read her mind, not really. He must have seen her rubbing her neck, she realized, and pulled her hand down to her lap. The prickling was getting worse; she needed to finish things up here. Pushing the image of a cat – those claws, unsheathed – from her mind, she made herself listen to what he was saying. 'I know you're a good kid. Really.'

He paused again, and Dulcie found herself thinking of a cat again. Not just any cat – a wide, grey face, green eyes flashing. Mr Grey: on alert and ready to strike. Her neck tingled and stung, and she wondered what she had done to displease her old friend as she waited for Rogovoy to continue. He was dithering, probably as overworked and tired as she was. She blinked away the thought of claws and considered ways to move the conversation along. Yes, she could say, she knew she would have to be available for questions. She'd probably have to sign something. Then, maybe, he would finally give her the tired nod that meant he was about to push his chair back and release her to go home.

Home. At the very idea, she was struck again by how tired she was. It wasn't yet four, the day outside still bright and sunny when she'd been driven over to the university police headquarters. But between last night's terrors and the horror of this afternoon, she felt like a year had passed since she had left Esmé in the kitchen. Since Esmé had made that odd comment about Mr Grey. What had the little tuxedo cat meant, anyway? And was there any chance Rogovoy would have one of the patrol cars give her a lift?

'And since they're involved, this has become much more complicated.'

'Huh?' Dulcie looked up. Rogovoy had been talking, but she'd been in another world. A quiet world of cats. 'I'm sorry. I didn't hear?'

'I said the Cambridge Police have taken over the investigation.' He was speaking slowly now, as if she were stupid or hard of hearing. Still, with the words that were coming out of his mouth, Dulcie felt like maybe she was. 'I am not the one in charge here.'

'Oh, I'm sorry.' The big guy worked so hard, Dulcie's heart went out to him.

He was shaking his head. 'No, it's not that. I have – well, I have my hands full this term anyway, what with the new security measures. After last spring, you know.' Dulcie did. In addition to the attack in her basement office, a combination of fraud and attempted robbery had exposed the vulnerability of the university library system. 'Ms Schwartz, I'm telling you this because it concerns you.'

'Oh, thanks.' Home. Home and more cocoa. Despite the unseasonable warmth, she decided, this day called for it.

She was trying to picture the kitchen cabinet, the box of hot chocolate. Had she and Chris finished it? She had a vague memory of Chris pouring some into a saucer. Esmé had sniffed at it, but had pulled away in disgust. She smiled at the memory and heard a gruff bark. Rogovoy, she realized, had cleared his throat. He was staring at her.

'What?' She forced a smile. 'Sorry, it's just been such a day.'

He grimaced. 'Well, I'll do what I can to make it better. You're still with that computer guy, right? If you give me his number, I'll call him. I mean, after I notify your mom.'

'My mom? No, really.' Lucy would not be useful in this situation. In fact, there was nothing Dulcie wanted less than to hear her mother's hare-brained explanations. Bad karma was certainly going to figure. And she could get herself home. 'And Chris might still be asleep. You don't have to disturb him. I'm fine, really.' Rogovoy was looking at her like he didn't believe her. 'Honest. And I can tell him when I get home.'

The big man before her shook his head, his meaty lips clamping shut. With one oversized hand, he rubbed his face. It didn't seem to help. When he opened his eyes, they looked just as sad, just as tired.

'You haven't heard a word I've said, have you, Ms Schwartz?' He looked around as if he'd never seen these white walls before.

The pain in the back of her neck was intense now. Forgot claws, this was like teeth – sharp feline teeth. Like a parent cat trying to carry her away. Like one of her bad nights, if Esmé or Mr Grey were desperate to wake her up.

'No, I'm sorry. I must have missed it.' She rubbed her neck again, pressing hard to ease the pain.

'That dean – the new guy. He's called the DA's office, the city cops, you name it. Considering that the victim wasn't a member of the university community, he has a case that this doesn't belong in my jurisdiction. But that means I'm going to have to hand this whole mess over to the city, and you're going to have to deal with them, Ms Schwartz. I can't tell you for sure what will happen, but I think that you should prepare yourself. It's likely you'll probably be charged – that means going to court for an arraignment and, well, they can hold you until this is all settled.'

He had the grace to look embarrassed. 'I'm going to be talking with the folks in charge, and I'll do what I can. I don't like being pressured. But one thing I know, Ms Schwartz – Dulcie – you can't just walk away from this. Unless, well, until we find out who did this, you're going to be in the spotlight. I'm afraid it's likely you are going to be arrested.'

SIXTEEN

I f one were ever going to faint, Dulcie told herself, now would be a good time.

In general, Dulcie was not a fan of fainting – either in real life, when it never seemed as glamorous as it should be, or in books. In fact, one of the reasons she'd become so fond of *The Ravages of Umbria* was because its heroine, Hermetria, had been a resilient, non-swooning type – whereas her enemy, the duplicitous Demetria, would go pale and keel over at the drop of a hat.

Right now, however, sitting in that claustrophobic white room, such a gesture might be useful.

It wasn't as though she felt fine. Although Detective Rogovoy's words had finally gotten her to focus, her headache had only grown worse – a tearing, biting sensation that had her blinking back tears. The pain was so intense, it left her breathless. It also left her more alert than she had been since, well, since before she had discovered the body in Dardley House.

'They can't just take me away,' she said, once she could finally form words. 'I am a member of the university community.' She had gathered steam and stood, banging on the table for emphasis. 'And I demand that the university represent me.'

'That's the problem,' Rogovoy had begun. Only then, as he began to explain, did Dulcie realize how much she had missed. The university had little say in this case, and the fact that Dean Haitner was pushing for charges to be pressed made the involvement of the city police necessary. 'We'd have started off looking at this as an accident, you see,' Rogovoy had concluded, his meatloaf hands palm up. 'No unexpected prints; nothing odd, in terms of forensics. But he'd already called the district attorney's office and made a fuss. Personal friend, I gather. He's claiming that you had a motive – that the murder was planned as part of a theft.'

'Ridiculous. Why would I . . .?' She paused. It was plausible, just barely. 'Look,' she continued, 'I can see what this looks like. This woman – Melinda – and I, we're in the same field of research. And, yes, it does seem like she was ahead of me in terms of publishing.' Dulcie paused. It was hard to think with the pain. 'But, Detective Rogovoy, it doesn't make sense that I'd have threatened her. I wanted to meet with her.' She stopped, an idea surfacing. 'Rafe, the head tutor, he can vouch for me there. He knew I was trying to talk to her.'

'We are talking with him.' Rogovoy's mouth was set in a tight line. Dulcie didn't need him to explain: Rafe probably had. He'd been asked to leave Melinda alone. Told Lloyd about the threats, but she'd gone up to meet her anyway. 'But the bottom line is: this book she wrote is gone.'

'I don't have it.' She looked around. The officer who had escorted her in had taken her bag. 'I don't even know where my bag is.'

'We know it's not on you.' Rogovoy said. 'It's not anywhere.'

This wasn't making sense. 'I'm sure there are copies around. Her publisher probably has one.'

He shook his head. 'We're not finding any. Her adviser at Ellery has been out with mono, says she's been working independently for months but that this gal was old school. Typed everything, and true enough, her computer only had some notes she'd pulled from online sources. The dean says he got to read it. He had to, he says, before he approved her visit, but he gave his copy back to her. Her editor had seen the opening chapters; that's why he agreed to publish it, but she says this Ms Harquist was determined to finish it before letting anyone read the whole thing. She wanted to tie up some loose ends, she said. Bulletproof it.'

Dulcie winced at the metaphor. At least the visiting scholar hadn't been shot. 'And we know she had it with her?' Dulcie wasn't good at lying. She thought back to the pages she had read and immediately tried to clear her mind of them.

Rogovoy must have seen something in her face. He grunted. 'She did. A big manuscript, like typed pages, all clipped together.' He sighed. 'I'm sorry, Ms Schwartz. The tutor saw it when he showed her the suite, and the dean is insisting that she had it with her, too.'

'That doesn't mean I—' Those footsteps. Rafe had said the door was supposed to be locked. 'Detective, I heard someone on the stairs, before I went in. And the door wasn't latched.'

He shook his head again. 'We've checked the log at the main entry. There wasn't anyone in Dardley House after noon who wasn't supposed to be there. Nobody, except you.'

Dulcie had collapsed back into her seat, her head throbbing like a time bomb. She rubbed her forehead. 'Detective Rogovoy, do you think I could get some aspirin?'

'Sure.' He grunted as he stood up, and Dulcie had the sense that the day was wearing on him, as well. He also, she noticed, locked the door behind him as he left. It was that sound – the sliding click of the latch – that did her in. Folding her arms on the table, she put her face down in them and sobbed.

'Mr Grey,' she called out. 'Why is this happening? What's going on?' And she heard nothing. Nor did the pain cease. If anything it got sharper, causing her to gasp. 'What – why are you hurting me? Ow!' Her hand went to the back of her neck. That bite – it had to have drawn blood.

And that's when it hit her. 'Detective! Detective!' She pounded on the door. 'Can you hear me?'

She might as well already be in prison. The door was so thick, her fists only made a dull noise. The door stayed locked, no matter how she rattled it. And Rogovoy didn't return.

'Detective!' She was yelling now. 'I figured it out – it's the blood!'

SEVENTEEN

'I can't believe they held you.' Suze, Dulcie's former room-mate was pacing. 'They had no evidence, no cause. Nothing. No, I do believe it. I am simply appalled by their behavior.'

They were back at Dulcie's apartment. Dulcie had crashed on the sofa, where Esmé had found her and immediately claimed her lap. Chris – last night's squabble at least shelved if not forgotten – had gone into the kitchen to make tea, leaving the old friends to hash things out.

'They had a body on their hands.' Dulcie wasn't sure why she was making excuses exactly. Maybe because Rogovoy had seemed so supportive, getting her aspirin and nodding as she tried to explain. Sitting here now, with the cat curled up and purring on her lap, it all seemed very long ago. 'And, well, I was the one there.'

She stopped petting Esmé to look at her hands. She had long since washed them clean of Melinda's blood, but they still felt sticky to her – sticky and odd. Esmé reached up, pressing her wet nose against Dulcie's wrist, and Dulcie went back to stroking her. 'I can't believe I picked up the statue.'

'That was fine.' Suze stressed the word. 'That's a perfectly *normal* reaction of an innocent person who has walked into a room where a piece of statuary is lying on the floor. The police have to see that. I will make sure they see that.'

'What do you mean, you *will* make sure?' Dulcie stopped petting in mid-stroke, and Esmé grunted in protest.

Suze looked at her with eyes full of pity. 'Oh, Dulcie, I'm worried that this won't be the end of it.'

'But they let me go. They didn't charge me.' Rogovoy was on her side. She'd explained everything.

'That doesn't mean they've stopped looking for evidence.' Suze's voice was soft. 'They don't file charges until they have everything they need to make their case. They get one shot at you. They want it to be their best.'

Dulcie sat there, open-mouthed, unsure of what to say. Suze may have graduated from law school, but she still hadn't passed the bar. However, she was clerking for one of the bigger public-interest firms in Boston, and she had been the one to show up, insisting that Dulcie be released immediately, just as Dulcie was outlining her theory to the burly detective.

'I'm just glad Chris reached me.' Suze seemed to be running out of steam. Chris, meanwhile, had come in with a tray. Dulcie's excruciating headache had disappeared as soon as she had her breakthrough, but the smell of mint tea reminded her of how hungry she was.

'Do we have any cookies?' Chris nodded and went back to the kitchen. Dulcie sipped her tea; Chris had added honey, just as she liked it. 'I can't imagine they'll charge me,' she said to Suze. 'Because of the blood.'

'What?' Suze looked up, distracted, and Dulcie felt a twinge of guilt. Between work and studying for the bar, her old friend didn't need all this aggravation.

'The blood, that's what I was trying to tell Rogovoy.' Dulcie took another sip, her stomach beginning to growl. When Chris came back with the box of Chips Ahoy, she grabbed two. 'It was tacky when I picked up the Poe bust,' she said, speaking around the cookie. 'On the ground, around – well, on the ground, it was already turning dark.' She swallowed hard, her mouth suddenly dry. 'She – ah – she had been there a while.'

As logical as it all seemed, recounting the scene was still difficult. The tea helped, and she tried another bite of cookie, a smaller one this time. 'She must have been killed while I was teaching.'

'Humph.' Suze took a sip of her own tea and grimaced. Chris must have put honey in hers, too. 'I don't know, Dulce. That room was warm, what with the sunlight off the river. And there's enough wiggle room on the timing. No, I still want to make sure you have a good defense team. You are not – I repeat, not – talking to anyone about this without counsel present.'

Dulcie nodded and ate another cookie. Suze was right, but possibly a little overprotective. 'Maybe there won't be any more to it, Suze. Maybe they've realized it's an accident. A simple, horrible accident.' She thought of the bust. It was heavy. The house was old. 'There were people running up and down the stairs. Doors slamming. It could have fallen on its own. And Melinda could have been in the wrong place at the wrong time.'

'I don't know, Dulce.' Suze took another sip of the tea and put it down. 'And what about the manuscript?'

Dulcie shrugged. 'With all the people in and out, it got knocked off the shelf. I'm sure it fell behind something. It's got to turn up.'

Suze looked at her. 'I'm not saying that isn't what happened, but they are going to investigate. They have to. And that dean of yours? He's making quite the fuss.'

'He's no dean of mine.' Dulcie could almost laugh about it now. 'He's the one who got me locked out of the Mildon – who gave her access to the materials I need.'

'I wouldn't share that with anyone.' Suze kept her voice low, as if even the walls might have ears. She glanced at Chris, warning him as well. 'You don't want to suggest more motive.'

'I'm not. I mean, I didn't.' The pain might be gone, but the day was wearing on Dulcie. With the warm tea and cookies inside her, she felt like she could curl up on the sofa beside Esmé and go straight to sleep. 'And maybe I can help them. After all, I know something about her thesis. I might even know why someone would want to steal it.'

EIGHTEEN

Neither of them believed her. Esmé had jumped off her lap by the time Dulcie got done explaining. Even Chris, who had been the one to hold her all those nights when she had woken from the terrible nightmares, declined to comment when she finished and sat there, looking at her two dear friends, waiting for support.

It was Suze who finally broke the silence, sounding more like the lawyer she was becoming than the friend Dulcie had bonded with in sophomore year. 'It is an interesting theory,' she said, speaking slowly, as if to a child. 'The problem, of course, is proof.'

'We believe you,' Chris broke in with what Dulcie thought to be a suspect vigor. 'We do! Only, well, you can't really tell the dean – or the police – about your dreams.'

'It's not just my dreams,' Dulcie tried again. 'I believe the author was involved in something, something just like this.' She couldn't say murder, not yet. 'I think that's why she went underground. That's why one of her books hasn't been found, maybe wasn't published under her name. I think, maybe, she was accused, too. Accused of murder, and this lost book might hold the key.'

There, she'd said it. She looked at them, waiting for a reaction. They looked at her, but stayed silent, and Dulcie was struck by the sharp sense that this must be how Esmé often felt. Hadn't she been clear? What didn't they understand?

She tried again. 'If I could get back into the Mildon, I think I could get proof. I mean, the one page I got to read was quite graphic. And if Melinda had more – more proof – well, I'm sure that it would explain everything.' Even as she said it, she hesitated. The dream images of a body had become so real to her, in the wake of today's horror. But the missing book was fiction. A novel. Dulcie suspected that it was based on real life, but could she be sure? Maybe what Dulcie had been seeing at night was simply the author's imaginings. A scene from a particularly gruesome Gothic.

'At least, I'm pretty sure it would help.' Honesty compelled her to admit that much, but that was enough. 'I think.' Suze and Chris exchanged a glance. Chris reached out to put his hand on her knee. When he spoke, his voice was at its softest.

'Honey? We believe you; we do.' Beside him, Suze nodded vigorously. 'Only, you see, you don't yet have the proof in hand, and the way things are going, you may not get it anytime soon. So maybe you should just let it lie? Just be happy that the timing exonerates you – and let the police do their job?'

Suze opened her mouth, then shut it. Dulcie knew what she'd

been about to say, and ignored her, pointing out that she'd helped the cops before. And that if she was right about Melinda's missing manuscript and the clues it might hold, it could not only explain why she had been killed, but also settle a centuries-old case. It had been hard to think of her recurring dream, in the wake of what had happened in Dardley House, but she made herself do it – visualizing the candlelit room, the books. The blood. There were clues here too; there had to be. Something that connected with what Melinda had written; something that would explain the missing book by *The Ravages* author.

Unless everything she had dreamed was simply a made-up scene from a lost novel. Or, worse, the result of late-night pizza. Dulcie closed her eyes and sank back into the sofa, admitting defeat. If she couldn't convince these two – if she couldn't convince herself – what hope did she have?

The silence was broken by a soft thud. Esmé had jumped on to the sofa and set to work kneading Dulcie's leg. Without opening her eyes, she reached out to stroke the soft fur and was rewarded by a resounding purr. After several minutes of this, Suze finally cleared her throat.

'Well, I guess I should be going. I told Ariano I'd call him when I knew what was going on.'

'Oh, of course!' Dulcie could hear Chris get to his feet. 'We shouldn't have kept you. I can't thank you enough for getting her – for getting her out of there.'

'Thanks,' Dulcie murmured, the rhythmic pulse of the kitten's action lulling her into sleep. 'Really, Suze.'

'Don't mention it.' Suze leaned over and kissed Dulcie's cheek, and Dulcie managed a smile. She could hear Chris walking her out. Undoubtedly the two were making some kind of plans together to keep her out of trouble. They meant well, she knew, but she'd have to find a way around them. She might not be sure of anything, not yet, but she wasn't going to leave this alone – not when she, and her author, were both somehow implicated in a murder.

For now, though, she was more concerned with the little cat. Esmé had ceased her kneading and now lay sprawled across Dulcie's lap. She could feel the cat's breath on her hand as she inhaled and exhaled, the tone of her purr rising and falling.

She also felt the warm softness of the comforter Chris was pulling over her, tucking her in. Another kiss, this one lingering, and she was out.

NINETEEN

B *lood. There was so much blood. The precious ichor stained her still, mocking her attempts to cleanse herself. Her hands, no longer soft, no longer white, now held further defilement, the mark of mortality sunk into every crevice and joint. Her skirt, she had found, was stained with the taint of it, as dark as her own curls falling forward, as if to shield her from any inquisitive soul, heavy and stiff where she had kneeled, hoping. No, praying, to find her senses wrong. It was no use. The life essence that had drained from him lay still and cold, marring the red-gold of his hair. So, too, lay the young aristocrat – the man who had pursued her. The one who would have ruined her beyond that pallid infamy named by society. The one, she realized, her horror growing ever larger, whose power had increased, e'en as his lifeblood ebbed away. She could run no farther. He had her now.*

Dulcie woke with a start, disoriented and breathing hard. A soft 'mew' of annoyance beside her caught her attention and brought her back. She was not trapped in some grisly snare, entwined with the fate of a dead or dying man. She was lying on the sofa, with Esmé perched on the pillow behind her. She was home. She was safe.

Apologizing to the cat, Dulcie sat up and checked the clock. Almost nine, Sunday morning. Chris must still be at work, she realized. The vague memory of him tucking her in came back, and she smiled. The comforter really was quite cozy, a gift from Chris's mom and softer than the commune-made quilt Lucy had sent off with Dulcie when she'd come east. She drew the soft fluffiness around her, more for comfort than for warmth. The morning was already heating up, but for now the air was balmy

and gentle, like the memory of that kiss. Clearly, Chris had let
their quarrel go. It was the dream that wouldn't leave her alone.

Wandering into the kitchen, Dulcie put the kettle on. She would
need some sustenance if she was going to make sense of the
nightmare's latest iteration.

'Mrrrrup?' Esmé leaned against her shin.

'You too?' The feel of the little cat started the work the cocoa
would do, calming Dulcie. 'Hang on.'

Reaching into the cabinet, she found the bag of treats. She
and Chris had talked about this. Esmé didn't seem to be growing
any more. Or, to be specific, not growing in length or height. In
order to keep her at a healthy weight, they'd agreed that the
chewy fish bites were to be a once-a-week treat.

'Mrrrrow?'

Sometimes, Dulcie decided, a girl needed something beyond
the necessities.

Dulcie knelt and held out her hand. The rough warmth of the
cat's tongue made quick work of the fish-shaped treats, and Dulcie
was considering pouring out a few more when the kettle started
to whistle. Luckily, the hot cocoa was where she'd remembered
it, and even if it wasn't seasonally appropriate, she wanted some.
Soon she was seated at the kitchen table, Esmé bathing on the
place mat in front of her, as she waited for the drink to cool and
went over the horror of the dream.

One possibility, the one she liked least, was that the original
dream had been somehow prophetic – a preview of what
happened in Dardley House – and that now it simply lingered.
'Lucy would have a field day with that,' she told the cat. Esmé
didn't even look up. Unlike her mother, Dulcie didn't give
most psychic phenomenon much credence – nothing beyond
talking ghost cats, that is.

There was another possible linkage between yesterday's tragedy
and her nightmare. Perhaps, somehow, her anger had spurred the
dream. 'Is that possible?' She stirred her cocoa and sipped. Too
hot. 'No.' She shook her head. The nightmare started before she
had ever heard of Melinda Sloane Harquist.

She took another sip. Maybe her unconscious was merely
playing out her scholarly instincts. After all, in her dreams, she
now saw the victim looking like he did in that handwritten

fragment, as opposed to how he had been described in the printed page she had found. Was that significant? Did it relate, somehow, to a real crime that the author was describing? Or were her dream senses simply set to analyze any text, much as she did during her waking hours?

Dulcie looked around for a pen. When she didn't find one in the kitchen, she was neither surprised nor deterred. However, her desk was suspiciously free of any writing implements, too. As was Chris's. And, while she was looking, Esmé had made herself scarce.

'Esmé?' The little cat did not respond. At least she wasn't sleeping on the laptop again. 'Esmé, would you mind leaving me just one pen? Or a pencil?'

Dulcie wasn't expecting a response. Some crimes really were just what they seemed. But, perhaps to prove that clemency, if not reform, was always possible, a soft rattle broke the morning quiet.

'Esmé?' Dulcie got down on the floor to investigate – and found a beaten-up red ballpoint. Chewed-up, actually, she realized as she examined the mashed plastic casing. And not by the cat, either. Dulcie smiled to herself as she remembered chomping on the pen. She'd been grading papers – and trying to diet – and had bitten the end of the plastic pen down to the ink cartridge inside, rendering it unusable. She, not Esmé, had been the one to toss this particular writing implement against the wall.

'You're not off the hook for all the others, you know,' Dulcie called out. But although she waited, hoping for an answer, none came, and after a few moments fingering the useless pen, she reached a decision. 'I'm going out,' she said to the apparently empty room. All she was doing at home was spinning her wheels. She might never understand her recurring nightmare, but if she could answer just a few of the questions rattling around her brain, maybe she'd sleep better tonight.

Fifteen minutes later, she was on her way out. Esmé had appeared while she was dressing, attacking her sneaker lace as if it were the enemy and almost dissuading Dulcie from her plans.

'You're adorable, and you know it,' she said to the cat, gently removing claws from canvas. 'And I bet Chris told you to keep an eye on me. But really, you don't have to worry. I'm just going to the library.'

Esmé looked up at her person, her green eyes bright. 'I promise,' Dulcie said, as the black and white face tilted, the tufted ears alert. It must simply be the memories of the day before, she told herself as she grabbed her bag and headed toward the door. That and the cat wanting to play. Dulcie knew Esmé was a special cat; the young feline had proved it only yesterday. Still, there was no reason for her to look so worried about Dulcie. All she was going to do was some research.

TWENTY

'Oh, Ms Schwartz!' Thomas Griddlehaus was wringing his hands.

'Good morning to you, too, Mr Griddlehaus.' Dulcie had gone straight to the Mildon Collection upon arriving at Widener. With Melinda Sloane Harquist out of the picture, there was no reason for the collection to be on lockdown any longer, and the sight of the slight clerk, blinking behind his oversized glasses, was doing her more good than that cocoa.

'Ms Schwartz, you're not . . . We're closed.' He was biting his lip now, as well as wringing his small, pink hands.

'I thought on Sundays you opened at nine.' She looked around for the scheduled hours. 'I know it's early, but I couldn't sleep. I . . . You must have heard what happened.'

He blanched, and she immediately felt guilty. Thomas Griddlehaus was a sensitive soul. 'She was so young.' He was examining his hands. 'Just starting out.'

'Yes, she was.' Dulcie gave the clerk a moment to collect himself. 'And I am sorry. But since she won't be needing special access any more, maybe I can get some work done? Maybe you can let me in while you set up?' A small squeak alerted her. 'Wait, this isn't just that you haven't opened the Mildon yet, is it? This is something new?'

He nodded. 'I'm not supposed to know the details, but everyone is talking about it. All the library staff, at any rate. At first, as you know, we had been told that everything *she* had requested was on lockdown. Then, this morning, we got a text message that the Mildon itself was closed until further notice. The dean had the temerity to suggest that this wouldn't be a big deal, because today is Sunday. You would think a dean of *research* would know better.'

Dulcie shrugged. She had not had any opinion of the new dean before this week. The one she was garnering now didn't prompt her to jump to his defense.

Thomas Griddlehaus, perhaps emboldened by his confession, leaned in close again. 'You were there,' he said, his voice barely audible. 'When they came by to search her materials, they told me.'

She nodded, unwilling to elaborate.

'They told me you were questioned.'

Dulcie sighed. She wasn't going to be able to avoid this. 'I told the police everything I knew, which wasn't much. They don't know what happened, and I don't know either. It could have been an accident . . .' She heard her voice trail off and knew she hadn't made a convincing case. That's when it hit her. 'Wait, you said – you said she was young. Too young. You met her? You got to meet Melinda Harquist?'

He nodded and glanced up. Dulcie didn't think she was imagining the blush on his pale cheeks. 'She wasn't what I expected at all. Not after what I had heard, you know. She was, oh, younger. Prettier.'

So 'Mellie Heartless' had made another conquest. Dulcie waited, knowing the story would unfold.

'She came by, you know. Yesterday, late in the morning. Only hours before . . .'

He blinked, and she resisted the urge to take his hand. Then, although they were alone, Griddlehaus leaned in as if afraid of being overheard.

'She came here first, before she checked in,' he said, his voice so soft she could barely hear. 'She hadn't even dropped her bags off, so I put them under the counter. She only had an hour, she told me. Then she was due at Dardley House. But she wanted to come here as soon as possible. She wanted to see –' here he dropped his voice still further, and Dulcie had to lean in to hear him – 'the fragments.'

Dulcie closed her eyes, letting the weight of the clerk's words settle. 'And she had time to read through them?'

Griddlehaus shrugged. 'She didn't take long. She seemed quite pleased with herself. But, Ms Schwartz?' He looked up at her again, waiting.

'Yes?' Her own voice had gotten soft again.

'She didn't see any papers that you haven't studied already. But she seemed to feel like she'd found just what she was looking for. She even said something out loud. I believe she said, "Proof!"'

TWENTY-ONE

*S*he didn't see any papers that you haven't studied already. The clerk's words were ringing in Dulcie's ears as she made her way across the Yard. *She said, 'Proof!'*

The implications made her head spin, and she paused in her walk. Around her, the campus was waking up. A gathering of freshmen plowed right by her, discussing the wild party they had attended at Kirkland House the night before, and Dulcie stepped off the path into the dappled shade of an oak to think. Proof! Proof in the papers that Dulcie had already read.

No wonder Melinda was – had been – a rising star, and Dulcie was still at work. There was something in those boxes, something she had overlooked. The question was: what? What had Melinda seen? And what had Dulcie missed?

She started to walk again, a little aimlessly. The day was once again fair, more summer than fall, and she had a lot on her mind. Maybe walking would help spark an idea. Help her uncover what she had missed. But as she passed the grey stone administration building, she realized it was hopeless. Without access to the Mildon, all she had were her dreams.

If only she had noticed something.

Or – she stopped short – maybe she had. Maybe she had noticed something and simply not realized its importance. She might not have that excerpt – and, no, she couldn't keep blaming Chris for that – but she did have other notes. Before Thursday, before that one providential box of fragments, she'd had leads – inklings of what might be found. She'd made some notes to herself, then, she recalled, copied down with one of the Mildon-approved soft pencils. She remembered using a yellow legal pad – but not where she'd left it.

Standing in the shade of a towering oak, she searched her bag, hoping to see that pad. Hoping, if she did, that her notes wouldn't be completely illegible. If only she had transcribed them, Dulcie thought with regret, moving her laptop to peer behind it. Then again, if she had, maybe they'd be lost too.

So where had she left those first, rough notes? Not in her carrel in the stacks of Widener. As a senior grad student, she had a lovely quiet space, but the molded desk and bookshelf, while great for study, was open to passers-by – not the kind of place to leave notes, even illegible ones. Home? No, after the fire that had prompted her move, Dulcie had been cautious about taking work home – and shy about cluttering up the apartment she and Chris shared. Then she remembered. The pad was in her bottom desk drawer in the basement office she shared with Lloyd. At least, she was pretty sure it was.

It had to be. She began to walk again – toward Memorial Hall and her office. And there had to be something in those notes. Something she'd missed before. She sped up, eager to get to the office. Some phrase. A reference or a word. And if she, Dulcie, could find it, she could make the proof that Melinda hadn't had time to make.

'*Because she died, Dulcie.*' The voice stopped her in her tracks, and without thinking she turned around. A bright-eyed squirrel froze on the nearest tree, staring at her. '*Because she was killed.*'

'I didn't do it,' she addressed the air. 'It *might* have been an accident.' The squirrel began twitching his tail and chattering to warn his fellows there was a predator around. 'OK, Mr Grey. That was a cop-out, I know that. But would it be so bad if I profited from her discovery? I mean, I know her book will turn up, and it will probably still be published. But if she only just discovered the proof, she probably didn't get a chance to write it in.'

'*Are you sure, Dulcie?*' The voice was gentle, but stern. '*You're making assumptions here, connecting factors as you see them. There may be a different perspective . . .*'

The voice faded out, but Dulcie had taken the point. She didn't think Melinda would have had a chance to change anything. Maybe she just wanted that to be so, though. She thought back and it hit her: There had been notes on that manuscript, handwritten in the margins in a distinctive, slanted style. Melinda was still clearly working on her book. Griddlehaus had said she'd been there yesterday morning. The day she'd been killed. Maybe she had already amended her manuscript to reflect her discovery in the library. Maybe she had already added a final, finishing touch.

'No, I'm not assuming anything,' she admitted. 'I don't have enough information.' Suddenly all the drive drained out of her. If it weren't for that squirrel, she'd have slumped against the tree. Instead, she sank to the ground and sat, cross-legged in the damp grass. 'That's the problem, Mr Grey. I don't know what she knows, or what she was focusing on. That's why I was going to talk to her.'

'*I know, little one. I know you didn't mean her harm.*'

'Well, I was pretty angry,' Dulcie confessed. Already she was feeling a little better. 'And I did sneak in. I mean, the door was unlocked, but—'

'*You don't have to explain, Dulcie. You never have to explain yourself to me.*'

'Thank you, Mr Grey.' A thought rose in her mind, one she had put aside. 'Mr Grey, would you tell me something? I thought, well, I thought you might warn me that something like this was going to happen. That you might, I don't know, have let me know that someone was doing the same research I was. You know, give me a head's up.'

'*So you could do what, little one? So you could have concerned yourself with her progress, rather than continuing your own research?*'

Dulcie shrugged. 'I don't know – maybe.'

'*As if there is only one thesis to be written? Only a finite amount of research to be unearthed for publication?*'

'Well, not exactly.' There was an edge to the voice, the touch of claws in the velvet fur. Something she wasn't getting. 'But it seems like she and I were doing such similar work.'

'*And then, perhaps, it might have been your thesis that*

disappeared.' The voice was growing fainter now. *'And your blood staining that carpet . . .'*

So they were connected, and Mr Grey hadn't warned her in order to protect her. Dulcie felt warmed, as well as warned, by her spectral pet's concern. She also felt confused. What could be in that thesis that someone would kill for? No, the only answer would be to find out what it was that Melinda had discovered. Then she could decide what to do about it, what to do *with* it. Finding that clue was key.

TWENTY-TWO

As Dulcie made her way through the brick gate, her phone rang. She ignored it. It was too early to be Chris. While she hoped he'd stumbled home by now, Dulcie knew he'd be non-verbal till at least noon. Even Esmé seemed to know to let Chris sleep after his overnight shifts.

The phone rang again, but Dulcie just walked faster. She couldn't afford to lose her focus now. Ten past ten and the student body was beginning to wake. As she began to make her way through the throngs at the entrance to the freshman union, she paused. With her ID, she could run in and grab a coffee – or even another hot cocoa. That was one advantage of having an office in the basement of the cavernous brick building. Then again, she might run into one of the students from her section. No, better to postpone the caffeine and get to work.

This time, the card reader worked, and Dulcie clattered happily down the stairs. Despite the crowd above, the hall of offices appeared deserted. However, a pale rectangle of light showed that her own office door was ajar.

She hesitated. The new security gate was supposed to be a safeguard, but really, how safe was it? Anybody could be lurking. Waiting for her to come down that dark hall and into the tiny office. Dulcie stood and listened, her own breath loud in her ears. Was that low rumble coming from upstairs? The sound of a hundred hungry freshmen? Was it, perhaps, a purr?

A peal of laughter interrupted her speculation, a particular hoot that Dulcie knew well. Raleigh, Lloyd's girlfriend. For an elegant young woman – and the first-year grad student really was stunning, with a natural grace – Raleigh Hall had the most discordant laugh. Dulcie progressed toward the office with a light step. That laugh really was one of her favorite things about her former student.

'Hey, kids,' Dulcie called out as she pushed the door fully open. If she was hoping her announcement would give the couple time to recover from any potentially embarrassing scenarios, however, she needn't have. Lloyd was sitting at his desk, and Raleigh was standing by the bookshelf, her warm brown hair highlighted in the sun from their one high-set window. But although she was still grinning, tears of laughter showing in the corner of her eyes, Lloyd was not.

'Dulcie!' Dulcie couldn't tell if her office mate sounded surprised or relieved to see her. She looked to Raleigh, but the younger woman just shrugged and shook her head. 'You're . . . you're OK.'

'Of course I'm OK.' Dulcie put her bag down on her own desk. 'Wait,' she turned to Raleigh. 'You heard?'

'Lloyd told me – and that the police took you away.' Raleigh pulled up the office's one guest chair and sat facing Dulcie. 'We were afraid that you were somehow implicated. He told me about her book,' she said, lowering her voice. 'And how it might overlap with your thesis. But really . . . I mean, I haven't started writing my thesis yet, but, well, the suggestion that you'd hurt someone because of it seems a little extreme.'

'It's more than just the thesis,' Dulcie admitted and brought them up to speed. 'The fact that her manuscript is missing is actually in my favor, I guess. I mean, when the cops questioned me, they went through my bag. I don't know what they thought I would have done with it.'

'Thrown it out a window?' Lloyd suggested.

'That's actually a good idea. I wonder if the police checked.' Dulcie toyed with the idea of calling Detective Rogovoy, then remembered her missed phone call. 'Excuse me.' Digging into her bag, she found her phone and clicked to see the origin of the last call: University Hall, home to most of the academic offices.

Almost by reflex, she turned it off, shoving the small device back in her bag.

'Bad news?' Raleigh looked concerned.

'Your mom?' Lloyd knew something of Dulcie's family life.

'The dean,' Dulcie confessed. 'I just don't want to talk to him right now.' Her friends looked at each other then back at her. She hadn't told them that Dean Haitner had wanted the police to press charges. 'I found out something about Melinda's research,' she said instead. It was true. 'Something she said to a clerk at the Mildon, and, well, I just wanted to get on it, you know?'

'So you came here to work?' Raleigh asked. Dulcie nodded and waited. Raleigh wasn't one to repeat the obvious. 'Well, maybe you didn't.'

Lloyd and Dulcie both turned to her.

'Maybe you left the Mildon but stayed in the stacks. In the library, your phone would have been turned off. You might be there all day.'

It was Lloyd's turn to smile. 'And we didn't see you. You were never here, and we'll swear to it. To anyone but Chris, that is.'

'Thanks, you two.' She smiled and reached for the drawer. 'I'll just grab my notes and be out of here.' She opened the drawer and looked down into a mess. That wasn't so odd. Dulcie knew that her habit of pulling the bottom drawer out to use as a foot rest meant that a lot of stray bits of paper – anything that fell off her desk, really – ended up in there. Even at her best, in the apartment with Chris, for example, she tended toward clutter. 'Creative chaos,' Lucy called it, largely, her daughter suspected, because she was the worst offender of all. And Dulcie knew that with two people, sometimes three, in a small space, things got knocked around.

Still, she reached in and pulled out her paper-clip holder with a slightly confused air.

'Has anyone been in here?' She replaced the black plastic cube in its usual spot on the desk corner. 'Did the police search my desk or something?'

'No, why?' Lloyd looked worried now, his brow bunched into premature wrinkles. 'Is something missing?'

'I'm not sure.' Dulcie dug down a bit, pulling out a loyalty

card for Lala's that she'd been sure had been in her purse. And
another, for the coffee shop by her old apartment. Why would
that be on the top of the drawer? Just as she was beginning to
panic, though, she saw it. A yellow pad, the space between the
green lines filled with slightly smudged hieroglyphics.

'Never mind, I've got it.' She sat up, holding her prize. 'I
guess my own mess is getting to me. And I should get to work.'

TWENTY-THREE

'I may be messy,' Dulcie said to herself as she unpacked her
bag. 'But I am not *sloppy*.'

It was with a great sense of relief that Dulcie unloaded
her bag on to the molded desk top of her library carrel. Three
floors down in the Widener stacks, with its strangely plastic
surface and uncomfortable chair, this little study nook was known
territory. Her space, she thought as she smoothed out the pads.
Her bag, *her* notes, *her* carrel – every iteration of the possessive
gave her a little sense of herself back. 'It's not that I'm a control
freak,' Dulcie explained to her pencil, as she lined it up next to
the new rollerball pen she'd splurged on only a week before. 'It's
just that I work better when I feel grounded.'

As she settled into that strangely formed chair, Dulcie waited
for the slap. She knew she was stretching the truth a bit. However,
when no swipe came – no hint of claws – she thought maybe her
exaggeration had been forgiven. Besides, a cat should understand:
after the last few days, maybe she was allowed to feel a little
territorial.

'Is that it, Mr Grey?' She looked up over the edge of her
carrel, but nothing appeared. 'Or maybe it's that I'm finally
getting back to my thesis?' The low whirring of the venting
system seemed to grow a little louder, almost purr-like, and so
she got to work.

The first thing, Dulcie decided, opening her laptop, was to
transcribe these notes. She'd made them a week or so earlier, after
finding that printed page. She'd recognized the style right away.

Known it for the missing work, but at the time she'd only filed the notes, knowing that the prize – something with attribution or written in the author's own hand – was still ahead.

Now, looking at her own cramped handwriting and the soft lead of the pencil, she knew she'd be lucky to get through half of these. 'Murder must oil,' she read. '*Be* oiled?' She squinted at the line, which had been made even more incomprehensible by the smudging of the lead. 'Most foul,' she decided finally. It wasn't what she remembered, but it was the only sensible possibility.

'Ded head?' She'd underlined this. 'Like, the Grateful Dead?' The paper didn't respond, and Dulcie realized she was muttering. Thoughts of the hippy demigods had Dulcie thinking of her mother. Lucy had done her best, Dulcie knew. Essentially a single mother, once Dulcie's father had taken off on his 'spirit quest', Lucy had tried to reconcile her own spiritual needs with the practicalities of raising a growing child. She'd made a home for them, of sorts, in the commune, and although she never seemed to understand her daughter's intellectual curiosity, she hadn't tried to stem it either. Instead, she'd passed along the small library she had somehow retained from her own, more staid upbringing – most notably a beaten-up Riverside Shakespeare. And she'd gotten Dulcie a library card for whenever one of their small group went into town.

The only thing she had been adamant about was Dulcie's preference for using her right hand. 'You can't be my daughter and be so left-brained,' Lucy had scolded more than once. 'You have the maven's blood in you. It's just not possible.'

Try as she might, however, from the first days of non-petroleum-byproduct based crumbly crayons onward, Dulcie simply couldn't form the shapes she wanted unless she used her right hand. And now, she thought as she perused another incomprehensible line, she clearly didn't do much better with her preferred hand, either.

Lucy and her opinions. Sometimes, Dulcie realized, her mother seemed determined to change reality simply by force of will. Like her refusal to see that Dulcie's hair was, essentially, brown. Yes, it turned coppery in summer, sunlight bringing out the red highlights. It would never, however, be the brilliant red-gold of Lucy's own hair, a color she said had passed straight through the maternal line ever since, well, the days of the goddess, if Lucy were to be believed.

'Maybe that's why I dream of the author as a brunette,' Dulcie thought to herself. 'And the victim as – ah! A redhead!' That was the detail that had been changed before the book's publication. *'Those red-gold locks, besmirch'd by life's gore.'* She struggled to recall the rest. *'Drenched in life's ichor, he lay broken on the rug . . .'*

But she had only found the manuscript on Saturday, and the victim in the typeset scene wasn't a redhead – his hair was described as black as a raven's wing, as she recalled. So why in her dream, that recurring nightmare, did the victim always have red hair? Long before she had read the handwritten fragment, Dulcie had 'seen' her author writing that scene – coming up with a gory description about blood darkening in red-gold hair.

Sometimes, Dulcie thought, our subconscious can be so obvious. Granted, she didn't know the full story, but she suspected that she herself had made the switch, maybe because of some lingering anger toward Lucy – and all the grief she had given her only child. Well, a nightmare image was a harmless outlet for emotions, Dulcie decided. In truth, her mother had done her best, and for someone who was so intent on shedding her past life, it was really rather touching that she had tried to will her genetic inheritance on her daughter.

There was more though – all this talk about the maternal line had obscured the obvious. The victim wasn't even a woman.

This was interesting for several reasons, and Dulcie started flipping through pages to find more. In *The Ravages*, male characters had been largely peripheral. There'd been the standard mad monk, as well as an avaricious nobleman and a young knight, who had been pure at heart and, honestly, a bit of a milksop in Dulcie's reckoning. But the main drama had been between two women. Hermetria and Demetria had been cooped up together in Hermetria's ruined castle. Their dialogues, which went on for pages, had basically outlined the arguments for and against women's rights as they stood in the late 1700s.

Had the author started writing from a male perspective? No, Dulcie thought back. There was nothing to indicate that the point of view of the scene was from a man. She looked through her pages, unable to believe she hadn't made a note of this. She was sure – almost sure – that in the nightmare text, the one she could see over the author's shoulder, the onlooker had been a woman. Was there something about '*skirts edged in blood, darken'ng the very lace*'?

Yes, she found it. '*I stepped back with a gasp, my skirts already edged in blood . . .*' Then more about the blood, about how the color changed. It was almost as if the narrator had watched the man die.

A wave of dizziness swept over Dulcie. This was a little too real, a little too reminiscent of the scene she had walked in on yesterday. She lowered her head to the plastic desktop. That spoke well of her author, she told herself. That woman could sure write a murder scene. It was almost as if she had been there herself.

Had she?

'Excuse me.' A voice broke into her thoughts. 'Are you OK?'

'What?' Dulcie hadn't realized her eyes were closed, but she sat up and smiled automatically. The woman in front of her was familiar. She definitely looked concerned, and Dulcie struggled to place her. Dark eyes, chocolate skin – for some reason, she thought of Chris. 'Darlene!' She smiled in earnest now. 'I'm Dulcie, Chris Sorenson's girlfriend?'

'Oh, yeah.' The girl leaned on the edge of the cubicle. 'I think we met at the open house?' Dulcie nodded: The computer science open house was a new idea and a good one, giving some of the university's most isolated students a chance to mingle with their colleagues' non-applied science friends. She and Darlene hadn't met that night, but it was a convenient excuse. Dulcie wouldn't have to explain that she'd witnessed the fight with Rafe. Which, all things considered, was just as well.

'What brings you to the bowels of the beast?' Dulcie asked. 'I don't think Chris has ever been down here.'

'Oh, it's for Rafe.' She ducked her head, her natural color insufficient to hide the blush that crept up into her cheeks. 'My boyfriend.'

'He's exiled you to the depths?' As soon as the words were out of her mouth, Dulcie wished them back. That argument had sounded serious, and Dulcie had only been guessing that they'd made up.

Darlene, however, was smiling. 'Nah, I offered to help out. He's working on a paper. Something that could be really big, but, well, he's been tied up. There's been a lot of stuff going on.'

'I know.' Dulcie stopped her with a raised hand. 'I was there.' Better to be honest than for this young woman, Chris's colleague, to think she'd been hiding something.

'You were?' Darlene leaned in. 'I hear it was pretty horrible.'

Dulcie nodded, a lump rising in her throat. 'It was.' She swallowed hard. 'Have there been –' she paused, unsure of how to phrase her question – 'any developments?'

Darlene smiled. 'Just now. And it's good news!' She was smiling broadly, and Dulcie felt the relief wash over her. It had been an accident, just as she'd thought. A tragic case of unstable statuary.

But Darlene was still talking. 'They found a page,' she said, and although for a moment, Dulcie wondered if she'd wandered into some Elizabethan farce, she quickly realized the other student had misunderstood her – and vice versa. 'You know,' Darlene was blinking at her. 'A page of the stolen manuscript?'

'Ah.' Dulcie digested this. 'So they're definitely saying it was stolen now?'

Darlene shrugged. 'I gather that's what they're thinking. It was stuck in a rain gutter. The latest theory, at least according to Rafe, is that whoever killed her threw the manuscript out the window to retrieve later. Only a page got ripped off on those old slates. The police are keeping Rafe busy, going through everything that shows who might have been there that day. He's not getting any of his own work done at all.'

It all seemed extremely curious to Dulcie. Chris was fond of telling her that nobody knew what was going on in a relationship besides the people in it. Still, having your girlfriend do your research was iffy at best. 'So, you're helping him?' It was a leading question. She knew it, and mentally she apologized to Chris.

The other girl nodded eagerly. 'I feel like I'm on a treasure hunt. I mean, I never get to come in here.'

'It is pretty cool.' Dulcie felt herself warming to the girl.

Maybe they should all go out sometime. That is, if she and Chris weren't covering each other's shifts. 'What's Rafe working on, anyway?'

Darlene looked around. It was such a stagey move, Dulcie almost laughed. Then she realized the other student was serious. 'I'm not supposed to talk about it.'

'Fair enough.' Dulcie felt an itching in her hands, almost a prickling. Claws, it had to be. Both Chris and Mr Grey would want her to mind her own business. 'I won't ask.'

But she wasn't imagining it. She couldn't be. The way the other woman leaned against the cubicle wall, she clearly wanted to talk. To tell someone. Dulcie was, after all, only human. With a silent apology to both her boyfriend and her guardian feline, she took the bait. 'Unless you want to tell me?'

She was right. Darlene's face lit up in a smile, and she crouched down to be closer to the seated Dulcie. 'He's found something,' she said in a dramatic whisper. 'It has to do with attribution.'

'Attribution?' Dulcie heard herself asking. 'Was the work . . . misattributed?'

'Something like that,' the other girl said. 'It was marked as anonymous. Author unknown. But Rafe, he's pretty sure he has proof that somebody famous wrote it.'

Dulcie could feel her heart pound. This was too close to be coincidence. She had to keep going. 'And you're down here, on C level. So it's got to be pre nineteenth-century British or American?'

The other woman shrugged. 'Yeah, kinda. But it's no good. I'm helpless down here. I can't find anything he asked me about.'

How could she resist? 'Do you want some help?'

Darlene shook her head. 'He'd figure out that I told someone. I'm probably in the wrong place anyway. Thanks, though!'

Dulcie felt like a heel. She smiled up at the other woman as she stood and walked away. She hadn't offered to be helpful. She had offered because only too late had she remembered what Rafe's specialty was and why he had been one of the creators of the English 10 syllabus. For so long, Dulcie had thought of the ocean as a great divide. Now, however, it seemed eminently cross-able. Rafe Hutchins had published his thesis on serialized fiction in post-colonial America. The book he was looking at could easily be the one Dulcie was looking for, too.

She had to find it – or at least find the proof that it existed. If Melinda had uncovered something . . .

Dulcie stopped, caught up short in the middle of her thought. Rafe was busy. He'd sent his unassuming girlfriend off to do his errands. If that was all that had happened, Dulcie would be happy. She'd even be content to battle with him over that lost work.

Darlene had looked so engaged, she'd undoubtedly said more than she should. Clearly, it hadn't occurred to Rafe's girlfriend that her tutor boyfriend might be busy with something other than helping the police voluntarily or overseeing the cleaning up of the visiting scholar's suite. That the police might be holding her boyfriend for any other reason. Or that he might have sent her off to research something that he had read in that manuscript, before he tossed it off the roof.

TWENTY-FOUR

'Dulcie, I love you, but don't you think you're grasping at straws?' Driven by hunger, as well as the need to confer with Chris, Dulcie had ducked back out of the library and called her beau. She hadn't woken him, at least that's what he said, and so, standing in the shelter of the Yard's brick wall, she laid out her theory. 'I mean, do you really think Rafe killed Melinda Harquist for her manuscript?'

'I don't understand why *anyone* would. But if someone did, then why not him?' Leaning in toward the red brick, she lowered her voice as she outlined her reasoning. 'The senior tutor position goes with the postdoc, but it's not tenured. He's got to find something. And this could be big. Could be a breakthrough!'

The silence on the other end of the line could have been disheartening. Dulcie, however, knew that Chris was eating. Eating and thinking. 'I don't know, Dulce.' She could hear him crunching. 'Along those lines, people could say you did it.'

'That's just it! People *have* been saying that, Chris. Only I know I didn't – and I think the cops believe me. Besides, the evidence shows that she'd been dead at least a little while before I got there. And who else would have done it?'

'I don't know.' More crunching. 'Do we even know that it was murder?'

'That's what Darlene said.' As she named the senior tutor's girlfriend, Dulcie realized that she hadn't told Chris the most important part. She filled him in on the argument she had witnessed. 'Something was going on. I'm sure of it. Darlene was jealous. Why would she have been jealous unless Rafe had been spending time with Melinda? Talking with her? Maybe even . . .' Dulcie paused as a couple passed by and turned to stare. In her excitement, she'd been talking louder and louder. Now she dropped her voice to a near whisper. 'Maybe he was arguing with her. Maybe she caught him reading her manuscript. Maybe that's what they fought about.'

'Dulcie, I know you've had a really rough couple of days . . .' He paused and she could hear liquid – coffee – pouring. 'But are you sure you're reading all this correctly?'

Dulcie paused before answering. Mr Grey had hinted at something similar – only he'd been talking about the manuscript. 'I'm not sure of the details, Chris,' she acknowledged finally. 'I do know there's something going on. For starters, the original manuscript of that book – the lost novel – it's here. It's in the Mildon, at least enough of it to make an identification, and I think we were both on its trail, too.' She stopped. Chris was her boyfriend. She trusted him, and he knew about her nightmares. Should she tell him about the other connection – between the dream scenario and what she had stumbled upon? No, until she could sort out fact from fiction, she would leave it at that. She already had enough of a motive. 'A newly discovered novel would be a prize worth, well, fighting for if not . . . Anyway, I think I can get to the bottom of all of this.'

'If anyone can, Dulcie,' he slurped, 'it's you.'

Dulcie was so happy, she wasn't even tempted to correct her boyfriend's tortured phrasing, and instead went off in search of her own lunch.

The counter at Lala's was crowded, and as she waited for someone to finish, Dulcie scanned the crowd. Between word of mouth and the succulent aroma of spice that escaped whenever the door opened, it didn't take long before the eatery made devotees of each new class of students. Sure enough, two familiar faces were sharing a table over in the back. Thalia and – could it be? – the handsome Andrew. Brains and beauty. And both from her English 10 section. Dulcie ducked her head and considered leaving – but only briefly.

'Dulcie!' It was Lala herself. The owner-chef had emerged from the kitchen and was gesturing with both hands as if landing a plane. A big woman, with heavy black brows that could have made her look threatening were it not for her proportionately sized smile, she nodded as she gestured, reassuring Dulcie of her intentions. Drawn as much by that nod as by those large hands, Dulcie made her way over through the frankly envious crowd. 'You sit.'

A stool suddenly appeared, brought out by one of the many similarly beetle-browed young men – sons, nephews, perhaps – who staffed Lala's kitchen. A damp white rag swept over it once and the young man was gone, back into the kitchen. Lala pointed. Dulcie sat.

'You need to eat something.' Coming from Lala like that, the pronouncement was more command than question, but Dulcie nodded anyway as the big woman turned and disappeared back into the kitchen. She had been a regular long enough to have a passing acquaintance with the proprietress. She had never merited such special treatment, though. It was, she thought as she waited for Lala to return, a little intimidating.

Although she could feel eyes on her, Dulcie refused to turn around. Instead, she buried her face in the menu that she already knew by heart. It was yanked from her hands a moment later, as a bowl of steaming, mud-colored liquid was shoved before her.

'Lentil soup.' Dulcie was about to protest. Lala knew her order: the three-bean burger special, with lots of hot sauce. But one look at those dark eyes stopped her, and instead she reached meekly for a spoon.

'Oh, good.' Despite its unprepossessing color, the soup was thick and rich, reminding Dulcie that she hadn't eaten a real meal since yesterday's breakfast. 'Thank you,' she said, looking up. Lala, however, had disappeared.

'Now you can have.' As soon as she'd put the spoon down, a plate appeared, this time with the familiar burger. 'Here.' Lala turned to retrieve a squeeze bottle of sauce from the station behind her.

'Wait!' Dulcie called before her benefactor could disappear again. 'Thank you, Lala. Really. But why are you feeding me like this?'

One eyebrow rose in a question.

'I mean, it's fantastic. You know I love your cooking.'

A nod. Dulcie had passed muster. 'Working here, I hear things.' Lala crossed her heavy arms across her substantial bust. 'I know you are in trouble.'

'What did you hear?' Dulcie started to ask, as a commotion broke out in the kitchen. Lala spun around and slammed through the door, cutting off the sight of what looked like shooting flames. When no screams issued forth, Dulcie picked up the burger. Lala would come back in her own time. There was no point in letting her efforts get cold. She took a bite, closing her eyes to fully savor the juice and spice.

'Wow, I didn't know you were such a big shot.'

Dulcie turned, suddenly aware of the hot sauce in the corners of her mouth. Andrew Geisner stood behind her stool. Thalia was nowhere to be seen.

'I'm not,' she managed to say, mouth still full. 'Bad day.' She swallowed and desperately stretched for the napkin dispenser. 'Sorry.'

'No problem.' With his longer grasp, he reached over her, grabbing a handful of paper napkins to hand her. 'I heard what happened.'

She swabbed her face. 'Is everyone talking about it?' She looked around again for Thalia. Maybe it had been a working lunch.

He was shaking his head, his sun-bleached hair falling across his face. 'I don't think so. Not yet. I think they're trying to keep it quiet. Bad publicity for the visiting scholar program.'

She nodded and reached for the water. 'To say the least. But you heard?'

'I have a work-study job in the dean's office.' He shrugged, surfer-cool. 'Keeps me busy.'

'I bet.' She didn't want to ask a student to leak information. It was wrong on so many levels. Still, he had brought it up. 'Dean Haitner?'

He nodded. 'They're going nuts. As you can imagine. I mean, on top of the whole thing being horrible, you know the dean had personally invited her.'

'I know they were close.' She remembered him yelling, his bereaved cries.

Andrew seemed less impressed. 'She wrote him last spring, and they've been talking a lot,' he said. 'He gets enthusiastic.' He shrugged, his usual blasé self, dismissing the topic, and then leaned in close. 'You know about the manuscript?'

'I heard about it.' Andrew's easy-going charm invited confidences, but with an effort, she stopped herself from saying more.

'The dean is convinced that it's the key.' His eyes were blue. Very blue. 'He thinks that someone in the university didn't want her to publish it.'

A few hours before, Dulcie would have dismissed that idea as mad. Then again, a few hours before, Dulcie had not thought of Rafe Hutchins as another rival. She swallowed. 'Does he have any idea who?'

Another shrug. 'He seems to have some ideas. All I know is that he was saying something about how the chronology is wrong, that the cops are missing the point. Hey, is that your phone?'

Dulcie looked over at her bag, which was buzzing. 'Yeah, I've been ignoring it while I eat.' The phone vibrated again, as if to show up her white lie, and her messenger bag trembled like a scared animal.

'It might be the dean.' Andrew nodded toward it. 'I should warn you, your name came up.'

'Great.' She heard the sinking sound of her own voice and smiled to make up for it. 'Sorry, it's been rough, and I did just want to have an uninterrupted lunch.'

'Finish your burger then.' Andrew stepped back. 'Sorry to be a bother.'

'You didn't—' Too late. With a nod, he'd turned and his long legs had already taken him out the door. To make matters worse, Lala was in the kitchen doorway, arms crossed, staring at Dulcie.

'He's a student of mine,' Dulcie said. She knew how Lala felt about Chris, and that the chef had appointed herself the custodian of Dulcie's affairs. 'From one of my sections. Honest.'

Lala's glare moved from Dulcie's face down to her plate. In response, Dulcie hefted the big burger. It had cooled, and the spicy drippings were beginning to separate on the plate. Under that fearsome scowl, however, Dulcie didn't dare complain. She took a bite, and then another. Only when the burger was completely done did Lala nod once, sternly, and turn back into the kitchen.

Dulcie grabbed another half dozen napkins on her way out the door, her impromptu seat having already been snagged by a hungry diner. Only then did she dig around in her bag, looking for the now-silent phone.

Three new messages. Great. If she were lucky, they'd be from Chris, she told herself. The first call was the one she had ducked in her office, from University Hall, and she skipped the message. Her eyes lit up when she saw the next number – home – and she hit the key for playback.

'Hey, Dulce,' Chris said on the recording, 'just me again. Thought you'd still be at lunch. Well, Esmé told me you'd be hiding out in the library today. She said that was the place for you to be. Give me a ring though, OK? You've gotten some calls I think maybe you would want to answer. Love you.'

Esmé had told him? Dulcie shook her head. Chris had a dry sense of humor and from a message she couldn't tell if he was joking or not. Maybe the kitten had picked up her intentions. Then again, maybe the kitten had thought she ought to stay in the library all day. Easy for a house cat to say, thought Dulcie. Esmé had a bowl of dry food to dip into whenever she felt the slightest hunger pang.

She was about to move on to the next message when another interpretation hit her. The library was the place she was supposed to be. Maybe Dulcie was supposed to run into Darlene. Maybe she was also supposed to be following up on the other girl's search, uncovering the lost link to the unknown author.

No, it was bad enough that she'd peeked at Melinda's manuscript. Bad enough that she was using what Griddlehaus had told her, trying to retrace the dead woman's footsteps. Coercing information from a colleague's girlfriend was beyond the pale. Dulcie didn't need Lucy with her Wiccan 'rule of three' to tell her that would be worse than dishonest. It would be unethical on several levels. No, if she was supposed to be in the library, it was because she was supposed to be doing her own work.

She hiked her bag up on her shoulder and looked across Mass Ave. The back of the library loomed, a solid beacon in a shifting world. Melinda, the dean . . . she was sorely tempted to turn the phone back off and cross over to the cell-free zone. Who had been ringing her? The dean?

As if on cue, her phone buzzed again.

'Hello?' It was hard to hear on the crowded sidewalk, so with a twinge of regret she turned away from the library, leaning up against a wall. 'Is anybody there?'

'I *said* I've been trying to reach you!' Whoever it was, wasn't happy.

'I'm sorry.' She couldn't place the voice. 'May I help you?'

'Well, yes!' The voice took on a peevish quality she recognized. 'We're waiting for you now.'

'Mr Thorpe?' She glanced down at the phone display. University Hall? 'You're with Dean Haitner,' she realized suddenly. 'I'm sorry, I only now saw that you'd called. I'll be there in five minutes.'

So much for her dream of getting back to work. At least she'd gotten to eat, thanks to Lala's stern generosity. She looked up now, through the diner window, and saw the big woman pointing at something – a dirty table, an empty hot sauce bottle – as she gave commands. The woman ran a tight ship, and she clearly knew more than she let on. At her gesture, a busboy had gone scrambling.

Dulcie smiled at the sight. As if she could sense that smile, Lala turned, and their eyes met. For a moment, though, Dulcie had the weird sensation that the eyes looking into hers weren't Lala's. Weren't human at all, and instead featured slit irises set deep in glowing green.

'Watch it!' The woman who knocked into her barked at Dulcie as if it had been her fault, then turned away, cell phone plastered to her ear. Dulcie looked up, but the spell was broken. Lala was just a big woman running a small business. And Dulcie was late to a meeting.

She looked down at her own phone. Clearly, it was too crowded out here for calls. Still, the voicemail was blinking at her. Three calls, and she'd only listened to that one message from Chris. Watching the traffic carefully, Dulcie waited for her moment to cross and, as she did, she hit 'play'.

The third message began. 'Ms Schwartz? This is Detective Rogovoy. We are going to need you to come in and answer some more questions. As soon as possible, please.' He repeated a number she knew too well.

With a sigh of resignation, she hit 'play all'. That first call had been from the University Hall number. The voice, however, belonged to her adviser, Martin Thorpe. 'Ms Schwartz? We need to talk. It's urgent, very urgent. There's been a matter – an accusation. I'm sure it's nothing, and this can all be easily cleared up. But you need to come in. Dean Haitner is looking for you. We both are. He has some questions about the research you've been doing, about your most recent article. He says there are some issues surrounding it. Issues of academic ethics, of the most dire kind.'

TWENTY-FIVE

It was just as she'd feared. Dulcie trotted through the Yard with her head down, thinking. She should never have tried to find out what Melinda was working on. Should not have gone down to the Mildon this morning, and certainly should not have tried to meet with the visiting scholar before her talk.

She'd have to explain that she hadn't been trying to steal the dead scholar's research. Instead of trying to hitch a ride, she had simply been driving along a parallel path. Of course, she had wanted to know what Melinda had uncovered – but more so that she could stay out of her way, find her own area to focus on. After all, until, well, until her unfortunate end, it was clear that Melinda would publish before Dulcie would. And once her book was out, it wasn't like Dulcie could steal her research.

Maybe it wasn't about Melinda, Dulcie thought as she

approached the administration building. Climbing those white
marble stairs had never seemed so hard before, and she paused
for a breath before pulling open the heavy outer door. It was a
good thing she hadn't pressed Darlene any more on Rafe's
paper, she thought with relief. The respite was short-lived, new
doubts appearing with each step along the carpeted hall. The
call – that first one – had come in before she'd seen Darlene,
but maybe it didn't matter. Maybe Rafe had told some story
about her just to get her out of the way, knowing they were
going to be competitors.

She had arrived at the dean's office and stood facing the oversized door, struck motionless by a sudden revelation. Rafe
wouldn't run to the dean to get the edge on research. No student
would. Unless, of course, he – or she – had something bigger to
hide. Something like murder.

'Ms Schwartz! There you are.' Before Dulcie had time to
follow through on her own thought, she was facing her adviser.
Mr Thorpe had opened the door in front of her, and she found
herself staring at the slight, balding man as if she'd never seen
him before. Then the moment passed, and Dulcie found herself
smiling. For all his nervous tics, Thorpe wasn't a bad guy.

Her adviser didn't smile back, though. Instead, after
ascertaining that the person at the door was indeed his student,
he lowered his eyes. Ducking his head down meant he gave
Dulcie a better view of his shiny and somewhat dented pate.
It wasn't that which worried her, however. It was the fact that
he wouldn't meet her eyes. As if her glance could convey some
contagion, she thought following him into the large and sunlit
room. Or, she amended the image, as if she had already been
tried and condemned.

She stepped into the room, wondering why she suddenly
felt so trapped. It couldn't just be Thorpe. She was used to
him ducking his head. He didn't even like taking responsibility
for her progress reports. Then it hit her. Her feet had sunk into
a deep blue pile of the carpet, silencing even the soft slap of
her sneakers. The high windows that captured the afternoon
sun were covered with a gauzy curtain, giving the warm light
a diffuse look. The room was as hushed as some kind of divine
anteroom. Instead of feeling elegant, the overall effect was,

well, spooky. The kind of muffled chamber her heroine would
have made into the torture room of a depraved lordling. The
place where bones were kept.

This was ridiculous. Yesterday's events were getting to her.
She turned toward her adviser, determined to break the silence.

'So, Mr Thorpe, would you tell me what all this is about? I've
been going through my notes, seeing what I have there and if I
can start another chapter of my dissertation. Until I can get back
into the Mildon—'

'I don't think you'll be going back to the Mildon anytime soon.'
Dean Haitner had entered the room by a smaller side door, and
now closed it behind himself with a small click. He was a short
man despite his girth, Dulcie noted, but he managed a swagger
as he crossed the thick carpet and took his place behind a large
wood desk. 'I don't think you'll have to worry about your
dissertation either.'

'Mr Thorpe?' Dulcie turned to her adviser. He was, after all,
supposed to be her ally.

The tutor muttered something, staring intently into the carpet.

'Ms Schwartz, you will need to answer these charges directly.'
Dulcie looked up. From the scowl on his face, the dean had not
appreciated her turning toward her tutor. 'And none of your
so-called friends are going to be able to help you this time.'

This time? Dulcie tried to rally her thoughts. Of course her
friends had come to her aid before, as she had to theirs. 'Sir?'
It was all she could manage.

'I know you've managed to charm the university police. God
knows how, or what wiles you've employed.' The way he said
it made Dulcie feel dirty. Even more so when she realized he
was talking about Detective Rogovoy. 'They seem to hold you
above blame.'

'Sir? If you're talking about the accident – the death – about
Melinda Harquist, sir, I believe that's all been cleared up.' She
didn't know how to phrase it, but surely there was something
official – maybe a coroner's report – by now. 'They saw how I
couldn't have been the one . . .' He had to have heard.

But he didn't seem to. 'Huh.' He threw his well-coiffed head
back with a derisive snort. 'Yes, I know the investigation has
moved on, for now. I wouldn't be surprised if that were to change,

however. I have it on good authority that the investigators are looking at the missing thesis. And those of us here on the academic side of university life can clearly see who would stand to benefit if that manuscript were never found.'

'But, no . . .' All of Dulcie's prepared speeches about parallel tracks and which train would be first into the station faded away, leaving her with the most basic truth. 'I knew she and I were writing about the same author. But I didn't take her thesis. I wouldn't have.'

'That,' said the dean, suddenly looking down at his desk, 'is a police matter. For the police to decide.' He brushed several papers aside, then selected one, which he pulled out to look at. 'Nor do I particularly care what you may have done with the missing thesis. No, my concern is with issues within my authority as the dean of research for the university.'

He scribbled on a paper and held it out. Thorpe, head still bowed, came forward as if be prearrangement, and took it. Nervously licking his lips, he walked over to Dulcie. She watched as he lifted the paper toward her. He didn't say anything as she took it. Across the top, she read the line: NOTICE OF ACADEMIC PROBATION.

'The police will deal with criminal matters. That's their job; that's what they do best.' Dean Haitner was talking again, but to Dulcie he sounded very far away. 'I deal with academic issues. Issues of ethics – and ethical violations. And I am presenting you with this letter today, Ms Schwartz, in the presence and with the full knowledge of your adviser and acting head of your department, to put you on notice. Based on the evidence of the salvaged page of Melinda Sloane Harquist's thesis, you have been accused of, and will be investigated for, the most serious offense in the university canon: plagiarism.'

TWENTY-SIX

Plagiarism. The word echoed through her mind as she stood there, mouth hanging open. The dean had left, letting himself out of that same side door by which he'd entered, and she had turned to her adviser, trying to form the words to all the questions that came rushing into her mind. Trying to put together a defense against charges she had not expected. Trying to make some sense of it all.

'Mr Thorpe, I didn't . . .' Nothing was making sense. 'From one page? But I've only published one . . . I don't know how to . . .'

'Don't panic, Ms Schwartz.' Her adviser had been bending over a chair, packing papers into a leather briefcase. For a brief moment, Dulcie thought he was trying to comfort her.

'I don't expect you'll have to prepare your defense for at least a few weeks yet.' He wasn't. Instead, Dulcie realized as he shoved a handful of papers into his bag with uncharacteristic careless-ness, he was telling her not to fuss at this moment. He no more wanted to deal with an emotional student then he would with any other kind of mess. 'Now, I'm sure we'll both be hearing from the dean's office in good time. You've got the notice there, and that has a little explanation of the process—'

'Mr Thorpe!' His blatant desire to flee, as much as anything else, had broken Dulcie out of her stupor. He was her adviser. He was supposed to be her ally, her teacher, the one to lead her through the bureaucratic maze of the doctoral program. The sight of him rushing to abandon her sparked something inside her. Dulcie envisioned Mr Grey, his silky fur rising in anger, and she found her voice. 'Mr Thorpe, I am not a plagiarist. I am innocent!'

He turned at her outburst, and she found herself facing a man she barely knew: white-faced and wide-eyed, he looked like a ghost. And not a friendly feline one.

'Ms Schwartz!' He stumbled a bit over her name, and she saw that his lips were trembling. It dawned on her that he was terrified.

'Mr Thorpe?' This was a complication she hadn't foreseen. For a moment, she almost forgot that she was the one under suspicion. 'Are you OK?'

Maybe it was her words. Maybe it was her tone of voice, a little worried and solicitous. The balding scholar had taken a deep breath. At the same time, his color had gone from deathly white to red, and, once his lungs were full, he let go with an angry outburst.

'In case you didn't remember, Ms Schwartz, I am the acting head of the department.' He paused to take more air in, turning even redder as he did. 'Acting! And while the administration has been quite content to have me fulfill the duties of your former adviser, the great Professor Bullock, it has been loath to grant me the full title, or the requisite compensation that should come with the job. Until today, I had great hopes that this semester would change all that. That my contribution, sizeable as it has been and will continue to be, would be recognized, and that I would be granted the title with all the benefits that confers.'

He had run out of steam by the end of his little tirade, but Dulcie had no response to make. Instead, she stood there, watching his narrow shoulders heave up and down from the exertion, and wondered how he had become the injured party in all of this.

'Mr Thorpe,' she finally managed, working to keep her voice steady. 'I am the person who has been falsely accused here.'

'*Falsely?*' He started to inhale again, and Dulcie rushed to correct herself.

'Wrongly, then,' she amended. 'But really, Mr Thorpe, I didn't do anything – anything unethical.' For a moment, her doubts sprang up. Her attempt to meet Melinda, the manuscript, Darlene. That moment of doubt must have shown in her face, because Thorpe took the occasion to pounce.

'Really, Ms Schwartz. I know how anxious you've been, and clearly I should have been keeping a closer eye on your research procedures. I do not know with any certainty what lengths you would go to. What I do know is that through the randomness of an assignment, my professional career is now staked to yours. I trust that by the time you are called to account, you will have a better defense than "I didn't do it".'

With that, he shoved what looked like a day planner into his bag and buckled it shut. With a nod to his charge, he walked up to the main door of the office and out – leaving it open as the broadest possible hint that she had no reason to remain.

In retrospect, Dulcie would wish she had. Left alone in the dean's office, she could have looked at the papers on his desk. Perhaps uncovered some trace of who had accused her – or what evidence they claimed to have. At that moment, however,

Thorpe's dramatic exit seemed to take all the oxygen out of the room, and Dulcie grabbed up her own bag and stumbled, gasping, out of the office, down the stairs, and back into the improbably nice day.

TWENTY-SEVEN

'I don't believe it.' Lloyd was shaking his head. 'I mean, I know you aren't a plagiarist, Dulcie. That wasn't even a question. What I don't believe is that anyone thinks you are.'

'Thorpe does.' For Dulcie, it was still sinking in. Sitting here, in the Science Center café with her friends, she was beginning to accept the reality of the charges. 'He actually questioned my research methods.'

'That bastard.' Trista was drumming her fingers on the tabletop, barely able to sit still. 'There's only one cure for sadists like that.'

A part of Dulcie wanted to follow up on Trista's intriguing statement – a very small part. Knowing Trista, the 'cure' would be almost as nasty as the accusation, but likely more physical. Most of her, however, was still stunned. Despite the rapid gathering of her friends, and the liberal application of both cocoa and chocolate chip cookies, Dulcie still felt dazed.

'What exactly are you accused of, anyway?' Lloyd reached for the letter. Dulcie had shown it to her friends, and they'd all read the charges. 'It just says "plagiarism". It doesn't name any example. I mean, your article went through peer review, right?'

Dulcie nodded, her head heavy. 'I don't think it's the article. I think it's what I'm working on with my thesis.'

'But that hasn't been published yet.' Lloyd looked at Dulcie, who shrugged. 'This is beginning to sound like a thought crime.'

'Maybe it is.' Dulcie had no other answer. 'He's my adviser. He's read all my roughs. I gather they talked about it.'

'I can't believe Thorpe didn't defend you.' Lloyd pushed the plate of cookies toward Dulcie. She broke off a piece, and then crumbled it into crumbs. 'No, I'm sorry. He's a coward. I can imagine him not standing up to Haitner. What I can't see is anyone thinking you are capable of that kind of dishonesty.'

'Well, he did – *they* did – so get over it.' Trista, who had fallen suspiciously silent, had been building up a head of steam. 'I'm sorry, Lloyd. This makes me so mad.' She looked up at Dulcie. 'You called Chris, right?'

'As soon as I got out of there,' she told her friends. 'I left a message.'

'I'm sure he'll call,' said Lloyd, trying to sound reassuring. Somehow that made it all worse.

'Of course he'll call,' Dulcie snapped. She hated their skewed schedule and never knowing where her boyfriend was. 'Sorry.' She slumped further in her seat. 'It's the new semester. I don't know his schedule yet, and I just felt so alone.'

'So you called us,' Trista broke in. 'Which was exactly the right thing to do. The question now is – what is our next step?'

'I don't know if there is a next step,' said Lloyd, absently breaking off a piece of cookie. 'I mean, isn't Dulcie supposed to wait until she's notified of a hearing?'

Trista glared at her fellow Victorian. 'She can't just sit there, and we have to help her. Right, Dulcie?'

Under Trista's ice-blue gaze, Dulcie drew back. But the effect was bracing. 'I want to,' she said, almost in a whisper. The full weight of the accusation was sinking in. Plagiarism. She'd be expelled, her academic career over.

Worse, she would never get back into the Mildon. Never get to finish tracking down the remnants of that lost book. She thought of Griddlehaus, of their cozy routine. There would be no more uncataloged goodies to go through. No more orderly procession of boxes, archival or otherwise. 'I don't even know where to start.'

'That's where we come in.' Trista leaned in. 'First, one of us – not you, Dulcie – has to find a way to track down who made this accusation.' Lloyd nodded, engaged. 'It has to have come from the department so we've got to be careful who we talk to and what we say. Lloyd, you find out who else is working on the Gothics. I'm going to see if I can get anyone to show us the paperwork on this. I mean, this place? There's got to be forms filed in triplicate, and I know some of the support staff.'

Trista's words sparked a memory. 'One of my students works in the dean's office,' she said. 'Andrew Geisner. He's a sophomore in my English 10 section.' She pictured the surfer-blond sophomore. He'd been friendly enough at lunch.

'Do you trust him?' Trista was so focused she was squinting.

'I don't know. He's a nice guy, though. Smart, and he's doing well in the class.'

'Damn.' Trista slammed back in her seat and blew up into her own blonde bangs. 'So you don't have any hold over him.'

'Tris!' Dulcie almost laughed. 'The whole point of this is to prove that I'm ethical.' Her friend only raised one pierced brow. 'But he is sympathetic. He came up to me at lunch to say something.'

'So he knows?' Lloyd was a little behind.

Dulcie shook her head. 'He was sympathizing about the whole Melinda thing. Dear goddess,' she put her head down in her hands. 'That was only yesterday.'

'Don't worry, Dulcie.' She felt the warmth of Trista's hand on her shoulder. A half second later, and Lloyd's was on her back too, patting her gingerly. She felt like a cat. 'We'll figure this out,' he finished.

'We will.' Now that she had a plan, Trista's anger had turned to a more confident form of energy. 'Dulce, I want you to follow up with this student of yours. Say you need to speak with him. Tell him it's not too early to be looking for a junior paper topic and that you should talk. He'll be flattered. You can use that. Lloyd, see who you can find in the department who might know something about the source of this complaint: Goths, eighteenth-century British fiction, anything like that. Me, I'm going to see what I can find out about Thorpe and the dean. Let's talk tonight.'

With that, she pushed back from the table and stood to go. Lloyd started to get up also, but paused to look at Dulcie. 'You OK? I've got office hours, but I can cancel.'

'I'm fine,' she said, and then corrected herself. 'Well, I'll *be* fine. You guys are the best.' She meant it, and managed to smile. She'd monopolized her friends' time enough over the last few days. Besides, she wanted to think before she spoke to Lloyd again. It had hit her, when Trista had given him his 'assignment', that he should be looking at American fiction writers from her period, too. And that meant Rafe – Lloyd's friend. Rafe who only a few hours before she had suspected of crimes worse than mere plagiarism.

Was the senior tutor somehow involved in all of this? He'd been in the library, with the EMT and the distressed dean, as Dulcie had been ushered out. In that chaotic time, anything could have happened. Or was it simply that the tragic death had everyone looking for the worst in each other? She needed to sort out what she knew before she raised more accusations. In the meantime, her friends were looking out for her.

Dulcie felt the first surge of optimism she'd had since that summons. As Trista and Lloyd traded names, she finally ate a piece of cookie. The chocolate chip, still warm and half melted from the oven, tasted good. It tasted, she decided, like hope.

TWENTY-EIGHT

For a woman who dealt with great works of literature, coming up with a plausible fiction was a surprising challenge. Dulcie had remained at the café table after her friends had taken off, ostensibly to finish the cookies. But the crumbs were long gone now, and Dulcie sat there still, trying to plot out her next move.

Despite Trista's suggestions, Dulcie couldn't imagine leading Andrew Geisner on with the promise of a junior tutorial. Or – she felt her cheeks go warm at the thought of the handsome undergrad – anything else for that matter. No, she'd have to come up with an honest way to solicit information from him. Or semi-honest, at least.

Which meant, she feared, tracking him down in person. The question was: where? From her seat, she could see the light outside beginning to fade. Here in the Science Center, the foot traffic had slowed. A few diehards made their way down to the computer lab, a small group trotted by with a basketball, laughing. None of them even looked like English majors to Dulcie's admittedly biased eyes.

Sunday afternoon, and if she had nothing else pressing, Dulcie would have been in the library. For a moment, her spirits soared. She'd go back to Widener and lay in wait for the tall sophomore. In the meantime, she could return to her notes. Maybe she could make some progress in tracking down whatever it was she had missed. Maybe, once she had her *own* proof, these ridiculous charges would be dismissed.

And maybe Esmé would have her next chapter drafted by the time she got home. No, as much as she'd love to dive back into her work, Dulcie knew it would be a cop out. Besides, she really didn't want to run into Darlene again. The flush burned up her cheeks, hotter now. She really had been close to the ethical edge with Chris's colleague, pushing her for information about Rafe's work. Too close for her own comfort, though not – she was sure – anywhere over the line. Still, the idea of running into the young woman again wasn't an appealing prospect. Mentally, Dulcie crossed Widener off her list.

Dulcie looked around. The café was mostly empty, despite the glorious aroma of those cookies that still emanated from the kitchen. She could, she thought, have just one more. That would at least postpone the decision. But she and Chris had planned on making dinner, and, really, except for the little bits Lloyd had eaten, Dulcie had consumed three of the oversized treats already.

Thinking of Chris, Dulcie realized that she hadn't talked to her boyfriend since the bomb had dropped. She'd called him as soon as she'd left University Hall, but he hadn't answered. Checking her phone, she saw that he had called her back. His message was too short and too cheery: 'Hey, sweetie! Hope you're feeling better!' She couldn't blame him for that, however. As far as he knew, her life was getting back to normal. She played the message again. Somehow, just hearing his voice helped.

A warmth like the brush of soft fur came over Dulcie as she listened to the brief message a third time, and she found herself shaking her head at her own stupidity. 'Thank you, Mr Grey,' she said to the empty café. 'I can't believe I didn't think of it.'

This time, instead of the number for 'replay' she hit the one for 'callback', and felt her heart racing in anticipation as the familiar digits beeped along.

'Hi, you've reached Chris Sorenson . . .' Her spirits plummeted, but by the beep Dulcie had rallied.

'Hey, sweetie. I'm returning your call.' She paused; that wasn't entirely true. 'Actually, I have something I could use your help with. Well, a couple of things really. It's been . . .' She searched for the right phrase. He was such a dear, and after her last surprise she didn't want to worry him overmuch. 'It's been a big day. I guess I'll tell you about it over dinner. See you soon!'

Dinner. Dulcie looked up at the clock – barely past four. Too early to go home, and she'd ruled out the library. If she were still an undergrad—

That was it! Dulcie sprang up, and ran her dirty plate back to the counter. Sunday afternoon tea was a ritual at Dardley House. As the leader of a section, she'd be welcomed. She'd also be besieged by students, which is what had kept her from the social hour before. Still, the tea – which really drew the undergrads with a variety of more solid snacks – would give her a perfect opportunity to buttonhole Andrew Geisner. If he wasn't there, she'd think of something tomorrow. Chris would undoubtedly have some ideas.

With a lighter step, Dulcie crossed the Yard and headed back toward the river. September's late-afternoon light was just beginning to fade to a golden glow. Its warmth – as well as the promise of seeing her sweetheart soon – filled Dulcie with more optimism than she'd felt all day. Those charges were ridiculous. She'd done nothing wrong, and the dean would see that soon enough.

Her mood lasted as she made her way through the Square, weaving through the taller pedestrians and somehow avoiding the eye of the few freshman she recognized. They were still getting their bearings, she realized as she ducked down to pass one she knew. They were probably too busy looking for street signs and trying to remember if it was Bow or Arrow that would take them straight to the indoor track.

It was only as she started down the familiar narrow path that she hesitated. By now, the shadows were lengthening, and Dardley House, with its six turreted entries, loomed like a castle over the pedestrian walkway. Not that medieval fortresses were usually constructed of red brick, Dulcie reminded herself, making herself take one step, then another, toward the undergraduate house.

Hermetria's castle had been stone, grey and cold. Not warm like the brick edifice before her. This building was red like the sunset. Like a fire in winter.

Like blood.

The cold chill that ran over her had nothing to do with the weather, Dulcie knew. The late afternoon had cooled down a bit, but her light sweater was more than adequate. It was nerves, and that was all. And as much as she'd like to think that there was a preternatural element to her alarm – a heightened sense, perhaps, or a friendly caution from a certain spectral feline – she did her best to banish that thought. She wasn't Lucy, to take every anxiety as a divine warning. Sometimes, she told herself sternly, a case of the nerves was just that and nothing more.

And so it was with steeled jaw and a determined step that she let herself into the main entrance to Dardley House. 'I'm here for the tea,' she announced to the startled student on duty, only belatedly hearing the force of her own voice. 'I mean, I teach a section here,' she amended, more softly and with a smile.

'Ms Schwartz, yeah, sure.' The young man glanced at her ID and nodded. 'I took English 10 last year with you.'

'Oh?' Dulcie didn't like to ask for compliments. Still, it was nice to be remembered. Maybe she'd made a difference in this undergrad's life.

'Yeah,' he said, half to himself, as he handed her ID back. 'Realized I don't like reading that much. I'm concentrating in statistics now.'

Dulcie muttered something that she hoped sounded encouraging and shoved her wallet back into her bag. It wasn't her teaching, necessarily. Not everyone was cut out to be a literature and languages scholar. At any rate, she had other duties to think about, and as she stepped into the courtyard one more time, she took a deep breath to help her think, and gasped when she realized what she'd walked into.

The tea was always held in the junior common room. The long wooden table would be loaded with baked goods, the over-sized industrial urn holding down one end, along with cream, half and half, and all the other additions necessary to make the over-brewed beverage palatable. That room, however, was part of F entry, in the hallway leading up to the visiting scholars' suite. She had peeked into it, had seen the sun shining off the table's polished surface before proceeding on to . . . Dulcie stood, rooted to the spot. She hadn't thought this through. She couldn't – she wouldn't go back there so soon.

'Ms Schwartz?' A familiar voice broke into her funk. Andrew Geisner stood in front of her, holding that familiar urn.

She looked up at him and down at the pot-bellied silver. 'The tea?'

He nodded. 'Moved.' He nodded toward the dining room. 'We're taking over the private dining room instead. The senior tutor just thought to change it, and we're running a bit late, so you didn't miss anything.'

'Thanks.' Her relief must have seemed out of proportion to the problem.

'See you over there.' He took off, and Dulcie realized she'd missed one more opportunity. Ah well, he had been in a rush, and she still hadn't figured out how to broach the subject. There'd be enough time over a warm cup to grill him about his boss, the dean, and any knowledge he might have of a certain upcoming disciplinary hearing.

Dulcie made her way over toward the dining hall. Inside the high French doors, the chandeliers were lit, but the door to the cafeteria line was still closed. Students were making their way through the big room, however, heading for the small, private dining room beyond. As she watched, one of the kitchen staff came out with a metal cart and began putting trays of beets, carrots, and broccoli on the salad bar. Well, not everyone filled up on cookies, Dulcie reminded herself. And with that thought in mind, it was time for her to eat her own metaphorical vegetables. Or, she amended, silently admitting that her previous analogy had been pushed beyond the point of strain, for her to do what she'd come to do. Then she could go home.

Dulcie took a deep breath and let it out slowly, all the while trying to picture Mr Grey. She had first adopted the grey longhair – or he had adopted her – while an undergrad living here. Of course, his presence in the suite she shared with Suze was utterly against the rules, and so he had never sauntered into the dining hall, as she was preparing herself to do. He had, however, always conducted himself in a dignified manner, more the honored guest than the trespassing intruder, and the image of his stately self-confidence seemed to be what she needed.

'Calm,' she told herself. 'Serene, even.' Sadly, thoughts of Esmé kept breaking in, the younger cat's antics making a polar opposite image to the one Dulcie had conjured. But the idea of the little tuxedo cat careening around the living room made her smile, and with that, she found the courage to proceed.

Nobody questioned her as she crossed the dining room. Now that the salad bar was loaded, dinner prep seemed to be in full swing, making Dulcie even more eager for her own supper, a few hours from now. Maybe they'd make spaghetti. Maybe chili. She couldn't remember what they had in the fridge, but on days like this, when Chris slept in, he'd take care of the shopping. Cheap and filling, that was the key, but with her sweetie there, no haute cuisine could be more tempting.

'Watch it!' Her reverie was broken by the yell and the subsequent clatter as a white-clad worker knocked a metal steam tray over. Another aproned man came running with a mop, and Dulcie sped up her own pace, crossing the wide dining hall to the small private room that opened off its far corner.

'Ms Schwartz!' Thalia, teacup in hand, stood in the doorway, eyes shining behind those large glasses. 'I'm so glad you're here. I was thinking about the reading, and—'

'That's great.' Dulcie cut her off. 'I'm glad to hear it.' She brushed by the eager student into the room, leaving her open-mouthed in astonishment.

'Cookie?' An older woman, obviously a motherly type, was holding out a silver tray. Dulcie smiled and took one, just to be polite. 'I'm Lynn Crawford,' the woman said. 'Co-master of Dardley House.'

'Dulcie Schwartz,' Dulcie introduced herself. 'I teach the English 10 section on Saturdays.'

'Lovely,' the matron beamed. 'I'm so glad when teaching fellows come by. We want to foster an atmosphere of congeniality and mutual learning.'

Dulcie was saved from having to respond by an arm. Reaching between her and the tray, it grabbed several cookies and forced her to step back as the house co-master turned toward the eager eater. Undergrads, Dulcie thought, nibbling on her own cookie. If only they were as insatiable about their reading lists.

Under the guise, not entirely fake, of looking for a napkin, Dulcie made her way around the crowded room. It had seemed odd, almost off-putting, that the co-master had been so jolly. 'Atmosphere of congeniality?' When a visiting scholar had been killed right across the courtyard? Now, as she made her way through the milling students – careful never to step between them and the table, which held slices of pound cake and what looked like pfefferneusse, she began to understand. For the residents of Dardley House, life went on. Melinda Harquist had been a stranger, a temporary visitor to their college residence. The masters' job was to make that residence feel like a home, albeit a temporary one, and if that meant piling on the cheer and sugar, so be it. Dulcie was in no danger of forgetting what had happened, or why she was here this afternoon. If only she could find Andrew and talk to him, then maybe she could enjoy the gathering. She would even be willing to chat about the assignment with Thalia, she decided. If only the tall sophomore would show up.

She had just about made a circuit of the crowded room when a burst of laughter caught her attention. A knot of tall men – rowers, by the looks of them – were crowded around an open doorway. The party must have flowed over into the masters' residence, she realized, and made her way up to the door.

'Excuse me,' she said. They were laughing and didn't hear her, and so she reached up to one sweat-shirted arm. 'Excuse—'

There, she saw him. As tall as the jocks in the doorway, if a little thinner, Andrew stood over by the far wall of the next room. This would be perfect, she realized. Despite, or perhaps because of, the knot of muscle whooping it up in the doorway, the smaller room looked fairly empty. Where Andrew was standing, leaning against a bookcase, would be almost private, cut off from the main party by the laughter of the jocks.

She put her hand on a muscle-bound arm. 'May I?' Then she caught herself. As the jock had turned toward her, she had gotten a better view of the room beyond. Andrew was there for a reason. He was leaning forward, apparently in deep conversation with a dark-haired woman whose back was toward Dulcie.

Could it be? Yes, Andrew nodded and ran his hand through

his long, sun-bleached hair, a gesture Dulcie had seen him do often in class. The woman looked up – Darlene. For a moment, Dulcie was puzzled. Darlene was a graduate student, not a Dardley resident. And any sections she might teach would be in the computer lab, like Chris's.

Then it hit her: Rafe. Darlene was probably often around the house because of her boyfriend. It would make sense that she'd know some of the undergraduates, at least well enough to chat with them at a social event. All Dulcie had to do was wait until she'd moved on, and then she could buttonhole Andrew for a tête-à-tête.

As soon as the thought was formed, she saw Darlene turn and step away. The jocks had returned to their discussion, a little less boisterous than before. But the big one in the sweatshirt had shifted so as not to entirely block the doorway, and Dulcie began to sidle by him, then stopped.

Darlene was walking to the front of the room, to where an oversized potted plant was soaking up the last of the afternoon sun. And there, standing in the bay window, was her beau, Rafe Hutchins, the senior tutor of Dardley House.

This was a dilemma. For all Dulcie knew, Lloyd had already called his friend. They probably wouldn't have had a chance to talk yet, but Lloyd may have initiated a conversation. And if he had, he very well might have said he wanted to talk about what had happened, specifically as it affected Dulcie. Lloyd, bless him, was not a great one for subterfuge, and Dulcie hadn't told him her suspicions about his friend. At the time, she'd worried that she was being unfair, and then she hadn't had time to properly explain. Right now, though, that reticence seemed like a mistake.

Dulcie surveyed the room. Andrew was still leaning against the bookcase, apparently deep in thought. Darlene – she could see – was almost behind the rubber tree. If she and Rafe retreated any further – into the window seat or to another, more private room – she could still grab Andrew. As they stood now, she would feel too exposed. If only she knew for sure where Rafe stood, or if Lloyd had said anything to his friend.

Just then Andrew looked up. Darlene was calling to him. Dulcie couldn't hear what the black girl said, as the jocks had gotten loud again. But she could see her raised arm, hailing the undergrad – and Andrew went over. Between two of the jocks, Dulcie could see his back, standing next to Darlene. Light and dark, both tall and lean, they seemed still, as if listening to someone – to Rafe.

She had to know what was being said.

The crowd of jocks was laughing again, and Dulcie had the strange sense of being a tiny animal on the veldt. An antelope, maybe, something vulnerable, hovering for protection on the edges of a herd of elephants. But if they were shielding her now, they were also obscuring her view of the trio in the window, their laughter covering up any conversation that might concern her.

Excusing herself, she made to pass by one of the large young men. He turned, startled, as she squeezed under his arm, but she didn't want to walk straight into the center of the room. Hugging the wall, she felt a little less obtrusive, and luckily the large young man didn't do much else beyond glance down at her. If she could make her way up to the potted plant, she might be able to hear what was being said. At least then she would have some idea of how to proceed.

'That manuscript . . .' The voice, deep and masculine. It had to be Rafe. Or, no, wait, Andrew was speaking. 'Before it went missing . . .' Another explosion of laughter from the rowers drowned out the rest. Andrew looked up, the jocks were so loud, and Dulcie flattened herself against the bookcase, grateful for once to be short.

'But what about—?' Darlene was asking a question. Dulcie leaned in again, desperate to hear more. '. . . looking for it,' was all she got.

The clot of rowers was getting boisterous again, and it was at least a minute before Dulcie could hear any more. When Rafe's voice, a little softer than Andrew's, finally cut through, it chilled her to the bone.

'They're asking,' she heard him say. 'Asking everyone about Dulcie Schwartz.'

Dulcie froze, stuck to the spot by the sound of her own name, but her mind was racing. She imagined herself breaking in, demanding to know who was asking about her – and why. Then she remembered that she was under investigation. The charges might be unfair, but the process was legitimate. The tutor could simply be talking about the academic probation committee, and while Dulcie might wish he had more discretion, she had no right to demand it. Then again, if Rafe had been the one to really steal the manuscript—

Her thoughts were broken by a loud ringing, like an old landline phone. Her phone, with the volume apparently set on high. Andrew looked around, and Dulcie squatted to the floor as she reached inside her bag, fumbling to silence the offending device. The jocks burst out in laughter again, and Andrew's gaze went to them – and stayed about three feet above Dulcie's head. He turned back to the conversation almost immediately, but it took Dulcie several minutes before she stopped shaking enough to stand. When she could, she edged her way back down the wall, her head bowed, and managed to work her way behind the knot of jocks and out to the dining hall.

She didn't stop until she had crossed the courtyard and hurried – still walking, but as fast as she could manage – out of the house's main entrance. Down the long pedestrian way and around a corner. Only then did she collapse against a fence, panting with fear. This was making her crazy. She had to give it up. She was innocent; she should let the investigation take its course. She would, at the very least, hear what Chris had to say before she did anything else.

Thinking of her boyfriend, she reached for her phone. Maybe she should offer to shop. She certainly wasn't going to do anything else productive today. But when she checked her missed calls, she saw that two had come in. One from the police, again: Detective Rogovoy. Well, it was Sunday, surely tomorrow would be soon enough. The more recent one had been from Chris.

With a sigh of relief, she punched in the code. Of all the people who could have called, this was the best.

'Hey, Dulce, it's me.' His voice warmed her, and she realized how much she was looking forward to seeing him soon. 'I've got some bad news, I'm afraid. I can't do dinner tonight and, well, I've got to work straight through.' His voice paused, giving his words a moment to sink in. 'Darlene was supposed to do a double shift, but she's gotten called away. Some emergency, I gather. I'm sorry, Dulcie. I know you've had a rough couple of days. But this isn't negotiable. She's on some kind of special assignment, she said. Something that's all rush-rush and top secret for Dean Haitner.'

TWENTY-NINE

'*The essential ichor besmirched his raven locks. All life, all essence, lay there, turned now to cooling mass.*' Dulcie looked from the excerpt to her own note: '*Cooling mass? Ick!*'

Back at the apartment that evening, alone, Dulcie had decided to try to work – at least a little. But even as she read through her notes, she found herself concentrating on what wasn't there, wishing she had copied down more and kept her editorializing in check. 'What was I thinking, Esmé? It's bad enough I don't have access to the manuscript. Why couldn't I have at least copied out the page from the printed book?' The cat, whose back was pressed up against Dulcie on the sofa, didn't respond.

'*As black as sable, his lifeless head lay upon the carpet.*' Why she'd written that down, she had no idea. Might as well have written 'as black as Esmé's back'. She stroked her feline friend until a soft purr started up. One yawn – a white bootie stretching out for a pink-toed yawn – and the gentle rumble subsided. Esmé was asleep.

Dulcie watched her for a moment, the epitome of peace. If only her own slumber could be so undisturbed. Or maybe it wasn't: as she watched, Esmé's pink nose twitched and one front paw flicked, as if in a dream.

What did cats dream about? Dulcie watched her pet stretch slightly and settle more on her stomach. She looked almost like an all-black cat from this angle. Even the pink of her nose was hidden.

Color. Did cats dream in color? In her own night-time re-imagining, the victim had had red hair, the 'red-gold' of the handwritten manuscript rather than the 'raven' black of the printed version.

But there was something else, too. Dulcie turned from her too-brief notes on the book's page to the few she'd jotted down about her dream. '*Her own raven curls descended, shielding her face from the inquisitive light.*' That was how the dream had started, as if narrated from the author's own writing. Now Dulcie read aloud to the cat, who blinked at her sleepily. '*Black as raven's wings*,' she'd written. 'Black as Melinda's,' she added, and then fell silent as her eyes moved on to the next passage. She must have been half awake by this part of the dream. All she had were vague memories of a chase. She'd jotted down a few impressions: the heroine was assumed to be the killer, though clearly she had been set up—

'Wait.' Dulcie sat up, causing Esmé to jump to the floor in disgust. Dulcie barely noticed: this was getting too close for comfort. This was her nightmare. It might also be a dramatization of a crucial scene from the missing novel. But it was also what had happened – what was happening – to her. And for all that she'd always felt a connection to this author, 'her' author as she'd always thought of her, finding herself stuck in one of her more lurid plots was not fun.

If only she hadn't gone up to the visiting scholar's suite. If only she'd taken better notes.

Dulcie slumped back on the sofa and, in lieu of the cat, reached for the bag of Chips Ahoy. She'd picked it up in Central Square hours before, while waiting for her takeout order of dun dun noodles at Mary Chung's. Sunday wasn't her usual night for Chinese, but the woman who had taken her order hadn't seemed to mind, only smiling ever so slightly when Dulcie tacked on a *suan la chow show* and some stir-fried pea-pod stems for balance.

She'd called Chris first, in the vain hope that she'd misunderstood his message. When he worked the overnight, he still got to hang around for dinner. Her boyfriend sounded like she felt as he'd explained that, no, this was a particularly full night. Darlene had signed on for an open house, which meant answering questions from undergrads who, especially this early in the semester, had no idea how to maneuver around the university system. That ran till ten, and then the overnight shift kicked in.

'At least it's money, Dulce,' he'd said sadly. 'Maybe I can take you out next week?'

'Maybe,' she'd responded, sinking into her own slough of despond. 'Hey, what say I come by?' She often dropped in when he was working the overnight. It could be a lonely shift, and they both could use the company.

'I don't know, Dulce.' His voice sank even more. 'You know how September is. I've barely had time to breathe. I don't think I'll get to any of my own work till at least two. Speaking of, I should go.'

'OK then.' In the background, she heard her boyfriend greeting someone and inviting him or her to pull up a chair. 'Talk to you later.'

'See you.' And that was that. His sign-off, she knew, was simply a sign of the craziness around him, but she felt it like a cold wind. Dinner and comfort had turned to the faintest of farewells. She hadn't, she realized too late, even told him what was going on. That was when she'd called in her takeout order, and ducked into the convenience store next door for the chocolate chip cookies. She hadn't even waited to get home before she'd pulled the bag open.

Now, three hours later, noodles and cookies were all gone. Dulcie was trying to make sense of her notes – and nursing a touch of indigestion. And her author seemed intent on switching things around, not to mention invading her dreams.

'Red hair, black hair,' Dulcie pulled the earlier note back to her and reread it. 'Why did I write this down? What does it even mean?'

For lack of another cookie, she started playing with one of her own curls, stopping herself just as she was about to start chewing on its end. The summer sun had left it coppery, Dulcie noted, pulling one ringlet in front of her eyes. Still, it was a far cry from the red-gold that Lucy thought it should be. The color of a real heroine. Or, she noted, of this victim. Maybe she ought to be grateful. Maybe—

'Esmé, please!' Just in time, Dulcie grabbed the lamp. Fully rested, Esmé had begun to career around the living room like a rubber ball. 'What is it with you?'

'Mrrow?' As if in response, the little tuxedo cat turned and mewed, looking up into Dulcie's face as if she expected an answer.

'Look, I know you can talk.' Dulcie resettled the lamp and reached to haul the cat up into her lap.

'Nnnow!' Those white feet kicked out, scratching Dulcie's outstretched hand, and Dulcie dropped her.

'Ow.' Dulcie shook her hand as Esmé bounded away. A thin red line had appeared along the ball of her thumb. 'Esmé, can't you play nicely? I've had a hell of a day.'

'Wow.' The sound, coming as it did from the kitchen, sounded almost apologetic, and Dulcie smiled.

'That's OK, kitty. I was just trying to make sense of my notes, and, well, there may just be no sense to be had here. I mean, why would I dream that the victim was a redhead when I had only read the final version, where his hair is black? Is this all just because of Melinda – and Lucy? And if it is . . .'

It took a bit of sorting. Lucy would say that she had sensed the author's original intent, that Dulcie had known the story had first been written with a red-haired victim in mind – and that her discovery of the manuscript page proved that. Then again, if Dulcie hadn't found that page, Lucy would undoubtedly have some other perfectly implausible explanation. Like maybe Dulcie had made the victim a redhead – like Lucy, like all the women in her family – because in her dream state she sensed that she, Dulcie, was somehow involved. Knowing Lucy, she would probably also be quite confident that it was more than an accident that Dulcie had been the one to come across the body. Either way, to her mother Dulcie's dreams always tended to prove that some form of psychic ability did run in the family.

'Like red – well, reddish – hair,' Dulcie said out loud. 'No, that's crazy.' Hearing your cats' voices was one thing. That was because of the strong connection she had had with Mr Grey, Dulcie had decided long ago. And Esmé? Well, in some way, Mr Grey had chosen the little tuxedo kitten to be his successor. It made sense that she could talk. When she wanted to, that is.

Still, even putting Lucy's dueling explanations aside, there had to be something else in the strange juxtaposition of victim and killer in both versions of the story and her dream. Unless – wait – Dulcie caught herself. The fragment she had read, both in the printed and manuscript version, hadn't contained much plot. A woman sees a man who is lying dead on a rug in a library. The scene had been described in detail, with the emphasis on grue-some features that distinguished the overblown fiction of the day. But it had been written with a precision many of its contemporaries lacked, full of lifelike – or deathlike – particulars and showing a command of language that Dulcie had instantly recognized. And Dulcie had simply assumed that she was reading a horror story, a tale of murder or the like, as narrated by the killer.

But maybe the protagonist – the woman describing the scene – had not killed the man lying on the carpet. Maybe she was as innocent as Dulcie herself was, and this passage was an attempt to explain or justify her presence on the scene. If that were the case, would that explain the switch – Melinda's black curls for the gore-clotted red-gold hair?

'*Chase me!*' Like a black-and-white rocket, Esmé shot past, interrupting Dulcie's train of thought for the umpteenth time. '*Chase me!*'

'You finally speak to me, and that's what you say?' Dulcie laughed. The little cat was impossible to resist, and the flash of language – faint like the voice on a bad long-distance line – only made her antics more compelling. 'Do you want to tell me why?'

In response, the cat turned and stared up at her, tail lashing. Dulcie jumped up and went after her, calling her name as they dodged through the living room until this time the lamp nearly did go over.

'I give up!' Dulcie called, finally collapsing on the sofa. 'You're too fast for me.'

'*In that case,*' the voice came to her as two green eyes peeked over the end of the sofa, '*I'll chase you!*' And with that, the little head darted down, bit Dulcie's bare foot, and dashed off to parts unknown.

'Esmé!' Dulcie called out, grabbing at her foot. 'No!'

The bite, she saw, hadn't broken the skin. It did put an end to the game, however. 'It's not your fault, kitten!' Dulcie called after her pet. It was Chris's, she knew. He never could break his own habit of rough-housing with the little hunter, and by doing so he reinforced all her bad behaviors.

'*Bad behaviors, huh!*' The voice, like a distant sigh, barely reached her ears.

'Esmé, I've got to get back to work,' she called into the other room. 'There's got to be some sense to be found in here. There *has* to be.'

Her dreams, the story fragment, and Melinda's death. They were all connected somehow, and, no matter what her mother would say, Dulcie wasn't ready to believe that she had simply picked up on what was going to happen. She thought back on what Griddlehaus had said: Somewhere in these notes was a clue, an actual factual link to whatever Melinda had found. Maybe, even, why she had been killed. If she could find out what that was, she could clear her own name – and maybe finish her thesis after all.

With that, she dived back in, reading and rereading her notes. When that didn't reveal anything, she went back to her timeline. Where had her author surfaced? When had her silent period been? Somewhere in here lay the key, of that Dulcie was sure.

'*Why does she do that?*' In the hallway, the little black and white cat stopped playing for a moment to look back at her mistress, bent once more over her books. '*Why doesn't she listen?*'

'*It's as hard for her as it can be for you, little one.*' Another voice, deeper and quieter still, caused those white-tufted ears to perk up. '*She isn't awake yet to all the possibilities. Give her time, little one. Give her time.*'

THIRTY

'*T*was blood she fear'd. Blood. A pollution in the body that would haunt her, e'ermore. 'Twas this, and not the slights against her person that haunted her. Drove her, compelling her to e'er more desperate acts.*

In her sleep, Dulcie tossed and turned, her dreaming eye caught on the image of a dark-haired woman, pacing in a small garret room. Then she was that woman, and they were her thoughts, full of anxiety and doubt, that she heard.

Mayhap she should grant him what he wished, a visitation, nothing more. If reason were her ally, he would perceive the injury done her. The insult perpetuated with each advance. He would repent, as she had. She stopped, cold, her head turning toward the low wall, toward the fire, toward that which kept warm there. No, she could not lie. Not to herself, nor to the one who watched, still and quiet. She knew, she would always know. It was too late. There would be no repentance for her of this deed, e'en unto death.

'Death!' Dulcie woke for real then, sitting up so quickly that Esmé squealed. Dulcie turned to the cat, who in the bright morning light looked quite affronted by her sudden movement. '*There would be no repentance.*' The words echoed in her mind, even as she reached out to her pet in her own apology. '*E'en unto death.*'

'Oh, Esmé, it's worse than I thought.' Dulcie gathered the soft feline in her arms, and Esmé, as if sensing her mood, went willingly. 'My author – the author of *The Ravages* – she must have gone mad. All that talk about "pollution", Esmé. I think she really killed him.'

If Esmé could have answered, she didn't, and Dulcie was left with only the comfort of the warm animal beside her. To give full credit, Esmé did purr, and Dulcie was almost lulled back to sleep, lying next to all that soft fur. However, fear that the nightmare would return kept her from dropping off and finally she hauled herself out of bed.

'Might as well get ready for class,' she explained, as Esmé yawned and stretched out one white paw. 'Not that you have to worry about that.'

In truth, Dulcie wasn't sure if she did, either. As she started the coffee, she weighed the possibilities. Disciplinary probation wasn't something she'd ever worried about, and so she had never learned its rules. They couldn't bar her from teaching, though, could they? Then again, if they thought she might be ethically corrupt, they might fear her sullying young minds.

That letter – the one Dean Haitner had handed her. What had she done with it? Dulcie left the kitchen to rummage through her bag. She had a clear sense of Haitner handing her the letter, and of her showing it to her friends. And then? Too much had been going on.

'I can't believe all the crap I have in here,' Dulcie commented, pulling out a Xeroxed handout from the spring semester and three receipts from Lala's. 'Why do I even keep these?' she asked aloud, balling them up. Esmé declined to answer, but sprang to attention as Dulcie launched the ball toward the garbage. 'Don't worry,' Dulcie added glumly, when against the odds the projectile hit its target. 'There'll be more.'

Two more receipts and a takeout menu followed, before Dulcie spotted the dean's letterhead, sticking out from between the pages of one of her yellow legal pads. 'There you are.' Dulcie pulled at it and heard the paper begin to tear. 'Whoa.' She extracted the letter, pad and all, from the overstuffed bag. Something sticky – glue, honey, some of Lala's famous hot sauce – held them together, and she gingerly pulled the pages apart. As she did so, another piece of paper – white, with typing on it – fell out of her pad and drifted to the floor.

In a flash, Esmé had pounced, sending the errant page sliding under the table. Dulcie ducked to retrieve it, just in time to hear the front door open.

'Hello?' It was Chris, and Dulcie rose to meet him.

'Ow!' Too late, she'd forgotten exactly where she was. 'Hey there,' she said as she stood up, rubbing her head.

'You OK, sweetie?' Chris dropped his own bag and went to embrace her. He was, she could tell, exhausted. So she managed a smile and a shrug before hugging him back.

It had to be his fatigue, she knew, that kept him from following up. Disengaging, he threw his jacket over a kitchen chair and went directly to the refrigerator.

'Tough shift?' Dulcie didn't want to burden him. Then again, she did want to talk.

'Uh huh.' Chris emerged, holding bread, peanut butter, and strawberry jam. 'Fall semester, nobody knows which end is up.'

'I gather you didn't get any sleep.' Her hopes for a meaningful discussion fading, Dulcie settled for coffee.

'Not even time for dinner.' Chris didn't even wait to sit, taking a bite of bread as he slathered peanut butter and jam on a second slice. 'You feeling better?'

'Well, not really.' She should let him sleep, she knew that. But it had been such a miserable day. 'Chris, I've been accused of plagiarism.'

To do him credit, he listened, downing two more slices of peanut butter and jam as he did so. He declined coffee, when she offered him the rest of the pot, and so she drank the rest. After her troubled sleep, she'd need it to stay awake, she told herself. By the time she'd finished telling Chris about the dean's accusations, however, she could hear the edginess in her own voice.

'Oh, Dulcie, what a hassle.' Chris leaned back against the counter, his eyes closing. 'But it's so crazy. I'm sure it will all work out.'

'Work out?' Dulcie, who'd been leaning against the other counter, stood up suddenly. 'Work out?' She spat his words back at him. 'What do you mean, Chris? I'm being *investigated*. I'm on disciplinary probation!' Underneath the table, Esmé looked up at them both, her green eyes growing round with dismay.

'I know, I'm sorry.' Chris rubbed his face with his hand, getting strawberry jam on his cheek in the process. It stood out, red against his pale skin, and at any other time Dulcie would have found it endearing – and come forward to wipe it off, a move that would undoubtedly end in a kiss.

This morning, however, she was just a little too raw. 'You have jelly on your face,' she said, her voice flat as she turned to the table, where the detritus of her bag lay spread out. 'And I . . . I have this to deal with.' She grabbed the letter and shoved it toward him. He reached for it with a hand that, she saw, had more jam on it. Just in time, she jerked it away. 'And your hands are dirty too.'

'Sorry, Dulce.' He shuffled over to the sink. 'I'm fried. Look, I'm not the best person to talk to about this right now. There has to be someone, though, right?'

She shook her head, the flare of anger fading. 'Thorpe's thrown me to the wolves,' she said sadly. 'He's more concerned with how this will reflect on him than on whether I'm guilty or not.'

'Well, what about Rafe Hutchins? He's in your department, right? I can ask Darlene to ask him about, I don't know. Everything.' Chris was positively bleary eyed, wiping his hands on a dish towel. 'She certainly owes me one.'

For a brief moment, Dulcie's spirits started to lift. Then memory dashed them back. 'But she's working with the dean. You told me so yourself.'

A ghost of a smile showed on Chris's face. 'Even better. Who knows what she has access to? Between her and Rafe . . . what?'

Dulcie's head was hanging down, the tears gathering in her eyes. 'She won't help me, Chris. Not if what I think is true is true . . .' She looked up into his sad, sweet face. 'Chris, I think Rafe might be behind what happened with Melinda. I think maybe he stole her manuscript. Maybe even killed her.'

'Oh, that's ridiculous.' His voice was gentle, but the words were too much for Dulcie.

'You don't know, Chris. There's a – there's a whole conspiracy. Last night, I wanted to talk to one of my students. He's working with the dean. And I saw him meeting with Rafe – and with Darlene, too.'

'I told you she was on some special assignment.'

'At the Dardley House tea? That's what kept her away from working her shift?' A horrible thought hit her. It wasn't true, she knew it. She even knew she shouldn't ask. But the last few days had been so awful, and she was tired. 'You were covering for her last night, right?'

'Dulcie, I can't deal with this right now.' Chris shoved his plate into the sink and headed toward the bedroom. 'I need to get some sleep.'

'And I need to get to class.' Chris, halfway down the hall, didn't respond. 'Goodnight,' Dulcie called after him. The only one listening was the cat, who had emerged from under the table to rub against Dulcie's shins.

'Oh, kitty.' Dulcie reached down to the cat. She hadn't been exaggerating. She was running late. But after the night she had just had – after what could only be described as another fight – she wanted the comfort of a cat in her arms.

Esmé, however, had other plans. Eluding Dulcie's hands, she ducked back under the kitchen table, and as Dulcie knelt down she reared up to bat at Dulcie with her paws.

'I'm sorry, Esmé, I don't have time to play right now.' Another bat, this time with claws, and Dulcie sat back hard on the floor. 'Hey, what was that about?'

The tuxedo cat scampered further under the table, skidding as she landed on a piece of paper that served as a sled. Once she hit the far wall, she turned to watch her human.

'No, I'm not playing with you. Not when you're like this, and besides . . .' The cat, she realized, had skidded on a piece of paper. The same paper that been stuck to the dean's letter, inside her legal pad. On hands and knees, Dulcie crawled under the table, but paused as she drew near the cat. 'Esmé, no claws, OK?'

The cat was silent, but Dulcie had the strange sense she understood and so she reached past her to retrieve the page. Just then, she heard the church chimes, three peals of the bell. Quarter to – there was no way she could be on time for her section now. Shoving the page back into her bag, she headed toward the door. For a moment she paused. Should she call to Chris? Say something affectionate about talking it over later? No, she decided. If he wasn't asleep already, he was well on his way. She'd already made a mess of things this morning. They'd talk later, when he was awake.

Halfway to Mass Ave, Dulcie realized that she had never checked that letter. For a moment, she wished for the worst. If she didn't have to teach, she could go back to the apartment and cuddle up in bed with Chris. Their fight would be forgotten in no time.

Then she realized – if she was banned from teaching, she was probably banned from all academic activities. That meant no income and no research, nothing until this case was resolved. Stopping short, she reached into her bag. That paper had to be here somewhere.

''Scuse me.' A travel mug brushed by, filling the air with the smell of coffee. Dulcie looked up in time to see its owner run to embrace a red-haired woman.

'Darling!' The woman squealed with delight, and Dulcie bent back to her task. Right on top, she saw a page with type on it and pulled it out. But, no, this wasn't the letter. It was mostly blank, save for a few lines on top. The tail end of some essay or other.

Dulcie was about to shove it back in, when something caught her eye. '*Anonymous*,' she read. '*The anonymous heroine . . .*'

Oblivious to the busy Monday morning bustle around her, Dulcie stood and read. '*The anonymous heroine had clearly gone into hiding at this point, her flight from her no longer doting*

motherland of England seemingly not enough to protect this one
wildly wayward daughter from the overblown Ravages *of her*
own misspent life.'

Dulcie reread the sentence as commuters jostled her. The
church bell rang, and she ignored it. The reference in the text
she was holding was, to her, unmistakable, and yet, to her, totally
new. The tone was familiar though: arrogant to the point of
pomposity. And filled with pretentious alliteration.

'And if, as seems likely, our mysterious Anonymous was
involved in the scandal, then isn't it probable that in light of her
willful ways she caused *the scandal?'*

'Wildly wayward'? 'Willful ways'? That's when it hit her: this
was a page from Melinda's missing manuscript. The unpublished
book for which she had been killed.

THIRTY-ONE

Her own misspent life? Clearly gone into hiding? Standing
there, the sunny modern morning bustling about her,
Dulcie found herself transported back two hundred years.
Although Melinda's thesis seemed highly speculative – the phrase
'speciously speculative' came to mind – Dulcie could not discount
the possibility that her late rival had some new information. What
kind of scandal had her author been involved in? And how did
any of this relate to her dream? The dream – that phrase, 'pollution in the body' – had clearly haunted the writer.

More to the point, Dulcie wondered as she looked up unseeing
at the pedestrians around her, how had this page gotten into her
bag?

'There must be more.' Like a squirrel intent on last year's
harvest, she dived back into her bag, pulling out the other pad,
her wallet, and finally the only other sheet of white paper to be
found: the letter from the dean's office. That – and the church
bells – brought her back to the present day. Stepping, finally, out
of the stream of traffic, she skimmed it quickly, translating from
the official language as she read.

'"Serious import . . ." Yes, yes, I know. "Future proceedings . . ." Sure.' In the last paragraph, she found what she was looking for. *Members of the academic community placed on disciplinary leave may have both their duties and privileges curtailed, as determined by the disciplinary board.* In other words, they could do what they want.

Since they hadn't, however, Dulcie shoved everything back into her bag and broke into a trot. She'd have time enough to figure out how that page had gotten into her bag. While she still had a teaching gig, she should do her best to keep it.

An hour later, she was wondering if the job was worth the effort. The Monday section was a mix of upperclassmen and freshmen, which would be bearable by semester's end, but in September brought out the worst of both. The two juniors in the class had rolled their eyes as she'd burst in, breathless and sweating. She'd heard at least one muttered comment about 'lost weekends' and had been about to bark something back when the younger students started in.

'Are we really expected to do all the reading?' They peppered her with questions. 'What's going to be on the midterm?'

By the time she had calmed them down, another twenty minutes had passed, and she barely had time to bring up that week's assignment. Luckily, one of the juniors had actually read all three sermons and managed a reasonable contrast and compare. While the freshmen scribbled furiously in their notebooks, Dulcie looked around, hoping for one other alert face.

'Anyone want to comment?' She looked around the table. One hand, raised by a spotty young man. 'Dwayne?' She smiled to put him at ease.

'Is it true that you found a dead body in Dardley House?' His voice, quiet but high, carried clearly. 'And that you might be arrested for murder?'

By the time the section was over, Dulcie was exhausted. And by the time she'd cleared the room – yes, you do have to read it all, and, no, I fully expect to be here next week – it was time for her junior tutorial. Three students, all thesis-bound, who were looking to her to fulfill their requirement of a 'pre-1850' course. None of whom seemed to actually care about the books she assigned.

'I have an idea,' she said, as they took their seats. 'Let's try something different today.' The tutorial took place in the departmental offices, a rather rundown clapboard house on a quiet side-street. This early in the season, the office windows were open for the breeze, and Dulcie was doing her best to ignore a robin as she talked.

Julie, her best student, perked up. The other two were staring out the window, and Dulcie had to fight the urge to close it.

'To get more in the spirit of these books, let's try to imagine what life was like for an author in 1804. For one of the Gothic she-authors, for example. What would she be dealing with?'

'Sexism,' Julie chimed in. 'Family expectations. I mean, if she were married, she might have children.'

'That's true today, too.' Sheila turned toward her colleague, and Dulcie smiled to see her become engaged. 'Though at least we have birth control now.'

'Well, how many women really wrote in those days, anyway?' As the only male in the class, Damien tended to take a contrary viewpoint. 'And, really, what does gender have to do with what you write?'

This was fertile ground for Dulcie, and for the first time that morning she forgot her problems, talking about the rise of the women authors of popular fiction. 'You could say they set the stage for much of what is happening in publishing today,' she concluded.

'Depends how you look at it.' Damien didn't seem to think the subject was closed. 'I mean, back then, maybe a woman writer was killed in childbirth. But, hey, look at what happened to the visiting scholar over at Dardley House. You were there, right?'

Clearly, it was going to be a long day. At last, however, she was alone, the upstairs conference room a peaceful refuge from everything but her thoughts. For a moment, she closed her eyes. That robin was still singing, and with the warm breeze, she could almost pretend it was still summer break. Still last week, even, before her world had fallen apart.

There was no going back, however. Mr Grey had said something to that effect, and she knew it to be true. And so she opened her bag and took out the stray manuscript page once more.

Turning it over, she examined it – locating the sticky spot on its back. It wasn't, she realized with relief, blood. Instead, it felt like a glue stick or syrup, something that had caused it to adhere to her own pad. But when? Dulcie ran through the possibilities in her mind. Her pad had been in her desk, but she'd had her bag with her when she'd gone to Dardley House. And, yes, she had dropped her bag on the floor when she'd entered and first seen the Poe statue, lying on the floor. Had she picked it up then? Had it somehow adhered to something in or near her bag? Try as she might, Dulcie couldn't reconstruct how she had left that room – only the sound of her own horrified screams and the quiet steady voice of Mr Grey, telling her to flee.

Still, that was the only opportunity she could imagine for the page to have gotten into her bag. And hadn't the police looked through her bag anyway? She'd heard horror stories, but somehow she couldn't see Detective Rogovoy planting the page in there.

She read the page again.

'*Her own misspent life . . .*' A grim chuckle escaped her lips. The writer – Melinda – had most likely been referring to the anonymous author of *The Ravages*. Right now, however, Dulcie felt like it applied to her. If only she could flee. If only oceans were as big a barrier now as they were then.

Though maybe, the thought struck her, they weren't. Her author had gotten some attention for *The Ravages*, but then had fled the Old World, and gone into hiding here. Dulcie had always assumed the trouble was new, something to do with American politics. But maybe it wasn't. Maybe something – or someone – had pursued her. Dulcie shook her head. Whatever had happened, her author deserved better than Melinda's cheesy wordplay. This had been a woman in danger of her life, desperate to write – to let her voice be heard.

So why had she gone quiet all those years ago? When she'd first hit these shores, her essays had announced her presence. Her distinctive voice – and progressive opinions – had helped Dulcie track her down. Then . . . nothing! Granted, if there was indeed a missing novel, then maybe that was part of the reason. Dulcie had enough trouble teaching and writing her dissertation. Working on a novel and also selling political essays would be tiring, to say the least. But if that was the case, how did she live?

The Ravages had too much about poverty, about the hunger and scrimping that faced the impoverished, if noble Hermetria, for Dulcie to believe its author had been a wealthy woman.

Had she gotten a job of some sort here in the New World? Had she – Dulcie stumbled on a novel thought – married?

'Too often, those bonds cripple us, tearing all natural joys from our hearts, our babes from our arms, and our affections from all that we would hold dear. No, 'tis better for a woman to stand alone, for to be friendless is to know that which is true for our Sex.'

No, how could the woman who wrote such things about the legal standing of married women have allowed herself to be so enslaved? More likely she was a well-to-do widow, Dulcie told herself. Someone who had experienced the *'disequal bonds'* and lived to tell the tale.

If she had lived. Unbidden, the image of Melinda, her glossy hair all mucked up with blood, came to Dulcie's mind, pulling her back to the present. Any chance she would have of solving the mystery of her author, or of finishing her thesis, centered on getting this case cleared up. The police had cleared her of murder. Or had they?

Detective Rogovoy had been trying to reach her, she remembered with a twinge of guilt. And Suze had warned her that the investigation was still ongoing. But the big detective had seemed so sympathetic. He'd agreed that the timing didn't make sense, that Melinda had been dead for at least a bit before Dulcie had entered the library. Had he changed his mind? Her own department seemed to think she had stolen Melinda's work. And then, what? Killed her in a confrontation?

Dulcie sat back hard, struck by the realization. It did make sense, all of it. She could have had some kind of argument with Melinda, fighting over the research or defending herself from the visiting scholar's accusations. Then, if she had killed her, she could have left and then come back, only to 'discover' the body.

Granted, she'd have to be a much more cold-blooded type to pull off such a feat. But, well, someone had.

Voices in the hallway broke her out of her daze, and suddenly she looked down at the page before her in a new light. If anyone saw this, they would think . . .

'No!' With an involuntary shout, Dulcie shoved the paper back into her bag.

'Everything all right in here?' Martin Thorpe's balding head appeared in the doorway.

'Just dandy,' replied Dulcie, her voice unnaturally high. She swallowed, her mouth dry, and waited for the inevitable follow up. 'Looking over my notes,' she added.

'Fine, fine.' The head withdrew. Thorpe, she realized, was about as eager to talk with her as she with him. Still, he was her adviser, and before she even thought about calling Rogovoy back, she needed to find out where she stood with the university.

'Mr Thorpe?' Making sure her bag was securely shut, Dulcie ventured into the hallway. As the acting chair, Thorpe had his own office down the hall. 'May I come in?'

He looked up nervously. 'Yes?'

It was a question, not an answer, but she entered anyway and sat in the chair reserved for visitors, tucking her bag between her feet.

'I wanted to ask about the process for my – ah – hearing.' There, the words were out.

'Oh.' He looked down at his blotter, but apparently the answer wasn't written there. 'What did you want to know?'

'The dean didn't really explain what happens. Should I be doing anything?' Or *not* doing, she was tempted to add.

'No,' he said and shook his head. 'I don't think so. The dean will appoint a committee, and that committee will examine the suspected work, and then we will receive a ruling.'

Something struck Dulcie as odd. 'What work?' She didn't mean to be rude, but the question came out sounding abrupt.

'What work?' Her adviser seemed startled.

'Yes.' Dulcie was on to something now. 'What did I write that has supposedly been plagiarized? My paper was totally vetted before it was published.' She remembered the weeks of worry. Peer panels were notorious for acting on minor grievances and jealousies. 'And it was approved with very few changes.' A scholar at Princeton, she recalled, had objected to her use of the word 'feminist', calling it a 'contemporary, nay, *postmodern* reinterpretation of what was essentially a humanist argument.' She had hemmed and hawed about that one for a bit but finally, on Thorpe's urging, rephrased the offending sentence to avoid the word. 'As you may recall.'

'Well, they missed something.' Thorpe dismissed those weeks of work with a wave. 'I seem to have as well, because it has come to the dean's attention that some of your writing, some of the writing that would potentially make up your doctoral dissertation, paralleled the work of the late Melinda Sloane Harquist and—'

'My dissertation isn't finished.' Dulcie didn't mean to interrupt. He was still her adviser. This, however, was too much. 'How could he have read any of it?'

She stopped and watched as her adviser turned red. As the flush crept up his cheeks, her own warmed with the realization. Trista had been right. 'It wasn't just the paper. You showed him my work. You gave him the chapters I've been writing.'

'I . . . Well, that is to say . . .' Thorpe sputtered and grew even redder. 'He asked, Dulcie. And, I mean, he's the dean.'

'But, but . . .' Now it was her turn to grasp at words. 'But *why*?'

Her adviser shook his head. 'All he told me was that he'd been tipped off. That someone had said that you were planning on stealing Ms Sloane Harquist's work.'

His voice grew quieter, and he looked at Dulcie with what seemed like honest sympathy. 'You might ask yourself the same question, Ms Schwartz. You might want to look around, and see who your enemies might be.'

THIRTY-TWO

The page in her bag had to be an accident. Dulcie wandered away from the old house, repeating that like a mantra. It was sticky. She'd leaned on it, or put her pad down on it. Something. Nobody would have put it in her bag – why would anyone?

Could she really have an enemy – enemies – who would want to frame her for murder?

Despite her new-found discomfort with her adviser, Dulcie

had been temped to stay in the cozy clapboard. Thorpe might not be much for defending her, but at least she knew him. And once he'd gotten over the shock that her disgrace could bring to his career, he'd been, well, if not helpful, at least honest. Someone had accused her of plagiarism, he'd told her, and she believed him. Thorpe was too much of a sycophant to misquote a dean. If Haitner had told Thorpe that someone had tipped him off about Dulcie, then someone had. Someone who had access to her dissertation in the works. Someone who also knew Melinda.

Dulcie had reached the corner and automatically turned toward home. It was nearly lunchtime, and even if Chris weren't awake yet, Esmé would be better company than her own thoughts. Maybe Mr Grey would have some advice as to how to proceed. Maybe Mr Grey . . .

She stopped short, a vision of staring green eyes appearing suddenly before her. That gaze said it all, or should have. Mr Grey had been a hunter. He would want her to help herself. Dulcie could easily picture the large grey cat as he had been in life, grabbing a pen cap off her desk for a quick game of pen hockey. Or maneuvering the kitchen cabinet open so he could get at his treats. Mr Grey looked out for her, she knew that, but he was ultimately a cat of the Kipling style: a cat who walked alone. Dulcie wasn't alone, but she needed to do what she could to help herself.

Besides, she realized, she'd become all too reactive. The last proactive move she'd made had been to approach Andrew Geisner. She'd given up when she'd seen him meeting with Darlene and Rafe, and when she'd heard Chris's message – saying that Darlene was working for the dean – she'd been too distracted to pursue the handsome undergrad. Today, she had no excuse, and as she turned back toward the Square, her conviction was rewarded. There, just ahead, ducking under a hedge, was a large grey longhair. He turned to peer up at her, regal in stature, and with the kind of intelligent, pointed face that looked more Siamese than Persian. For a moment, he paused, fixing her with his intent green eyes. Then he lashed his tail and pounced on some unseen prey, and he was gone.

'Thanks, Mr Grey,' Dulcie said under her breath. She couldn't resist: she had stopped at that hedge and peeked under it. She'd seen nothing and hadn't really expected anything else. But she felt her resolve strengthen with a new sense of purpose – and feline support.

The question, she realized as Memorial Hall came into sight, was how to find Andrew – alone. Her original thought had involved running him down at Dardley House again, but she had no idea if he'd be there, or who he'd be with. For a moment, she wavered. It was close to lunch; maybe she should take a break first.

The ringing of her phone broke off her deliberations. 'Hello?' She answered without checking to see who was calling. 'Chris?'

'No, it's Lloyd. Are you busy?' Until she heard her office mate's voice, Dulcie hadn't realized how badly she wanted to patch things up with her boyfriend. For now, however, it would be better to let him sleep.

'Not really. What's up?' As soon as she asked, she had a second realization. She wanted this to be about office hours, or some mundane maintenance issue concerning the listing of midterms. Anything but what Lloyd said next.

'I managed to get a hold of Rafe. It was . . . interesting.' The pause in his voice was anything but encouraging. 'Do you have a minute to talk about it?'

'Sure,' said Dulcie. She was only a few blocks from their office. 'I'll be there in ten minutes.'

Enemies. Dulcie didn't know if the word was coming from Mr Grey or from her own fears. Her own dreams had hinted as much, and Thorpe himself had warned her. Now, as she walked, all she could think about was how silly she had been to not tell Lloyd her suspicions. If Rafe really was behind all her troubles, then taking him into their confidence had been a huge mistake. But Lloyd liked the senior tutor. Trusted him . . .

With a heavy heart and feet that felt similarly leaden, Dulcie passed through the security gate and clattered down the stairs to the basement corridor. At least, she realized as she walked up to their open office door, Lloyd was here alone. If he'd brought his buddy for a chat, she wasn't sure what she'd have done.

'Hey, Lloyd.' She shrugged off her bag, and took as much time as possible tucking it into that messy bottom drawer. 'What's up?' she asked finally.

Lloyd rolled his chair up toward her desk and leaned in before speaking. 'Something's wrong, Dulcie. Rafe is uneasy,' he said, his voice low. 'And he thinks you should be, too.'

'Huh?' This wasn't what Dulcie had expected. Unless it was all some kind of misdirection. 'Why should he be worried about me?'

'He thinks you're close to something. Something big.' Lloyd looked so serious, but Dulcie didn't buy it.

'That's nonsense.' She pushed back her own chair. 'I'm a graduate student studying an obscure book from a maligned discipline. Nobody cares about what I discover. Well, nobody except for Melinda.'

'That's just it.' Lloyd pulled his chair closer still. 'He thinks it's all about *The Ravages* author, and Melinda's thesis.'

'Lloyd.' She had to stop him, to explain. 'Look, I should have told you yesterday. I know Rafe is your friend and all, but I think he's involved – and not in a good way. I ran into his girlfriend in the library yesterday. He had her tracking down some quotes, basically, doubling up on books that I've been working on. I think we've been looking at this the wrong way, because we've thought of him as an American specialist, while my dissertation and –' she swallowed before adding – 'Melinda's is on a London-born author. But she came to the United States and she wrote here, too. And I think he's looking for the missing work himself.'

'Well, of course he is!' Lloyd's interruption stopped her short. 'He has to. He's under suspicion, too. I mean, I told you they used to go out, right?'

Dulcie shook her head. 'No, I don't mean he's looking for Melinda's thesis. I think he's looking for the missing novel – the one Thomas Paine wrote about. The one by my author.' Quickly, she filled Lloyd in on her research, the letters, the printed page she'd found, and the manuscript fragment she'd managed to read before the Mildon was closed to her. 'Didn't I ever tell you?'

'Sorry, Dulce, you probably did. It's just that . . .' He waved his hands, and Dulcie sank back in her chair again.

'You see? You're a fellow grad student, and it bores you. So why should I believe that my work is threatening anybody? Why should I believe that I'm in any danger? I mean, unless he means academically because he – Rafe Hutchins – is looking to beat me to the discovery.'

'But if you think he'd do that, then you must think . . . No.' Lloyd looked up at her, mouth agape. 'You think he killed Melinda. You think he killed her for her research.'

Dulcie shrugged. There wasn't a kinder way to put it.

'You've got it wrong. You've got him wrong.' Lloyd was getting worked up. 'I know him. Hell, Dulcie, I know what he's interested in. Early-eighteenth-century prose – not fiction, *prose*. Political tracts and the like.'

'She wrote those, too.' He had to see the connection. 'And why else would he have sent Darlene down to Level C? He was following up on Melinda's thesis.'

'Well, of course he was – he wanted to see what she had written.'

'So he could finish her work. So he could claim it as his own.'

Lloyd sighed and closed his eyes. 'Rafe doesn't have her dissertation. He never read it. He said he never saw it, and I believe him. Yes, he's been following up on her work, but only to find out why it was stolen. Why she was killed. Because, Dulcie? He's heard that there was something explosive in that thesis. And he wanted me to warn you, because if you're on the trail of the same missing manuscript, then you're in danger, too.'

THIRTY-THREE

Getting the rest of it was like pulling teeth. At first, Lloyd would only say he'd been sworn to secrecy. Then he admitted that Rafe had given his word, too. But Rafe, said Lloyd, wasn't happy hiding what he'd heard – and Lloyd wasn't either.

'It's his girlfriend, Darlene.' Lloyd had finally said. 'She's doing some special project for the dean. Something with computer security on the university interface, or, well, Rafe was vague about that.'

Dulcie nodded. She was vague on most of the stuff Chris did, too. But this sounded a bit more urgent.

'Anyway,' Lloyd was still talking. 'He seemed really uncomfortable with what she was doing, so I pressed him on it. Finally, he told me: Darlene read something. An email. He said she would never have intentionally read any email the dean had written, but this was in his out box. She meant to send it along, you know, figuring that it had just gotten tied up somehow. But in the moment before it got sent, she saw who it was addressed to – and what it said. Dulcie, it said, "This is too dangerous. Dearest please reconsider. There's too much risk for you and don't forget this Dulcinea Schwartz."'

'Dearest? He called her "dearest"?' For some reason, that was the detail that stuck with Dulcie. 'So the dean really was involved with Melinda.'

'The dean said "dangerous", too, Dulcie.' Lloyd was leaning in, intent. 'Don't you think we should focus on that?'

Dulcie shook her head. 'I'm not the one he was warning, not really. It's not even clear if his warning pertains to me, or he is referring back to something else he'd said about me.' She didn't like that idea. 'And, well, don't you think the key might be in their relationship?' She grimaced. 'Their romance?'

Lloyd opened his mouth, about to protest. Then, clearly, the idea caught him. 'It does make sense,' he said. 'I mean, he was giving her the run of the place. Treating her like a queen. And, well, she always was a heartbreaker.'

'Isn't he a little old for her?' Dulcie fought down a slight queasiness at the idea. 'I mean, I'd heard about his reputation. But, well, wasn't that years ago, like, at some other college or something?'

Lloyd only shook his head. 'I thought this kind of thing happens in your books all the time, Dulcie. You know, the lecherous old lord and the innocent young noblewoman.'

'Maybe.' Somehow, Dulcie couldn't bring herself to see Melinda as innocent, but Lloyd had a point. 'Actually, they're usually even more twisted than that. Like, the guy is a monk and supposed to be celibate, or it's really incest.'

'OK, enough.' Lloyd held up a hand. 'I get the idea. But, well, now we understand why he was so broken up. I mean, beyond the obvious.'

'I guess.' Despite the evidence, Dulcie couldn't see it. 'But doesn't it also make him a suspect? I mean, a dean fooling around with a student. He could have gotten into big trouble.'

Lloyd considered this for a moment before dismissing it. 'She wasn't a student here. She was a visiting scholar; that's different. I mean, could he have gotten in trouble for pulling a few strings? Maybe, but I bet not. From what Rafe says, he cares too much about his position to risk it for a fling.'

'Maybe it wasn't a fling?' She didn't have to believe it to follow up with the hypothetical.

'No, not Haitner,' said Lloyd. 'I remember when he came here, the Gazette ran his bio. He's never been married, no kids. Nothing. Says things like his legacy will be the work he does here. You know the type.'

'Midlife crisis. Gorgeous young girl . . .' Dulcie was warming to the idea. A little too much, perhaps, because Lloyd gave her a look.

'You really want this to be something, don't you?' He paused a beat. 'I'm not saying you're not on the right track, but shouldn't we be talking about the other bit of news? Dulcie, your name was in that note. Linked with hers. The dean thought you both – or, OK, at least Melinda – might be in danger. Now she's dead. Rafe thinks it was a warning about both of you, though. That's why he's has been trying to figure out what was going on.'

'So he says.' Dulcie wasn't ready to accept that. 'I mean, why doesn't he just ask about the email? Darlene made an honest mistake, he could ask the dean. Or she could.'

'Would you?' Dulcie paused at that. 'You don't trust him,' Lloyd continued. 'I see that, and, really, considering everything that's been going on, I don't blame you. But I've known him for years. He's a stand-up guy.'

This was supposed to reassure Dulcie. She knew that, and she knew Lloyd meant well. But as she looked at his earnest, pale face, she found that she had become convinced of only one thing: Lloyd trusted Rafe, and she didn't. And that meant she could no longer trust Lloyd. Her small support group was shrinking even further.

THIRTY-FOUR

'Hi, sweetie. Are you up yet?' Dulcie had hoped Chris would answer the phone. Even if he were still annoyed at her, it would be better to talk to him than to this machine. 'It's noon, and I was hoping we could talk.' She bit her lip. She didn't want to sound needy, even if she was. 'I'm sorry I got so wound up this morning, Chris.' This wasn't getting any better. 'Call me?'

Dulcie had left the office a few minutes before. After Lloyd had dropped his bombshell, they'd both fallen silent, and she had tried to work. The first student three-pagers had been completed the week before. If she was going to keep teaching it only made sense to try to keep up with them, but it was hopeless. First she couldn't find her favorite red pen, and then she had wasted ten minutes looking for the form she needed to renew her online grading access for the year. The form had turned up, and Dulcie knew it was only her current state of mind that had her looking for the form in the wrong desk drawer. But then she couldn't find her address book, and she knew she was licked.

It wasn't so much that she couldn't talk to Lloyd. It was the knowledge that she did not dare confide in him that hung over her, weighing down on every simple exclamation that she'd made – whether about that pen, the errant book, or her students' blatant disregard for dangling modifiers. Everything seemed to suddenly have import, and nothing felt casual or easy. It was, she decided, the better part of valor to flee before she ended up picking a fight with her office mate, as well as her boyfriend. It was also, she realized as she surfaced into the sunny day, time for lunch.

Hoping she could make peace as well as lunch plans, she'd called Chris. He might, she realized with a sinking heart, still be asleep. He might also be out already, leading a group of clueless undergrads through the logic of applied math. The semester was still too new for her to have his schedule by heart. Of course, she indulged in a dash of self-pity, he could be ignoring her.

'*Dulcie . . .*' She felt as much as heard the warning voice, a little tickle like the brush of whiskers behind her left ear.

'You're right, Mr Grey. I'm being overdramatic.' She fought the urge to reach up to pet him. He wasn't really on her shoulder, she knew. He hadn't been there for real in over a year now.

'*Now, now.*' The tone of reprimand had softened, and Dulcie found herself swallowing back tears at the unexpected comfort of his voice. '*You've been in dark places before, Dulcie.*' The voice was soft and low, the rumble of a purr underlying its gentle words.

'It's just that I feel so alone, Mr Grey.' She walked over to a tree, the better to hide the fact that she was talking to a creature who was not in any physical sense actually there. 'I mean, it was bad enough finding . . . finding Melinda. And then being put on "disco pro". But the loneliness is the last straw. First I fight with Chris, and now I don't know if I can trust Lloyd . . .'

'*And?*' She paused. He was right: there was something else bothering her, too.

'My author.' That was it. It was a relief finally to locate the heart of what was niggling at her. 'I don't know what happened, between that fragment and my dream. I'm afraid she wasn't . . .' Dulcie paused, unsure how to proceed. 'That she wasn't the woman I thought she was.'

'*She must have been tired too,*' said the voice. '*She faced hardship to come here, to accomplish what she did . . .*'

'You're right.' Dulcie found this encouraging. 'I guess I feel a kinship with her. Is that silly?'

'*Not at all, Dulcie. But remember . . .*' His voice was fading now, the words barely discernible above the purr. '*There are others close to you as well. Kinship goes deep, but it may demand from us that which we would not choose to give . . .*'

He was gone, but Dulcie felt relieved. It was true, she had people who cared for her, even if they didn't always act as she would prefer. Like Lloyd and his faith in Rafe. Or Lucy, for that matter. As she started walking across the Yard, Dulcie realized that she probably owed her mother a call.

'Lucy? It's me.' By the time Dulcie reached her mother, she was on the other side of the Square. She'd been heading to Lala's through force of habit, but stopped herself once her mother picked up. 'Ladybug Sweetwater said you were busy when she picked up the phone, but I was thinking we hadn't spoken in a while.'

'Nonsense, Dulcinea. We've been in constant touch.' Dulcie looked down at the phone in her hand, a little worried.

'Mom?' She swallowed. 'We haven't spoken since last week.'

'In the corporeal world, Dulcie. On the physical plane.' Dulcie calmed down. Her mother wasn't losing her mind any more than she already had. 'But this is a very sensitive time right now.'

'It is?' Dulcie wracked her brain, trying to remember what phase the moon was in. 'The equinox?'

'Exactly! The nights are growing longer, Dulcie. Which means this is the season for those who share bloodlines to reach out to each other.'

Dulcie nodded, then realized her mother couldn't see her. 'Did you hear from Dad?'

A snort of laughter answered her question. 'I'm talking about the matrilineal line, Dulcie. Don't tell me you haven't been feeling it, too.' Before Dulcie could formulate a proper response, her mother continued. 'Though maybe the touch has truly passed you by. I've always worried, ever since your hair started to fade. It was red when you were a baby, you know.'

'I'm not psychic, Lucy.' Maybe it was her mother's dismissive tone, but Dulcie decided to correct her. 'But I do have dreams – and I do feel connections to the past. Only they're to the literary past. To the author I'm studying. I dream about her.'

'A writer.' Dulcie could hear the disappointment in her mother's voice. 'A stranger you only know from books.' But Lucy Schwartz never stayed down for long. 'Maybe she's not a stranger. I assume she was a woman of power. Am I right, Dulcie?'

'In her fashion.' Dulcie tried not to laugh. 'But not in the way you mean, Lucy.'

'Well, how can you be sure? If you are having visions, dear, that could mean there's a deeper connection.'

'It's possible.' Dulcie could say that without telling an outright lie. After all, anything was possible. Then she paused. Her mother always talked about the connection between parent and child; now would be the time for her to ask about Dulcie's life.

'Well, you just keep an open mind, dear.' It was not to be. 'Now I'm hip deep in preparations for our next circle. And, yes,

I do mean that literally, since we want to hold a water ceremony before it gets too cold.'

'I wasn't going to question—'

'No, of course not, dear. Everyone knows how gentle you are. Lovely to hear from you! Glad you're doing so well.'

As she stood there, holding the silent phone, Dulcie remembered one of her childhood fantasies. In it, she'd been stolen away from the most rational family in the world, and Lucy, for all her good intentions, was no more her mother than Lala was.

THIRTY-FIVE

Everything looked better on a full stomach, Dulcie told herself. But after talking with Lucy, Dulcie knew she couldn't bear to run into any of her students, and so instead of Lala's, she headed toward the Baglery. Besides, she rationalized as she walked away from Harvard Square, she was having a hard day. She deserved an eight-dollar sandwich that would take a while to chew.

Her mouth, of course, was full when her phone rang, but she reached for it anyway. It wasn't too late for Chris to join her, especially if he was already in the area. That last bite of bagel almost choked her, however, when she heard Detective Rogovoy's gruff bark on the other end.

'Ms Schwartz.' He didn't wait for her to identify herself, undoubtedly part of his police training. 'Glad I caught you. Finally.'

Dulcie swallowed with difficulty, the dry bagel still a lump in her throat. 'Detective?' She reached for her diet Coke, as she counted back. Had she ignored one call? Two? 'I've been meaning to get back to you.' She tried to sound optimistic. 'Have you, uh, figured everything out?'

Another bark. This one sounded like a laugh. 'I wish. No, I'm calling you again because apparently you no longer return calls. And, Ms Schwartz, I'm afraid I've got to ask you to come in again. There's been a new development.'

Dulcie put the soda can down and ever so briefly considered hanging up. It would be the wrong thing to do. She knew that. She also suspected it would be futile. It was, however, tempting.

'Ms Schwartz?'

'I'm here.' She couldn't help the heavy sigh that followed.

He must have heard it. 'I am sorry, Ms Schwartz. I really am. I shouldn't say this, but I do feel like I've come to know you and, well, my daughters aren't that much younger than you.'

'Thanks.' She felt surprisingly comforted by his words and found herself wondering what the bear-like cop would be like as a father. There were so few men at the arts colony that Dulcie hadn't been ostracized by her lack of a dad, but the idea still tantalized. Maybe, she decided, living with Chris was changing her ideas of family. Or maybe it was Mr Grey.

A loud clearing of the throat brought her back to the moment. 'So, Ms Schwartz, when may we expect the pleasure of your company?'

'May I finish my lunch first?' The idea didn't seem that scary any more. 'My office hours start at two, but surely we'll be through by then.' The quiet on the other end brought some of her nerves back. 'Won't we?'

'The sooner you get here, the sooner we'll be able to figure that out.' The detective was back in police mode.

'Figure what out?' Her mouth had gone dry again.

Now it was her turn to hear a bellows-like sigh come over the phone line. 'We've been looking through the deceased's rooms, the ones she'd just moved into before the – ah – incident. And we found something that has been admitted into evidence.'

Dulcie waited. She had only been in the library, the outer room of the suite. There was no way this could be connected to her. 'Something,' she paused, fishing for the right phrase, 'that I might be able to help you with?'

'You could say that, Ms Schwartz. At the very least, we need to go over your statement again. Basically, we'd like to know if you can think of any reason why we should have found, under her desk, a leather bound address book that seems to belong to you.'

THIRTY-SIX

'Excuse me?' Dulcie was dimly aware of the voice on the other end of the phone, as Rogovoy went back over what he'd said. What she heard, however, were her own racing thoughts.

It was a set-up. It had to be. Dulcie knew there was no way she had brought her address book into Melinda's suite. In fact, the last time she had seen it was . . . She stopped herself. It had been in her desk. Only, when she had looked for it in the top right drawer, it had been missing.

Someone had taken it, she realized with a gasp. Someone had taken her address book, and at the same time planted the page of Melinda's manuscript. She was sure of it. She remembered going through her drawers, thinking everything was just a bit out of place. No, neatness was not her strong suit. Still, she hadn't put the grading form in the left-hand drawer. She *never* put the grading form in the left-hand drawer. It always went in the right, where she could pull it out when she needed to look up the procedure for filing the grades – and then she shoved it back. Only it hadn't been there. It had moved. And the manuscript page had been shoved down into her pad. And, clearly, her address book lifted.

'Well, clearly,' she started to explain, 'what happened . . .' She stopped herself cold.

Dulcie had been about to tell the detective all of this. About to explain her theory, with all the parts as evidence, when she caught herself. He knew her, he said. He had daughters her age, he said. But he also now had one piece of evidence that placed her closer to a murder victim than she had previously admitted to being. To tell him about the manuscript page was to give him another piece, a possibly damning piece. And for all she knew, all this talk of daughters could be a ploy to get her to confess.

Dulcie didn't buy into Lucy's paranoid world view. Detective Rogovoy might be a man, a man in authority, no less. That didn't mean he was 'The Man' or inherently evil. However, her years here at the university had taught her to recognize what she didn't know. Chief among those things was what a father might act like, if that father were also a police officer, and whether Rogovoy's statement of trust was consistent with paternal behavior or simply a way of handling a suspect.

She also didn't know who had gone through her desk. Whoever it had been had not cared much about being found out. Perhaps he or she had thought Dulcie wouldn't notice. In all fairness, she realized, she almost hadn't. However, whoever it was had a clear intent: putting her squarely in the frame for murder.

'I'll be down there soon,' she said, finally, and managed to get off the line. That was probably the best she could do, she realized. Afterward, assuming the police let her go after this interview, she would find out who was after her, and what other tricks he – or she – might have in store. The question was: how?

Taking another bite from her sandwich, she toyed with the phone. Chris would have ideas. Thanks in no small part to his academic discipline, he was a very organized and logical thinker. But she'd already left him a message. He would have called back if he'd gotten it. Unless – Dulcie didn't like to think about this – he was still angry. Once again, she found something stuck in her throat. Bagel, undoubtedly, she told herself as she forced herself to swallow and dabbed at her eyes.

Lloyd was off limits because of his faith in Rafe. This new information, Dulcie realized, might sway her office mate. After all, someone had gone into the visiting scholar's suite to plant evidence. Who better than the house senior tutor? Then again, Lloyd might hold firm. His loyalty was one of his better traits, one that Dulcie had relied upon in the past. No, she couldn't risk it.

Trista? Now that was a possibility. Dulcie was curious if the blonde Victorian had learned anything on her own, and this new info would certainly energize her. She wiped her mouth and reached for her phone again, only to have it ring in her hands.

This time, she looked at the caller ID before picking up. Not Chris, but not the police headquarters, either. Only after the third ring did she recognize the number: someone was calling from the office of the Mildon Collection.

'Hello?' She'd never gotten a call from the Mildon. 'Dulcie Schwartz speaking.'

'Ms Schwartz! It is I, Thomas Griddlehaus!' The little clerk's voice was soft, and she thought he had his hand over the receiver, but his palpable excitement made even his whisper oddly distorted.

'Mr Griddlehaus?' Dulcie paused, worried. 'Is everything OK?'

'Yes! Yes!' He was almost yelling, in a breathless kind of way. 'I've found it, Ms Schwartz! I was filing the sequestered material. You know, the material I'd set aside for the unfortunate Ms Sloane Harquist? Well, I was looking through the pages, simply to make sure I filed everything correctly, of course, and I realized that we'd been looking at something incorrectly. You must come down here, Ms Schwartz. As soon as possible! I believe I've found the missing key.'

THIRTY-SEVEN

Dulcie had rarely felt so torn. What she wanted to do was race down to the special collection and see whatever page or passage Griddlehaus had found, and then get right to work on it. What she had promised to do, however, was go talk to Rogovoy. She'd said she would. She'd been ducking the detective for days. And, considering that she seemed to be still under suspicion, it was the sensible move.

Or was it? A half-hour later, Dulcie wasn't so sure.

'Someone must have planted it. Isn't that obvious?' Dulcie was nearly yelling. Not a good tactic when talking to the police, she knew. However, she had never run into such a ridiculous situation. She had come in determined to defend herself, Rogovoy's last words ringing in her ears. However, she'd been so distracted by Griddlehaus's news that she'd failed to come up with a reasonable explanation. 'What's the alternative? That I killed her and left my address book in her room? I already told you, I think someone was in my desk—'

In front of her, Detective Rogovoy sat with a stone-faced young cop wearing the city of Cambridge's blue uniform. Rogovoy raised his eyebrows a fraction of an inch. It was as much of a hint as Dulcie was going to get, and she sat back down.

'Well, someone was. I can tell,' she said, trying not to squirm on the hard wooden seat. 'And what you're saying doesn't make any sense.'

Rogovoy opened his mouth – then shut it. The presence of his stony colleague was clearly having a dampening effect on his usually more voluble self.

'OK, then. Go back to the . . . the incident. You know the timeline.' Dulcie had a vague sense that she was digging herself in deeper. Unfortunately, she couldn't see any solution except to try to excavate a way out. 'You know that when I showed up, she – ah, Ms Harquist – had been, well, gone for a while.'

'And for the half-hour before the police were notified, you were . . . in the courtyard?' The other cop, younger than Rogovoy and leaner, sounded cool, like a shark. He looked down at a sheet of paper that Dulcie was sure he'd already memorized. 'You were "hanging out" after your class?'

'After my section, yes. Which I teach. I started to walk into the Square to get some lunch, and then I ran into a colleague and we returned to Dardley House.' Dulcie bit her lip. This young cop had a sharp-featured face and no familiarity with the trusting traditions of the university community. She turned toward Rogovoy. 'The detective here talked to me right after. He took my statement.'

'There are gaps,' was all her old ally said. His face, she now saw, was shut down like an old stone wall.

It was her own fault, Dulcie knew. She had arrived at the police station without a strategy – and without calling Suze. All she could think about was getting through this and returning to the Mildon to see what Griddlehaus had found. To make matters worse, she hadn't been fully focused on the questions the young cop had asked her. She hadn't seen the way the muscle on the side of his face clenched when she brushed off the timing discrepancy. And she hadn't seen the glint in his eye when he questioned her about Melinda's missing manuscript.

'So, you never saw the dead woman's book?' His voice had been as flat as a rock, a very cold, flat rock.

'No, never,' she had responded automatically. 'I mean, yes,

when I went in and found her, I saw it. I mean, before I found her. It was on the bookshelf. At least, I think it was. And then this morning—'

She'd caught herself then. She'd been about to tell them about the page that had appeared in her bag. The page that might implicate her. 'This morning, I was wondering about it again.' Even to her ears, it sounded lame.

'You were thinking about it,' the city cop repeated. Rogovoy shook his head, a barely noticeable gesture. It might have been unconscious, an expression of sadness or disappointment. She had always been a bad liar, she knew that. At that moment, however, she hadn't wanted to see his response as a sign that he knew she was holding something back. That he was disappointed in her. Rather, she took it as a warning – a subtle way of telling her to quit talking, at least while that other, sharper cop was there. That only made her more nervous.

'You see, she and I are researching the same author. Were. That is, I still am, and her thesis would have been interesting to me, if I had read it.' The young cop turned toward Rogovoy then and nodded. They knew, then. They probably knew she was on disciplinary probation, too. 'But I didn't. I was barely in there for a minute. Maybe even less.'

In response, Rogovoy fished something out of a folder he'd kept on his side of the table. A heavy plastic bag that he then pushed halfway across the table toward her. She looked down at it, and saw the missing address book inside, its scarred leather binding and one bent corner as familiar to her as any of Esmé's toys. Rogovoy then repeated what he'd told her on the phone. That her address book had been found on the floor of the suite bedroom. 'Like it had fallen out of someone's bag, perhaps when someone knelt down to search for something. Or to hide.'

That was when Dulcie had lost it. The whole situation sounded ridiculous to her. 'You can't really think I killed her and left, and then came back?' She looked from Rogovoy to the young cop and back again. Neither was giving her an inch. 'What? I was so overcome by guilt I came back just to raise the alarm?'

'Not exactly,' the young cop spoke. 'We know that you were in the process of leaving when the senior tutor and your colleague were coming up the stairs to look for you. We are considering the possibility that you were going to call for help. Raise the alarm, as you put it. We are also considering the possibility that you had been there before, and that you came back to retrieve what could be seen as evidence.'

THIRTY-EIGHT

A t that point, Dulcie had finally shut her mouth. 'I don't think I should say anything else,' she said, once she could again summon words. 'May I go?'

The city cop had nodded, and Rogovoy had heaved himself to his feet to escort her out.

'There's something you're not telling us,' he said as he walked her down the hall. 'And that's a mistake. I don't know if you're protecting somebody or if you think you know better, but, believe me, you really should talk to me.' He looked at her then, big eyes as sad as a spaniel's, and she was sorely tempted to spill it all.

It was a risk she didn't dare take. 'I didn't do it, Detective Rogovoy,' she'd said finally, her voice falling to a whisper. 'I didn't do *any* of it. I think someone is trying to set me up.'

'And who would that be?' He leaned in, and in that moment she realized her mistake. She'd grown used to thinking of the detective as her friend, the gentle ogre. He was in cop mode, though. All he wanted was information, and Dulcie knew that anything she could say would only damn her further.

Besides, all she had were suspicions. 'I don't know, Detective. I honestly don't know.'

Since they didn't seem to be charging her – goddess be praised – he had let her go then, along with all the usual warnings about how she needed to stay in touch and how they would likely have more questions. As soon as she was on the sidewalk, she realized how foolish she had been to go in there alone. She needed help. Legal help.

Suze answered on the first ring. 'Legal aid.'

'Suze, I've done a really stupid thing.' Walking down Garden Street, Dulcie confessed it all: from finding the manuscript page to going in to talk to the police without counsel. She'd been naive, she knew that. But Suze, she was sure, would commiserate.

'You didn't tell anyone about the manuscript page?' That wasn't the response she anticipated. 'And it appeared in your bag, when?'

'This morning,' said Dulcie. Something was tickling at the back of her memory.

'Did you leave your bag anywhere? You know, in a public place, unattended?'

'No, I would never do anything so silly.' The words were automatic, but she could hear the sharp exhalation of breath over the line. Her former room-mate and best friend clearly thought she could do something even more foolhardy, and that she had.

'Well, that's not useful,' Suze said after an overlong pause. 'Nor is the fact that you didn't immediately go to the police with this. You're lucky they didn't search your purse.' She paused again. 'Did you check to see if there was anything else in there? Anything potentially incriminating?'

'Of course,' said Dulcie, making a mental note to do so at the next available opportunity. She opened her bag now, and looked through it. Pens, her pad – that was it. 'But Suze, I don't know if the page was slipped into my bag. I think it was put into my desk. I picked up a pad from my office yesterday, and I had the strangest sense that someone had gone through my desk, you know? Also, I'm nearly positive that's where my address book was. Maybe someone went through my desk, grabbed my address book, and stuck this in my pad. Maybe I wasn't even supposed to pick it up.'

'That's possible.' Suze sounded a little more optimistic. 'And your office is probably more accessible, right? When are your office hours?'

'This afternoon.' Dulcie looked at her watch. 'In twenty minutes, actually.'

'Oh,' Suze paused. 'Well, who else has access to your office?'

'I share it with Lloyd, Lloyd Pruitt. He's been in there and so has his girlfriend, Raleigh.' Suze knew Lloyd and Raleigh. They'd both been guests at their old apartment in Central Square.

'And when are Lloyd's office hours?'

Dulcie thought a moment. 'Thursdays, from one to three. So . . . before this all happened.'

There was quiet on the line, and Dulcie realized she was biting her lip. 'Suze?'

'I need to think about this a bit, Dulcie, and I want to talk to one of the partners here, one of the real lawyers. There's a lot about evidence that I'm not really up on, and they deal with this kind of thing all the time. It doesn't sound good, I won't lie to you. But in the meantime, maybe you can do something, too.'

'Sure.' It sounded like Suze was calling in the heavy hitters. That had to be good, Dulcie told herself, trying not to feel even more terrified. 'Anything.'

'I need you to make a list of anyone who may have had access to your office at any point since the killing. Maybe you can find out if Lloyd had any visitors; maybe he left the door unlocked for some reason. It's all within the bounds of plausibility. But I also need you to prepare yourself for two possibilities.'

'Yes?' Dulcie's mouth had gone dry.

'One, that we may have to surrender this page to the police. It's too little, too late, and you definitely shouldn't go in alone, but it may still be the prudent move.'

'Uh huh.' Dulcie closed her eyes, and immediately pictured Detective Rogovoy, shaking his head in disappointment. 'And the other thing?'

'The other thing is that this may end up implicating Lloyd.' Dulcie started to protest, but Suze cut her off. 'If he's the only one who had access to your office and to your desk, you need to consider the possibility that he's more involved than you know. This is a murder investigation, Dulcie. We don't know who the cops are talking to – or who they suspect. But I can make suggestions about who you should or should not talk to, Dulcie. Right now, I don't think you can trust Lloyd.'

THIRTY-NINE

I t was with a heavy heart that Dulcie walked back to her office. Lloyd, her friend and ally so often before, had become first someone she couldn't confide in and now – what? A suspect?

Dulcie shook her head, then acknowledged the truth. Maybe not a suspect in the official sense, in the sense that the police would be questioning him. But he was someone she had to be suspicious about. Someone she needed to avoid talking to. She'd already had her doubts about his loyalty, but to imagine him actively betraying her was chilling.

Unless, the thought hit her with a happy jolt, he hadn't. Lloyd could be perfectly innocent of the whole set-up. Maybe he had left the office open – or let someone else, a friend, use their shared space for some reason. Dulcie found herself walking faster.

That could be it; suddenly it was all perfectly reasonable. Lloyd would have no reason to suspect anyone. Maybe he'd met a friend here. Maybe he'd run off to the bathroom while his friend waited. Not Raleigh, but . . . Rafe came to mind. Rafe, who Lloyd trusted, certainly enough to hang out in his office for a few minutes. Maybe Rafe had planted that page here. Or maybe he'd simply hoped to hide it, afraid for some reason to destroy it. Either way, if it had been stuck into Dulcie's drawer without Lloyd's knowledge, that would exonerate Lloyd. Suddenly, instead of dreading a meeting with her office mate, she was hoping he'd still be there. He'd explain. It was all so obvious, Dulcie practically ran the last block.

'Don't lock up!' She called down the hall. Lloyd had his key in the door as he looked up.

'Dulcie! You're early.' He checked his watch. 'Unless this is off.'

'No, no, you're fine.' Dulcie leaned on the door frame and tried to catch her breath. 'I was hoping you'd still be here.'

Lloyd raised his eyebrows. Office etiquette called for each to vacate the tiny space when the others' students might come by. 'Everything OK?'

'Of course.' Dulcie spoke too quickly and saw the puzzled look on her friend's face. He didn't know anything, she was sure. And then, suddenly, she wasn't sure. Suze's warning echoed through her mind. She couldn't just ask. Too much was at stake.

Lloyd, meanwhile, was staring at her. 'I mean, as much as it can be now,' she tried to cover. 'I just . . .' She looked at the door, unsure how to continue. 'You always lock this, don't you?'

'Of course.' He was definitely looking at her funny. 'Dulcie, is something wrong? Did something go missing?'

'No, I mean, I don't think so.' She sounded inane, and she knew it. Getting information without giving any was more difficult than she'd thought. 'I just thought maybe someone had been in my desk,' she came up with finally. It was weak, but it was better than asking outright. 'Everything was . . . messed up.'

'It's the mice, isn't it?' He was nodding. 'I should have told you. I left a bag of pretzels in my desk last week, and something gnawed a hole. Left some – ah – souvenirs behind, too. I brought my lunch again today, but I've taken all my trash. I've been meaning to tell you, but with everything so crazy . . .'

'Thanks.' She didn't know what else to say, and so she watched as her friend pocketed his keys. 'You think of calling an exterminator?' It was the best she could come up with. Maybe he had let custodial services in. Maybe they had let someone else come in while they were working . . .

'What? No way.' Lloyd turned back. 'It was just a bag of pretzels. Not something worth killing over. But, hey, I've got section.' And with that, he headed down the hall.

'It doesn't mean anything.' Dulcie was sitting at her desk, trying to decipher Lloyd's words. 'He's a gentle guy. And I didn't ask him straight out if he'd let anyone in.' That was the crux of it. Dulcie couldn't figure out how to ask, not after she'd said that nothing was missing. To tell him about her address book would be to tell him too much. And to suggest that someone had planted evidence would be even harder to explain. Besides, she still wasn't one hundred per cent sure that it had happened here. No, she hadn't dropped her address book at Melinda's. She was sure of that, but she couldn't really be sure where she had last seen it. And, yes, her desk had seemed rearranged, but really, that could have been her memory – or the mice.

Mouse. Griddlemaus – Griddle*haus!* How could she have forgotten? She looked at her watch and tapped her foot anxiously. Her office hours were about to start. This early in the semester, she ought to stay here. Students had problems, and the sooner they were addressed, the easier the rest of the semester would be. Not to mention that she was on probation. Accessibility to her students wouldn't make or break her case, but if she ran out during posted office hours, it couldn't help.

Her office hours were supposed to last until four. The Mildon closed at four forty-five, which really meant fifteen minutes earlier, as the library staff started sorting and re-shelving the various effluvia of the days. Still, the Mildon was right across the Yard. She'd have time to run over and find out what Griddlehaus had been talking about. Maybe even read whatever he had found, if he hadn't already started closing down the archives. 'Not that it matters,' Dulcie muttered to herself. 'Because four o'clock will never come.'

Neither, it seemed, would any students. Twenty minutes later, Dulcie felt ready to pull her own curls out. After the tension of her interrogation, the quiet was, well, murder.

She looked up at the shelves before her, at the raking light coming in from that one high window. She'd watched that beam of light since it had moved from Lloyd's desk to hers in a slow, silent course. But even with its warm illumination, she knew she wouldn't be able to get any real work done. A week ago, she'd have been unaware of the beam's passage, reading her notes and looking up only when the occasional student came in, lost and a little scared.

A week ago, she'd had plenty of students. It had been all she could do to be gracious, when her own work had been trundling along so productively. A week ago, everything had been different. If only she had never heard of Melinda Sloane Harquist and her stupid book.

The light had reached her hands now, where they'd been drumming aimlessly on her laptop. But instead of warmth, the afternoon sun felt strangely cool. Like the brush of leather, she realized. Or the pads of a cat's paw, dabbing softly at the back of her fingers.

'Mr Grey?' She looked up into the sunbeam, at the slow dance of dust caught in its light. 'Are you there?'

Nothing, and she looked down at her fingers again, at the keyboard. She'd been wasting time, really. About to call up a game of solitaire. But she'd been thinking of Melinda, of how little she knew about her rival. With a silent nod of thanks to her feline guardian, Dulcie started typing.

'*Melinda Sloane Harquist.*' She hit 'enter' and waited while the screen before her filled with options. The first few clearly referred to different people: Dulcie doubted that her rival ran a used car dealership in Toledo or had died in 1898. Others were vague: Had the dead woman been selling a used Toyota? Had she been looking for a room-mate in the Tri-State area? It wasn't until Dulcie was halfway down the second screen that she found anything vaguely academic, anything she could positively link to the woman who had died.

'*Melinda Harquist to receive Dashwood Prize,*' she read. The link was to the *Ellery Teller*, student newspaper for Ellery College. Dulcie vaguely recalled hearing about it – small and artsy, with a make-your-own curriculum program that supposedly allowed 'brilliant minds to flower'. According to the paper, this prestigious award, which Dulcie had never heard of, honored an undergraduate's library collection.

'What a strange prize,' Dulcie said to herself. 'All that means is that you have money to buy books.' A strange feeling, like the faintest puff of air, brushed her forearms. 'Or she could have inherited a collection.'

She scrolled down, and felt her heart begin to race. This was silly, she told herself. She was worrying about nothing, about a possible hint that a vague and unformed fantasy would prove to be invalid. Still, she couldn't help thinking about it: Melinda had information about the author of *The Ravages*. She had some kind of noteworthy private library. Could she have inherited something important? Could she even have inherited something from the author herself?

Dulcie read further. No, the Dashwood Prize referred specifically to bound books, not manuscripts. Still, it left her wanting to know more, and so she typed in a few more words: family, background. Home. While she was waiting, she did some quick calculations. Two hundred years would be ten generations, more or less. A rare book could have been passed along over that span. Of course, that would mean that her author had married. Several of her colleagues, even Thorpe himself, had suggested that her periods of silence could be explained away by family issues, including childbirth or rearing a family. But Dulcie had read her radical essays, comparing the institution of marriage to – what was it? – '*Slavery that enchain'd not only limbs but mind, taking o'er the last free exercise of the Female spirit.*'

No, despite her own fantasies that she, somehow, was descended from her nameless heroine, Dulcie couldn't see how she fit any kind of domesticity, happy or not, in with the composition of such fiery words.

'*Harquist, Melinda.*' Dulcie clicked on the link, expecting another item from the Ellery website. Perhaps an early article on the author of *The Ravages*, or on some other 'She-Author'. Instead, this seemed to be a who's-who type entry. Yes, she scrolled up, and saw 'Who's Who of Women in Academics'. Dulcie itched to go to the main directory. Was she listed?

Fighting off the urge, she scrolled back down and read. '*As the sole child of a single mother, I have always felt supported . . .*' Well, that explained it, Dulcie thought. This was some kind of vanity press that solicited entries from its 'honorees'. At a price, no doubt. '*Nor have I felt the pressing need for male approval of those raised with an overwhelming male presence.*' Dulcie could have laughed at that one. Tell that to Rafe – and to all the others she charmed. '*Indeed, never knowing my father has made my life singularly free to pursue academic excellence uninhibited by any male dominion.*'

That was sad. Dulcie sat for a moment. Her own father, Lucy's one-time 'soul mate', had been present for Dulcie's early life. He still wrote to her when his busy schedule of meditating or whatever allowed. At least, Dulcie thought with a sigh, she knew who he was.

Something tickled her memory. Her name – that was it. Hadn't someone said that Melinda had added the 'Sloane' because it was a family name? Maybe she found her father; Dulcie found the thought surprisingly heartening. But, no: '*As I proceed with my career, I have chosen to honor the mother who raised me and her mother before her, taking my maternal grandmother's maiden name as part of my own.*'

That didn't mean she hadn't found him, Dulcie told herself. She might have had time. But, no, she saw, the entry had been updated only the month before. Well, maybe that meant one less parent to mourn her, Dulcie told herself. Somehow, though, that just made it all worse.

FORTY

Subsequent searches proved fruitless. No articles, no early hints of that thesis topic. Nothing that could have warned Dulcie that her own work was about to be derailed, and Dulcie realized she was in no mood to dissect the life of the late woman. She was so disheartened that she was ready to call it a day and close up early when her phone rang.

'Chris!' In her joy, she didn't even want to let him speak. 'Honey, I want to apologize. I know I get upset, but I was out of line.'

'No, Dulcie, please,' he cut her off, and she waited, sure that his apologies would follow. 'I know this has been a really difficult time. Believe me, I know.'

That wasn't really what Dulcie had been hoping for, but in her current conciliatory mood, she was willing to let it go.

'I shouldn't take these things out on you, though.' There, she'd wanted to get that out. 'It's just, well, finding one of my colleagues dead and then being hauled before the dean . . .'

She let her voice trail off, waiting for her boyfriend to rush in with sympathetic support.

'So, she's your colleague now?' He chuckled, and Dulcie felt her stomach clench up. 'No, I know, it was pretty horrible. And I'm sorry, too, Dulce.' That was better, but before Dulcie could make her next move – offer to pick up dumplings – Chris continued. 'I know I've not been myself lately and, frankly, I know things have to change.'

'Change?' She was having an out-of-body experience. She had to be. 'Chris?'

'Yeah.' He drew the word out, his voice sounding tired. 'I was thinking—'

'Ms Schwartz?' Dulcie looked up. Thalia, her English 10 student, was in the open doorway. 'Are you free? Oh, sorry.' She backed into the hall.

'Thalia, give me a minute?' Dulcie put her hand over the receiver, but Chris must have heard.

'Dulce, it sounds like you're busy,' her boyfriend said. 'Look, I have some ideas. We'll talk later.'

'Chris, wait!' She couldn't let him go like this. Not with the dreaded 'we'll talk' hanging between them. 'Chris!' Clearly, however, he didn't want to linger. The line was dead.

'Ms Schwartz?' Thalia stuck her head in, her pale face lined with concern. 'Is everything OK?'

'What? Oh, yes, it's fine.' To give herself a moment, Dulcie grabbed a bunch of the many papers piled on her desk and started to shuffle them into shape, sending others flying. 'Come in.' Her head was spinning. She knew that with everything that had happened she wasn't being entirely rational. Still, she worried. She'd been difficult lately, maybe too difficult. Would Chris be having second thoughts about them living together? He wouldn't be breaking up with her, would he?

'Ms Schwartz?' Dulcie looked up – and then down again. Thalia was kneeling by the side of the desk. 'I think you dropped this.'

Dulcie took the sheet of paper her student had retrieved. At its top, like some offbeat letterhead, she saw the semi-circular ring of a coffee cup stain and felt herself blush. It didn't do for students to see how little respect she might have for their work. She glanced down at the type below the dark brown brand. *'Clearly, those who read "The Ravages of Umbria" would have little idea of the rationally radical ideas enthusiastically espoused by its anonymous author . . .'*

'Ms Schwartz?'

'Hang on, Thalia.' Dulcie stared at the paper in her hand. It couldn't be student work. This semester, she wasn't teaching anything remotely related to the Gothics, nothing in which one of her students would be writing about *The Ravages of Umbria*.

'In fine, if occasionally flailing, fictional format, we find a surprising syncretism of ideas, a coming-together of truly first-wave feminism and the new naturalism of the true Gothic, as embodied in the florid phrasing, "Much like her terror, like the screams frozen in her throat."'

It had to be hers. But, no, she would never have written that. Dulcie would never have assumed anything about the contemporary readership of the Gothic. After all, the author had been espousing total equality, and she didn't exist in a vacuum. That had been the point of her paper; that her author was a freethinker, an advanced thinker, but that she was speaking to a like-minded audience of newly educated, newly emancipated women. *Readers*.

'Should I . . .?'

'Just a moment.' Dulcie raised her hand as if to hold Thalia still.

Besides, Dulcie shook her head as she reread the sentence, she would never overuse alliteration like this. *Rationally radical? Fictional flailing?* And what was that about the scream? Wasn't that from the manuscript page? Then it hit her: this was another of Melinda's pages.

She shoved the page roughly into a desk drawer and tried to compose her features. 'So,' she said, finally. 'How may I help you this afternoon?'

'I, well, it's personal.' The thin girl in front of her colored, a dark flush reaching up to her large glasses. 'It's about one of my section mates.'

'Is there a problem?' Dulcie tried to remember the cursory training they'd all received. If someone had been harassing this girl, or worse, she needed to get ahead of it. 'You can talk to me, Thalia. Everything you say here will be kept confidential, but if someone is being unfair to you or pressuring you in any way, you have to tell me. We have to deal with it.'

Even before she'd finished her little speech, Thalia had begun shaking her head. 'No, no. I'm sorry, Ms Schwartz, I didn't mean to alarm you. It's nothing like that.'

Her focus now firmly on the student before her, Dulcie waited.

'It's, well, it's just kind of awkward.' A quick glance up showed large dark eyes behind those frames. 'I've been tutoring him, you see. Only, it's become something more.'

Dulcie smiled. This was an old story of a different, happier kind. 'And that's a bad thing?' she asked, keeping her voice soft.

A vehement nod. 'Yes, I think so.' The girl sounded determined, and drew a breath, obviously searching for the right words.

While she rallied, Dulcie readied a little speech, something about how a peer tutor is not in a position of authority. There was nothing unequal about their status, hence, there were no ethical issues involved.

'You see, I think he's doing wrong,' the dark-haired girl finally said. 'Something immoral, maybe even illegal, I don't know. And I don't want to report him. I . . . I like him too much. But I want to get him to stop before he gets into trouble. I mean, he could get me into trouble, too. You know?'

FORTY-ONE

I t had taken Dulcie a good half-hour to come up with an answer for Thalia. The girl refused to give any details about what was happening, and although Dulcie suspected who the girl was talking about – she had seen her with Andrew, after all – she couldn't do anything without confirmation. Or the girl's consent. And Thalia was adamant about wanting to handle this herself. Not even Dulcie's direst warnings about getting herself in too deep seemed to have an effect.

'I need to talk with him, that's all.' She kept coming back to that. 'If he thinks I've broken his confidence, he'll withdraw, and then he'll never get himself out of it.'

Ultimately, Dulcie had fallen back on the student handbook, referring her student to every section on ethics that she could find. Without specifics, it was the best she could do, and Thalia seemed a little more at ease by the time she left. For Dulcie, the entire interaction was frustrating.

At least, Dulcie thought, as she watched her student head down the hall, the student had been a distraction. Her watch showed that office hours were a few minutes to their close, and so she grabbed her bag, carefully locking the office door behind her as she left.

Climbing the stairs, she considered her student's issue. Andrew – it had to be Andrew – was doing something that wasn't quite on the level. Dulcie thought back to her interactions with the young man. He'd seemed above board, and Dulcie didn't want to believe that was an act – or that she was so susceptible to male beauty. However, she had to admit that looking more like a SoCal surfer than the usual pale Yard scholar might make short cuts easier for him. As she walked across the Yard, she tried to conjure up the possibilities. Had he charmed some teaching assistant out of a copy of a test? Had he smiled that killer smile when caught cheating?

It was probably nothing, Dulcie thought. Maybe he was pushing Thalia a bit, trying to get her to 'edit' his papers. She didn't want to think the handsome undergrad had courted the skinny girl just for her brains. There was no denying that she was a better student than he was, though, and such a suspicion would go far to explain Thalia's reticence.

As she strode toward the Mildon, Dulcie tried to put these issues aside. She'd done all she could for the girl. Now she needed to focus on Griddlehaus. He'd found something, he'd said, and Dulcie needed to put all her energies into her work.

She would not, she thought as she walked by the university administration building, allow herself to be dragged down by the dean. The words 'disciplinary probation' rose before her, and she ducked her head, eager to put the stone building behind her. He was wrong. His sources were bad. She would be cleared by whomever he assigned to investigate her case. Out of the corner of her eye, she saw the big doors open and she glanced up. Maybe she'd already been cleared. Maybe the dean was sending a messenger to find her now.

Something about the figure was familiar – the build, the way the tall youth loped down the stairs and took off. Dulcie spun around and watched as he disappeared around the corner of the building. It was Chris, she realized, and he was hurrying away from her.

FORTY-TWO

There had to be an explanation, a rational one, for Chris being in University Hall. Maybe there had been some mix-up with his registration, or with one of the students he shepherded through the computer labs. Maybe he had an appointment with another dean in the building. Maybe . . .

It was no use. Dulcie stood, rooted to the spot, and watched these excuses vanish like her departed beau. She and Chris had been registered for weeks, as had their students. Any problems that came up now, in mid-September, would have to do with grading or transcripts, and those offices were in the old Byerly Hall. As for other errands – Dulcie visualized the long hallway and the placards outside each office or suite: alumni affairs, varsity promotions. Something with environmental compliance happened down at the end; she remembered seeing some kind of celebration when the rehab of the Science Center had been completed. None of these were likely to have called her boyfriend in, and certainly any of them would have been worth mentioning.

No, there was no way around it. Either Chris had been called in to give evidence against her, or he was – the idea sprang into her mind – volunteering some kind of information. After all, he had access to all of her computer files, even the ones that were supposedly encrypted.

No, she wouldn't believe it. Lloyd she would keep her distance from – more because of his friendship with Rafe than anything else. Thorpe she already knew wouldn't lift a finger to help her. But Chris? There had to be an explanation.

'*We'll talk.*' His words echoed in her memory. She would just have to wait.

In the meantime, she could still salvage something of the day. With a lump in her throat she turned and started once again toward Widener and the Mildon Collection.

It was no use. Instead of bounding up the wide granite stairs, Dulcie felt each leaden step. The security guard took forever to examine her ID, and the elevator was slow. By the time she got down to the collection's special entrance, it was ten to five. Officially, the collection was still open, but, as she knew from long experience, too late for anything to be taken out of the archives.

When Dulcie saw the security gate – half down in preparation for closing – she was tempted to just collapse in the hallway and cry. She was, in fact, slumped against the wall when Thomas Griddlehaus saw her.

'Ms Schwartz!' He abandoned the cart he'd been pushing and ran out to greet her. 'Are you all right? Have you been hurt?'

'No, I'm fine.' Forcing a smile on to her face, she struggled to her feet. 'It's just been an exhausting day and I ran.' She gestured to the gate. 'Then, when it looked like I was too late, I guess I indulged in a bit of drama.'

'Perfectly understandable.' The little man gestured toward the opening. 'And in truth, I shouldn't be letting anyone in at this hour. But for you, Ms Schwartz . . .'

'Thanks.' The smile became genuine as she followed him into the collection's sterile, white anteroom. 'After your call, I confess, I've been looking forward to this all day.'

'Oh.' Griddlehaus began rubbing his hands together. Something was wrong. 'About that.'

'You . . . *didn't* find something?' Dulcie braced herself. This day could get worse.

'No, no, I did, I did. Only . . .' The little man paused to glance in one direction, then another. Since the library around them was silent, the effect was comical. In any other circumstance, Dulcie would have been tempted to laugh. 'I can't show it to you,' he concluded, his voice sinking to a loud whisper. 'It's been sequestered. Again.'

'What?' Her own voice sounded loud to her and clearly alarmed the clerk. 'But, why?'

'Well, you know, originally, I had pulled the material for Ms Sloane Harquist,' he said, leaning in. 'So I thought that, considering what had happened, it would be fine to re-file it. I had several documents and, of course, those boxes of unidentified writings, as you'll recall.'

Dulcie nodded. Melinda's request had covered everything, ranging from the Paine letters to the boxes Dulcie herself had only begun to sort through.

'I was in the process of replacing them, when I realized what had happened, and I became so excited that I called you right away. But then I was informed that I was to surrender everything that might pertain to Ms Sloane Harquist's thesis. The young man who had been sent insisted on taking the material with him.'

The little man looked around again before continuing, his voice heating up with outrage. 'I understand the need to investigate her unfortunate accident, Ms Schwartz. I do. Though how her thesis might be involved, I don't understand. And I certainly do *not* see the need to remove valuable, and fragile, documents from the one place where we can guarantee that they are properly maintained.'

They both fell silent at the dean's extreme breach of etiquette, and, for a moment, Dulcie felt a wave of relief. He hadn't mentioned the case against her. It was embarrassing to have her ethics questioned, and she wouldn't want Griddlehaus to doubt her. Still, she suspected that her case – rather than the murder investigation – had caused the dean to nab the documents. 'When did this all happen?'

'Less than an hour ago,' he said. 'I meant to call you after closing.'

The timing could have been coincidental, but Dulcie doubted it. She didn't think that Chris would be doing the dean's dirty work for him. Still, the timing was suggestive.

Her thoughts were interrupted by the little clerk leaning in closer.

'That isn't all,' he said, his voice so soft she barely heard him. 'I made a copy.'

'A copy?' Now it was Dulcie's turn to look around, though for a different reason. 'But . . . how?' The Mildon, she knew well, had nothing so mundane as a Xerox machine. The light, it had been explained to her, would have been too harsh for most of the papers in the collection.

'By hand.' Griddlehaus blinked up at her. 'I told him I needed to check out everything he was taking, so while I was copying his information down, I also quickly jotted down a few relevant lines.'

'Mr Griddlehaus, I love you!' Dulcie cried out. 'I mean, thank you,' she added at a lower volume.

The clerk turned away, blushing. He was flustered, Dulcie realized, and when he opened a drawer and started fussing, she waited for him to recover his equilibrium. But he was not simply covering his embarrassment, she saw, when moments later he pulled out the famous log book. Inside its leather binding, sheets of yellow tickets – and their carbon copies – made for a simple and yet very workable system. Anything that could be checked out – and not much could from the collection's rarities – would be noted here, with the borrower's name confirmed and countersigned by the clerk on duty. Ever since the problems of the previous semester, the library had been planning to update the system, and there was talk about palm-print technology or, at the very least, a swipe-card database. Ultimately, however, this anachronistic and low-cost system seemed to work best, provided that the clerk on duty was reasonably awake and honest.

Griddlehaus was both, and he had cleaned the house of any suspect characters on his staff over the summer. But Dulcie ignored the neatly printed names and instead looked where the clerk now pointed: at five lines of tiny, almost calligraphic script. She squinted and leaned in, and Griddlehaus rooted through the drawer to come up with an oversized magnifying glass.

Placing it on the page, she could now read: *Those red-gold locks, besmirch'd by life's gore, she now addressed. "The Sire of my troubles, and also of my deepest joy," proclaim'd she, though he would ne'er again respond.'*

It was the rest of the passage – the one Dulcie had started to decipher. Eagerly, she read on: '*Would have been better for this woman to stand alone, for to be friendless is to know that which is true for our Sex. 'Tis better far.'*

'The false hope of love!' Dulcie gasped. That last line, it was taken nearly verbatim from the essay she had been reading so recently. And the first bit, with the bloody head? 'Oh, Mr Griddlehaus,' she worked to keep her voice low. 'I think you're right. This *is* the missing link. If we accept that the "False Hope of Love" essay was written by the author of *The Ravages*, and I think I've made that case, then this links the book fragment to her, too. That means—'

He was nodding. 'You have it, Ms Schwartz. You have proof that your subject wrote another novel, perhaps the great work discussed in Mr Paine's letters. An Anglo-American Gothic.'

'A horror novel.' Dulcie's mind raced. 'But I have to find more. There has to be more. Mr Griddlehaus—'

'There is, Ms Schwartz.' The little man sounded ever so slightly smug. 'In fact, this is not even what I had called you about. There is more.'

'More?' She couldn't stop staring at the tiny translation. 'May I take this, Mr Griddlehaus? This is so exciting.'

'You don't have to.' He lowered his voice. 'I am afraid I took a rather large liberty.'

She tore her eyes from the scrap of paper to look at him, waiting.

'I'm afraid I did something of which you might not approve.'

Dulcie nodded, expecting another small breach. Perhaps he had been so bold as to copy some text out in pen.

'I snuck something into your folder,' he said finally, his voice barely audible. 'A page of the manuscript.' He stopped, and Dulcie stared. 'It wasn't like *she* was going to need it any more,' he concluded weakly.

'Wait, that was you?' The manuscript, Melinda – none of this was making sense. 'Those pages? Don't you realize they make me look guilty? Like I stole her work? Like maybe I killed her? What were you thinking?'

He blinked up at her, mouth open, and she realized she had it wrong. 'I'm sorry,' she said, as she saw his eyes fill with tears. 'You didn't mean *that* manuscript. You meant . . . I'm sorry, Mr Griddlehaus.'

It was too late; he had turned away and was already tucking the ledger into the drawer. 'I should have known better,' he said, locking the drawer. 'We have rules for a reason. Only, I thought in this case . . .' A large sniff, and he pocketed the key.

'No, it's me. There's . . .' She fumbled, at a loss to explain everything. 'There's something else going on. Melinda Sloane Harquist's dissertation has gone missing, and I've found what may be parts of it.'

It was no use. She was confusing him more.

'I'm sorry,' she said finally. 'You've done nothing but try to help me, and I made an assumption and yelled at you.'

'No, you were right.' He opened a door to remove a tweed jacket, and reached for the lights. 'Protocols exist for a reason.'

'Mr Griddlehaus, please,' she was practically begging. 'I am sorry, really, and I deeply appreciate what you've done for me.' She followed him as he turned off another set of lights, leaving the back rooms in darkness. 'May I see the page, the one you put in my folder? Please?'

'Well, perhaps when we reopen.' He punched in a code. 'Tomorrow.' And with that he ushered her out to the hallway, pulling the security gate down shut behind him. The exercise of routine seemed to have helped him regain his equilibrium, but it was definitely a stiffer, more formal Griddlehaus who pulled a cloth cap from his pocket and adjusted it on his head with a nod. 'Goodnight, Ms Schwartz.'

She watched him make his way down the main library corridor with a heavy heart. Griddlehaus had done nothing but try to assist her. He'd already given her a leg up with the fragment she'd started to read, and it appeared he'd identified an additional page of that handwritten manuscript, too.

In fact, she realized as she watched the elevator doors close on the small but devoted clerk, there might be even more he could have helped her with. Griddlehaus had signed out those pages to someone. If she hadn't flared up at him – if she hadn't spoken out of turn, he would have let her look at the yellow ticket. She could have found out exactly who had taken the documents. Who was looking through them for clues – and perhaps trying to frame her.

FORTY-THREE

S ome days were so long, they became a burden, Dulcie decided. When she'd left the library, she'd been surprised to see the sky still bright, the early autumn twilight just beginning to soften the shadows in the Yard. No matter what those trees said, however, it was time for her to head home. She was dreading whatever Chris might have to say, but she might as well get it over with. Besides, she could really use the comfort of a cat right about now, and if Mr Grey wasn't going to visit her, then Esmé would be called into duty.

The thought of the bouncy young feline cheered Dulcie, and she imagined how she'd love the Yard like this, the squirrels racing around among the shadows. The mockingbirds calling out their evening song somewhere high in the trees. Then again, if she did take Esmé out, she'd have to be careful, she realized. 'I wonder if she'd consider walking on a leash?'

The thought made her laugh, and her steps became lighter. Even the breeze seemed more optimistic, cool for a change but not chilly. She could almost imagine the soft rumble of a purr, somewhere around the vicinity of her hip. It took a moment before Dulcie noticed that something was buzzing by her side. She'd turned her phone on, automatically, as she exited the library, but she'd turned it to vibrate by mistake.

'Hello?' She was too late; whoever it was had hung up. With a mild sense of annoyance, she flipped over to voicemail and was shocked to see she'd missed four calls, the most recent from Trista. She hadn't talked to her friend since the cookie powwow, she realized with growing excitement. Maybe Trista had found something. Maybe she'd have the answer to all of this craziness. Dulcie longed to call her back, but the other three were from Lloyd and she paused. If he'd been trying that hard to reach her, she owed him the courtesy of calling him first.

Something must have been wrong with his phone, however, or with her voicemail. 'Dulcie, it's Lloyd.' That was the extent of the first message, before the call ended. The second, from the same phone, was a blank. On the third, she heard two voices, a woman's she didn't recognize and a man's that was vaguely familiar. She heard something falling – books? Papers? There was a thud, and once again, the call cut off. He must have dialed her by accident, she decided, at least after the first try.

With a free conscience, she dialed Trista.

'Hey, Tris.' The message had only said to call, but Dulcie was optimistic. 'What's up? Did you find anything?'

'Did I ever! Dulce, we've got to talk. I'm not sure what to do about it, just yet, but all information is useful, right?'

That didn't sound quite as good as Dulcie had hoped. Still it was better than nothing. 'Right,' she said, her own voice sounding a little too tentative. She looked around for some privacy. University Hall wasn't her favorite place, but at this time of day, even the dean must have gone home. Sheltering against the side of the white stone steps, she lowered her voice. 'Can you tell me what's up, Tris? I mean, it sounds urgent.'

'It is.' From the street noise in the background, Dulcie figured that Trista was walking – perhaps through the Square. 'But I don't know if we should talk on the phone. Can you meet me?'

Dulcie hesitated. She should go home. Chris would be expecting her soon, and now that she'd gathered the courage for that confrontation she was loath to put it off.

'Just for a few minutes?' Trista must have read her silence accurately. 'Where are you? I'm on JFK.'

Dulcie told her, and they agreed to meet at the Starbucks. It was only a slight detour. 'But I can't stay,' she said.

'That's OK, Dulcie. This is important. I mean, girl, you've got enemies.'

'Enemies?' It wasn't anything she didn't know. Still, to hear it confirmed made her stomach clench up. 'Tris, tell me, please.'

'Meet me.' The line went dead. Dulcie leaned back against the cool stone and closed her eyes. Rogovoy had warned her. She herself had her suspicions. Maybe this was good. She'd find out who her enemy was at last. 'Enemies,' she corrected herself. 'Plural.'

'Excuse me? Ms Schwartz?' She opened her eyes to find herself facing two cops. Dressed in the dark blue uniform of the City of Cambridge, the one addressing her was clean cut and stern. It was the cop from her interview with Rogovoy. Beside him stood a woman in the same uniform. She was holding, of all things, an oversized flashlight and a Manila envelope.

'We need you to come with us,' the male cop said.

'But, wait.' She had to meet Trista. She needed to go home. 'I've already spoken with you – and with Detective Rogovoy.'

The two cops looked at each other. The woman raised the folder, but almost imperceptibly her partner shook his head. 'Come along,' he said. 'We can talk at the station.'

'What's . . .?' She reached out for the folder, and the other cop jerked it away. As she did, the top flipped open. It was only for a split second, but it was long enough for Dulcie to see white paper, with typing on it. At its top: a coffee stain like a brand. The manuscript page from her desk was now evidence against her.

FORTY-FOUR

Lloyd must have been calling to alert her, she realized as she walked between the two officers. He must have wanted to warn her; maybe he saw what they had found and was hoping to give her a head's up. Unless, she thought, he had been the one to call them in. In which case, why phone? Guilty conscience?

It was all too complicated to sort out. At least, by herself.

'Excuse me?' she said to the female cop. 'I need to call my room-mate. Do you mind?' The woman had considered showing her the paper, she figured. She was sympathetic. Once again, however, the cop looked at his partner, and he shook his head.

'Sorry.' The officer sounded regretful, at least. 'Once we're at the station.'

She continued walking, phone in hand, when it hit her: she had Suze on speed dial. The phone was turned on. Feeling the keyboard carefully, she hit 'three'. At least, she hoped it was three – she really didn't need to have Lucy hear what was going on.

'Legal Defense.' The voice was soft, muted against Dulcie's palm, and she cleared her throat to cover it. Neither cop seemed to notice.

'I would like to know,' she said loudly, 'why I am being taken to the Cambridge Police Station. I believe it is my right to be told.'

'Dulcie!' She could hear Suze's voice before she hung up. 'I'm on my way.'

The male cop gave her a dirty look. 'I said you'd get your chance.' His partner smiled as she opened the cruiser door.

During the short drive, Dulcie's mind raced. This was more than someone just trying to get out from under a cloud, or help out a friend with a dodgy favor. This was a concerted attack. Not only had someone planted that page – both those pages, she admitted silently – but someone had also dropped a dime about where to find them.

That didn't clear Lloyd, she realized as the cruiser made its way toward Central Square. He might have reached out to her because the cops had shown up, asking which was her desk. Or it could mean that he knew something was wrong. Maybe Rafe had asked him to give her those pages, and he had done so, not knowing what they meant. Maybe . . . It was useless, Dulcie realized as the car pulled into a marked spot. As much as she wanted to trust Lloyd, to believe that he hadn't helped land her in this mess, the truth was that she knew very little of what had happened, and she understood even less.

What she did know for sure was that she was in trouble. And although she had no idea what a cat, even one on the spectral plain, could do for her in this situation, she found herself looking around as the female officer escorted her out of the cruiser. 'Mr Grey?' she whispered to the air. 'Any ideas?'

The female cop turned toward her, but Dulcie shook her head. Instead, his name on her lips, she glanced into the shadowy corners of the alley as the two officers walked her up to the forbidding stone building. 'Mr Grey?' Could it be that she imagined the breeze, soft as the touch of fur, that brushed her face as they made for the front door? Was there something in the small dust devil that rose up in the corner by the door, something with green eyes, perhaps?

Newly heartened, Dulcie prepared herself for the confrontation to come. She would, she decided, tell the police everything. Suze had advised her to come clean about the first page, and such a disclosure had to be better late than never, or so she hoped. Besides, if she explained about the first page showing up, stuck to her notepad, she could tell the cops her theory about Rafe. She knew he was a friend of Lloyd's, but really, as the dead girl's ex, as well as a potential academic rival, he had every reason to be put through the same scrutiny that she was. And if he had set her up, well, that only made him worse.

She wouldn't feel good telling tales about Rafe. For all she knew, he might be innocent. But someone wasn't, and whoever it wasn't, wasn't her. She paused for a moment, the syntax getting the better of her. But as the female cop turned to face her, she started moving again. Murmuring her question to the air – 'Isn't that right, Mr Grey?' – she allowed herself to be herded into the building.

Unlike its university counterpart, the city police HQ had nothing of the quiet office about it. Although the same dull fluorescent lighting illuminated a similar set up, with a tall wooden barrier serving as some kind of counter in a large reception area, everything else looked different. Older, grimier, from the stained linoleum to the three grey-haired men who sat on the reception benches, staring into space. But if she didn't see any trace of her beloved pet, Dulcie did catch sight of another face that was equally, if not more, welcome.

'Suze!' She jumped up and waved, causing both her escorts to whirl around. 'Over here.'

'You'll see your friend in a minute,' said the woman cop, in a not unkindly voice. Taking Dulcie's elbow, she walked her over to that wooden counter, and Suze disappeared behind a closed door. 'Let's get you signed in first.'

'She's not just my friend,' Dulcie couldn't help bragging. With Suze here, she was sure that everything would soon be straightened out. 'She's a lawyer.'

It took another forty minutes, however, before even her old room-mate could get to her. In the meantime, she was escorted through a glass-fronted door and down a long corridor badly lit by flickering fluorescents.

'Where are we going?' Dulcie wasn't too worried, not with Suze in the building. Her room-mate had seen her, hadn't she? Besides, she was getting hungry. Chris would be waiting for her, wondering where she was. 'When will I get my phone call?'

'Just a bit longer,' her escort said, though in answer to which question, Dulcie couldn't tell. 'Around here, please.' With her hand on Dulcie's elbow, she maneuvered her around a corner and toward an open door. 'Have a seat.'

Dulcie stepped into the doorway, then jerked back. 'Hey, wait.' She craned her neck down the corridor at a familiar sun-bleached mop. 'Andrew?'

He was gone, and the officer was losing patience. 'Ms Schwartz, please take a seat.'

'I know him,' Dulcie started to explain, as the cop nodded to an armless chair. 'He's one of my students. I don't understand—'

Then, suddenly, she did. Thalia had been trying to tell her, to warn her, when she visited. Thalia had said that her friend – Andrew – was involved in something that made her uncomfortable. Could that something have been planting evidence on her, in her office desk drawer? She pictured him at the house tea; he'd been pretty chummy with Rafe there. Would he be willing to do the tutor's dirty work? It almost made sense, but why?

And why wouldn't Lloyd have said something if the handsome undergraduate had dropped by? Lloyd was friendly with the senior tutor, but as far as Dulcie knew, he didn't know Andrew at all. Dulcie shook her head, more confused than ever.

Before she could puzzle it out, however, the door jerked open and Suze stormed in like a fury. 'Dulcie! Are you OK?'

'Suze!' Dulcie couldn't help smiling. 'Thank the goddess, you found me.'

Suze stepped aside to let in a faded middle-aged woman in a lumpy suit holding an equally lumpy canvas briefcase.

'This is my boss,' Suze whispered to Dulcie, pulling up the extra chair. 'I figured it would help to have someone who is actually licensed to practice in the state.'

'Thanks, Suze.' Dulcie looked up at the older woman, who was talking to the police woman in the doorway. 'I'm sorry to be such a bother.'

'Hey, it's part of my practicum.' Suze didn't seem at all put out. 'We agreed on the way over. I'll handle everything, and she'll sign off. It's great that I get real-world experience. In a way,' she paused when she saw the look on Dulcie's face, 'you're helping me out.'

'You really are a great friend, you know.' Dulcie had to give her that. 'So, what happens now?'

Suze looked up at her boss. 'Now we figure out what's going on. If you're simply here to be questioned, then you can leave. If they're going to press charges, well, then . . .' She paused and looked at her friend. Dulcie knew she'd gone pale, and Suze continued with more enthusiasm in her voice. 'If that's the case, then we tackle that.'

'Burn that bridge when we come to it?' Dulcie tried to conjure a smile.

'Exactly.' Suze patted her hand. 'Don't worry, if you can help it, Dulcie. I really don't think that's what's going on here. I mean, they didn't say anything to you about being arrested, right?'

Dulcie nodded – then quickly shook her head, and Suze, smiling, went on. 'And they didn't Mirandize you?' Another shake.

'They're just bluffing then.' Suze sounded so confident, Dulcie looked to her for more. 'Some of it is the usual town-gown tension,' her old friend continued. 'You know, they think the university is soft on its own. They think college cops, like your buddy Rogovoy, can't solve anything. And now that they've gotten their hands on a murder case—'

Dulcie put her hand up. 'Suze, please.' Her friend blinked, and Dulcie realized that she must look as green as she felt.

'I'm sorry,' Suze leaned in. 'I got carried away. There really isn't any reason to be scared.' She tried a smile, but Dulcie knew her too well. 'Elizabeth is the best there is,' she said finally.

They both looked up. Suze's boss was still talking, but as they watched, she turned and walked away. The cop remained.

'There's a lot of paperwork,' said Suze, sounding so blasé that Dulcie almost believed her. She had, however, brought up something Dulcie had wanted to discuss.

'Speaking of paperwork . . .' Now it was her turn to lean in toward her friend. 'They found another of those pages in my desk. I think maybe I know how it got there, and the page in my bag, too.' She looked up. The cop was still in the doorway, but staring across the hall. Dulcie dropped her voice further. 'One of my students, Andrew Geisner, is here, too. I don't know what's up with him, but he was one of the bunch talking to Rafe Hutchins the other night.'

'Who's that?'

'Rafe Hutchins, senior tutor in Dardley.' Dulcie mused on the connection. 'And Andrew's working for the dean. I'm wondering if the dean is investigating this independently. If he has someone down here to report back to him. But why? I know he wants this solved, and he's already got me on probation . . .'

Suze's voice was gentle as she took her friend's hand.

'Dulcie, I don't know what to tell you,' she said. 'From everything you've told me, it just sounds like this dean is out to get you. And it would be a lot easier to expel you if you were facing a charge of murder.'

FORTY-FIVE

S uze's boss, Elizabeth Ventner, might look like someone's kindly aunt, her grey-streaked brown hair coming loose from its bun. But despite the old-fashioned 'do and a round face that ought to have been jolly, the attorney did not give an inch. For starters, she insisted on accompanying Dulcie into the interrogation room. ('A discussion? Please,' her soft voice had dripped with sarcasm.) Even then, she barely let Dulcie answer any questions.

'But I have an idea,' Dulcie had turned toward her at one point, gritting her teeth with the effort of keeping quiet.

'May I have a moment, please?' Elizabeth had turned toward the detective who was doing the questioning. He had nodded and stepped out of the room.

'Are they listening?' Dulcie looked around the apparently empty room.

'That would be illegal,' said Elizabeth, in what Dulcie recognized as a non-answer. 'However, as your attorney, I would advise you, once again, not to say anything.' This had been a running theme of the past ninety minutes.

'But I think I know what happened. I think Andrew Geisner, my student, planted those pages for some reason. And now he's here, looking for dirt to bring back.'

The older woman silenced her with a gesture. 'Please, Dulcie. We're not looking to present an alternative theory here. That's what we'll do if this goes to trial. Once again, please, let's keep this simple. Straightforward and simple. Got it?'

'I've got it,' Dulcie said with a resigned sigh.

'Good.'

It was excruciating. Not being able to give the nuance and context that seemed so incredibly relevant, and yet not being able to tune out, either, as Suze's boss and the cop went at it, dissecting her life for the past few days. But after her first few attempts to explain, she gave up, falling back on the 'yes,' 'no,' and 'I don't know' that the lawyer seemed to want.

Back and forth, short questions and shorter answers, until Dulcie felt dizzy. The whole thing was like some verbal tennis match, in which lobbing the ball was more important than the truth. As she watched, they went back over Saturday, the day of the murder, and the timing of who had been where when. When they moved on to the paper in her desk, she'd leaned in, hoping to hear something about how the office happened to be searched.

The police were intent on gathering information, however, not giving it out. The search was presented as a fait accompli – no reason, no tip-off. Nothing. Simply something that had happened and had turned up a page that had been verified as belonging to the missing manuscript. It was maddening.

'What we'd like to know is how, if Ms Schwartz claims no prior knowledge of this page, did it find its way into her –' he paused to check his notes – 'bottom-right drawer.'

'Claims! I don't know how it got there.' She couldn't help herself. 'But I do have some ideas—'

'Now's not the time.' Elizabeth shut her down, her eyes hard in that soft, round face. 'You and I can talk later.'

'If Ms Schwartz wants to volunteer some information . . .' The way the cop said it made Dulcie feel dirty – and grateful for her advocate's quick response.

'That was a communication with me. That's all,' she said. Another volley returned. 'Come on,' Elizabeth said to her. 'We're done here.'

The cop at the other side of the table didn't respond, and so when Elizabeth stood, Dulcie did, too. At a gesture from the older woman, she walked toward the door, opened it and stepped out. Nobody grabbed her, and she realized she had been holding her breath.

'Here's my card.' It took Dulcie a moment to realize that the woman standing beside her was still talking. 'If you want to go over any of this, we can arrange a time for you to come in. And if the police call you again or want you to come down here again, call me immediately.'

Dulcie took the card and looked at it, unseeing.

'Are you OK, Dulcie?' The attorney's voice was gentler than it had been inside the room, and Dulcie looked up to see the round face lined with concern.

She nodded. 'This is just all so confusing,' she said. It was the best she could come up with. Even though Dulcie didn't think she'd said more than thirty words in total during the entire interrogation, she was exhausted. 'I don't understand any of it.'

'They don't want you to.' Elizabeth's mouth was set in a grim line. 'Come on, let's get you home.'

It was more than she could hope for, but Dulcie's heart leaped when she saw Suze. Her friend jumped up from the waiting-room bench and strode toward them. 'Dulcie! Are you OK?'

Dulcie nodded, as Elizabeth hustled them both out of the building. 'Thank you so much, Suze. And you, too.' Dulcie turned toward the older woman.

Under the harsh street lights, Elizabeth looked as tired as Dulcie felt. But she smiled as she unlocked a beat-up sedan and Dulcie piled into the back seat. Suze, in the front, leaned over the seat-back to talk. 'So, tell me, you've got to have some ideas about who's setting you up.'

Elizabeth looked over. She didn't say anything, but Suze responded to her silent admonition. 'I'm not saying Dulcie should share her ideas with the cops. But you've got to agree, if we can figure out what's really going on here, it will be easier to clear Dulcie.'

Elizabeth nodded slightly, and Suze turned back to her friend. 'Tell.'

'Well, there's Rafe.' She gave her friend the low-down on the senior tutor, including the house tea. 'Which reminds me, did you see Andrew Geisner?'

Suze shook her head. 'I don't know him.'

'Tall, surfer-dude handsome.' Dulcie had rarely felt at such a loss for words. 'Young.'

'No, I think the youngest guy who walked by me was about forty. Or maybe that was just his lack of teeth. But I don't think he'd qualify as handsome.'

Dulcie was forced to agree. 'Maybe that means something, though. Maybe he wasn't being questioned. Maybe he was giving evidence. Does the police station have separate entrances?'

Elizabeth glanced over at Suze. 'It does. Your friend has a point.'

'I have to talk to him, then,' Dulcie decided, despite her fatigue. 'As soon as possible.'

'No, you don't.' Elizabeth broke in before Suze could. 'You have to stay out of trouble – and that means not talking to anyone who's involved. This might be something Suze could take on.'

'Happy to.' She looked it, too, and Dulcie realized how frustrating it must be for her friend, not being able to help. Still, she wasn't thrilled with the idea. Suze didn't know Andrew. She didn't have a relationship with him. She didn't know Thalia, or what her student had said about her boyfriend.

'Dulcie?' Suze was looking at her, and Dulcie realized that her doubt must be writ across her face. 'You've had a rough day. Let's talk about this tomorrow, OK?'

'OK.' That was fair. Elizabeth was pulling up in front of Dulcie's building, when another thought hit her. 'Suze, did you get a chance to call Chris?'

Guilt washed over her friend's face and she bit her lip. 'I'm sorry, Dulce. I forgot.' She checked her watch. 'It's not that late, though. Tell him it's my fault, OK? And give him a big hug from me.'

Dulcie nodded as she got out of the car. The situation with Chris was more complicated than she was able to explain right now. Repeating her thanks to Elizabeth, she waved them both off and went inside to face the music.

'Hello! I'm home!' At the sound of her voice, Esmé came galloping, skidding the last few feet across the hardwood floor to plow into Dulcie's shins. Dulcie responded by dropping her bag and scooping up the little cat, suddenly aware of how much she needed Esmé's warm comfort. After a moment of nuzzling that soft white belly, she realized that the feline tackle was the only greeting she'd received.

'Hello?' she called as she carried the cat into the kitchen. 'Chris?'

Nothing, not even a note. Only the cold remains of some takeout. Dulcie saw what looked like congealed *yu shiang* eggplant, and her heart sank.

'Oh, hell.' She put Esmé on the ground and reached for her phone. Sure enough, Chris had tried her several times in the past two hours. He had not, however, left any messages.

Taking a seat at the kitchen table, she dialed his number.

'Chris? Hi, sweetie, I'm so sorry—' The line disconnected. Dulcie immediately hit redial.

'I'm sorry, honey. I can explain—'

'Dulcie, I'm kind of busy right now.' He was, she could tell. She could hear raised voices. One voice in particular, a woman's, sounded familiar.

'Where are you, Chris? What's going on?'

'The Science Center, where else?' She could hear fatigue in his voice. Something else, too. 'Look, I'll call you when things settle . . .' That other voice, saying his name. Was it Darlene?

'Chris, please. I need you to know: it wasn't my fault. The police—' But he was gone.

Esmé seemed to sense something was wrong and jumped up on the table as Dulcie reheated the leftover Chinese. While the microwave whirred, she texted Chris, explaining about her detainment in short, unsatisfactory bursts. It was far less gratifying than telling him in person; she couldn't even be sure he'd read them. But at least he'd know what had happened, and maybe some of that coldness would turn to sympathy by the time they next spoke.

'If there's a next time,' she said, wallowing in the gloom. Then the timer pinged, and she allowed herself to be distracted by eggplant, dumplings, and the remainder of something that might be shrimp. Esmé stood watch but chose not to comment on any of it.

It wasn't until after eleven that Dulcie remembered her missed meeting with Trista. Her blonde friend, she was reasonably sure, wouldn't hold it against her. In fact, Trista might even sympathize – as Chris hadn't, Dulcie thought. Besides, maybe she'd have some good news.

Dulcie reached for her phone once again and dialed her friend.

At first, she was convinced she'd gotten the wrong number. Throbbing music, all bass and drums, forced her head away from the phone. 'Trista?'

'Hey, Dulcie!' her friend yelled back. 'What happened?'

'I was picked up by the cops,' Dulcie shouted. More noise, so she tried again. 'The cops got me!'

'That sucks!' her friend yelled back. And while that sentiment beat out the cold and tired response she'd gotten from her boyfriend, Dulcie began to despair of having a meaningful conversation. Just then, the volume cut out. 'There, that's better.' Trista was back.

'Where are you?' Dulcie had neither the money nor the inclination for dance clubs, and she'd never heard the People's Republik be that loud.

'Following up a lead, my friend.' Trista paused, and the music got louder again. 'In fact, I shouldn't linger in here or I'll lose him.'

'Him? Who? Trista, you said you had information for me?'

'Yeah, I think so.' In the background, a toilet flushed, and for a moment the music got louder again. 'Now I'm not so sure. That dean? He definitely had an interest in Melinda. I've got proof. But tonight he's out with someone else. A woman his own age. I don't know. Maybe he was cheating on her, and she found out?'

'I don't know. It sounds pretty weak to me.' The noise level was rising and falling behind Trista, and Dulcie wasn't sure what she'd heard. 'That was it?'

'I don't know,' her friend said. 'I know he was keeping tabs on her, and I think he— Oh, sorry!' Her voice took on an unnaturally perky tone. 'No, I'm not waiting. All yours.'

The music grew louder as Trista headed out the ladies' room door. 'Dulcie, I'll call you tomorrow. Gotta go. Stay safe.'

FORTY-SIX

'*B*lood, so much blood. She'd never known the human corpus could contain so much blood. The brightness of his copper hair now dull'd, matted with the darkening gore of life, now cooling—'

The pen scratched on the paper and stopped. A moment's

pause, a breath held, and it went back. Scratched out some words and started again. 'The luster of his coal-black hair now dull'd,' the pen wrote again.

Better to dissemble. Better to disguise the act, the crime. The sire of all her desires.

Dulcie woke with a start, confused, and sat up, disturbing the cat. She'd had the dream again, only this time it was different, a hodgepodge of older dreams and the more recent nightmare. She'd seen her author again, at her garret desk, writing. Only, this time, the scene didn't fade to the scene of horror. And the story had changed again, ever so slightly. Was this the result of the previous day's turmoil – or of finishing that iffy shrimp? Dulcie looked at Esmé, but the little cat turned away and began to wash.

A mumbled grunt from beneath the comforter caught her attention: Chris. Her boyfriend must have come home early that morning, but Dulcie had been out cold. Looking at him now as the morning sun filtered in through the blinds, she considered waking him. Maybe that grunt was a sign of a nightmare, in which case, she'd be doing him a favor.

'*Dulcie . . .*' The familiar voice had the edge of a growl in it, a low rumbling warning.

'No, you're right, Mr Grey,' she whispered to the empty air. He hadn't woken her, and she had no right to disturb his sleep. As if in confirmation, her boyfriend sighed and shuffled, and then seemed to drift off into a deeper and dreamless sleep.

'At least he came home,' she whispered to her feline companion as she slipped out of the sheets. 'At least he didn't, I don't know, go to sleep on the sofa.'

'*Dulcie.*' This time, the tone was admonishing, and Dulcie paused, waiting to hear what would come next. '*Is anger that important? Is fear? So many mistakes may be made under those influences.*'

'You're right, Mr Grey. It's just hard to know sometimes what's real and what's not.'

'*You're so afraid of mistakes, my dear.*' The voice had softened. '*Of going wrong. And yet your heart knows what matters – that even missteps may bring us closer to love. Your heart already knows this, Dulcie.*'

'So I should let Chris sleep?' She meant it as a joke, at least in part, mollified by the feline spirit's gentler tone. A low rumble, part purr but part growl, was her only answer, and Dulcie moved on to the kitchen, with Esmé galloping to catch up.

'It's just that Chris and I haven't had a chance to speak, Mr Grey.' Dulcie kept her voice low as she spooned out the coffee. 'I mean, I haven't had a chance to explain. And I really want to.' There was no point in trying to hide anything from her spectral pet.

Something much closer to a purr rumbled close by, and she felt the brush of fur on her bare shins. Looking over, she could see Esmé on the other side of the room, staring.

'We exist in relation to each other, Dulcie. We are here for each other, because of each other. All else is illusion.'

'Does that mean that you're only here because I need you?' As the coffee began to drip, Dulcie looked down. Esmé had taken Mr Grey's place at her feet, and she bent to pet the sleek black back. 'What about Esmé?' She asked the empty air. 'What is your relationship to her, or hers to you?'

'Mrrup.' Esmé responded in classic cat, but Dulcie got the hint, opening a can for her. 'Maybe I just exist to feed you,' she said as she put the dish down. Esmé, who managed to purr while she ate, declined to respond further, and Dulcie retreated to get dressed.

'You be good,' she said to Esmé, as she re-emerged ready to start her day. Dulcie had made enough coffee for two, but when the aroma hadn't woken her sleeping beau, she'd filled her commuter cup. Now she stood by the door, reluctant to leave. 'Don't wake Chris with your rampaging.'

Esmé looked up at her, and although the little cat didn't comment, her eyes seemed to glow with understanding. Dulcie hesitated, on the brink of saying more. If only the little cat would converse with her, as Mr Grey did. At times, Dulcie felt more like her pet's landlady than her person, or maybe her housekeeper and cook, and Dulcie would have loved to enlist her aid with Chris. Well, her boyfriend had undoubtedly gotten her texts from the night before; he had come home, after all. And she'd left a brief, affectionate note by the coffee maker.

She checked her watch one more time. If she waited, she'd

probably end up waking him. Besides, if she left now, she just might be able to sneak into the Mildon before her ten o'clock class. The special collection didn't open until nine forty-five, but if Mr Griddlehaus were there – and if he were better disposed toward her this morning – she knew he'd let her in a few minutes before.

'Maybe that's what Mr Grey meant,' she mused out loud as she shouldered her bag. At the very least, she could work on repairing that relationship, she decided, and headed out the door.

Leaving distracted as she did, she didn't see how Esmé had responded to her last words. Didn't see the little cat rise up on her hind legs and reach out with her mittens. As the door closed behind her, the little cat sank back down to the floor, a look of dejection on her sweet, furry face.

'*She doesn't get it, does she?*' The voice, high and clear, was so soft as to barely stir the silent air.

'*She will, little one,*' the other voice, deeper and full, replied. '*She's begun to feel the connections, and that is more than many can. Give her time, little one.*'

'*But does she have time?*' the younger cat asked the empty air. And when no answer was forthcoming, she began to bathe.

FORTY-SEVEN

By hurrying, Dulcie got to the library in record time. As she dashed up the wide stone steps, however, she realized that her slight breathlessness was not so much because of her speed as her nerves. Through her own carelessness, she had insulted the very person who had been most helpful to her. And it wasn't, she realized as she opened her bag for the guard to peruse, just that Griddlehaus had given her access to some of the collection's relevant rarities. The little clerk had become a friend, as well. Someone who understood her love of research and the written word, as Chris never would.

That thought gave her a twinge of guilt, but she brushed it off as she made her way to the elevator. She loved Chris, and he loved her, too, she repeated for reassurance. They might be going through a rough patch, and they might have different interests, but their hearts were joined. Perhaps, she mused as the elevator – empty this early – descended, that was what Mr Grey had meant.

Maybe this was a good thing, she thought, brisk walk and caffeine combining for an unusual bout of optimism. Maybe she should make the effort to expand her friendship with the library clerk. But as the elevator opened on the Mildon corridor, the combination of the overhead fluorescents and her own imagination got the better of her. Somehow, she couldn't see the fastidious clerk joining her crew for a pint at the People's Republik. Couldn't imagine having him over for dumplings from Mary Chung's either. Well, she thought with a sigh, at least I can return kindness with kindness, and let things progress as they may.

Unless they couldn't, that is. As she rounded the corridor to the special collections entrance, she saw the security gate still down and locked tight.

'Mr Griddlehaus?' She knocked on the metal barrier and leaned in, the better to hear any scurrying within. 'Are you there?' She knocked again. Her watch showed twenty of ten – still not officially opening time – but Dulcie had been at the Mildon often enough over the last few months to know that the gate would usually be up by now. And while other staffers might tow the line, keeping her out for another five minutes, her friend the chief clerk would usually let her in.

Unless, of course, they were no longer friends. 'Mr Griddlehaus?' She tried again, rapping softly with her knuckles, and then louder, to get the attention of anyone inside.

'He's not in yet.' A voice from further down the hall made Dulcie start, and she turned to see a beefier, younger man, probably a student, pushing a cart up to the closed elevator. 'I usually see him in the mornings,' the chubby man said. 'And I didn't today.'

'Is everything alright?' Dulcie couldn't help it. The last few days suggested all sorts of horrible alternatives.

'Why shouldn't it be?' The young man stood and looked at her, his face as round and red as a berry. 'Do you know something?'

'No, no.' Dulcie shook her head. 'I just worry.' She tried a smile to soften her words. 'He's a friend.'

'Huh.' The round-faced man seemed unimpressed. 'Well, I can't help you.' The elevator opened and without another word, he pushed the cart in and disappeared.

Unsure of what else to do, Dulcie waited another five minutes. By ten of, however, she had to face the inevitable. Mr Griddlehaus was not at his usual post, and nobody was going to open the Mildon, at least not in time for her to make her class.

As she hurried across the Yard, Dulcie couldn't help thinking about the library clerk. She knew very little about him. Only that he loved his job and took any slights on the collection personally. He had also, as far as she knew, never missed a day of work. On occasion, he had other staff scheduled, but it was a rare day that he did not also drop in, at least to open the collection. Still, for all their time together, she had never found out the most basic information about him.

Did Thomas Griddlehaus live alone or with someone? Did he have cats? For all Dulcie knew, he could be lying ill or injured somewhere, and she would have no idea how to find him.

When her phone rang, she grabbed for it. Maybe it was the little clerk, calling to explain. He'd been delayed by a missed bus, he'd tell her. Or maybe by a well-aimed hairball. But, no, she saw as she dug the cell from her bag. Still, this was almost as good.

'Trista!' She kept walking, one eye on the Memorial Church clock. 'I didn't think you'd be up so soon.'

'Why?' Trista sounded puzzled. 'Anyway, I'm on my way to a seminar, but I wanted to let you know. Something is up with your pretty-boy student, but I don't think it's what we thought.'

'Huh?' Dulcie stopped walking, hoping that would make Trista's sense clearer. 'I don't understand.'

'Well, I was going to talk to that boy, Andrew, but I thought I'd ask around about him first. And guess what? He does work for the dean, but I'm thinking that in his off-hours, they were rivals, not colleagues, if you get my drift.'

'Tris, I don't.' The church bells started. Dulcie's section would be gathering.

'Well, the dean? I saw him at the Harvest, chatting up some

woman. That's why I followed him to that dance club last night.'
Dulcie wanted to ask her friend what she'd been doing at the
pricey Square boîte. After all, the restaurant's bar was a notorious
pick-up spot for the tenured set.

'I dragged Jerry with me.' Trista must have sensed something
in Dulcie's silence. Lucy, she knew, would have a different
explanation. 'I mean, sometimes I want to go to a place that can
mix a Martini.'

Dulcie resisted the temptation to comment. Instead, she listened
as the bells finished chiming the hour. She was definitely going
to be late.

'But when I saw Dean Mack Daddy, I knew I had to check
him out. Dulcie, he was all over this woman. The good thing
was, she looked age appropriate for him. I mean, she was old
– like forty, at least. Though kind of nice looking.'

'Tris . . .' Dulcie needed to get moving.

'But what got me was, this guy wasn't acting like he'd just
lost his lover, you know what I mean? I mean, everyone else I
talk to says that he and Melinda were like this – and now he's
already replaced her? Of course, he could be a psychopath.'

Dulcie didn't know when Trista's seminar started. She did know
she needed to get moving. 'So that's it? The dean has moved on?'

'Well, or we read it all wrong. Because, well, I told you I was
asking about Andrew?' Dulcie nodded. Trista didn't need any
encouragement. 'Well, it turns out he was asking about Melinda
– talking to anyone who knew her back in the day. Doing some
pretty sophisticated online searches about her, too, using the dean's
all-university access.' Dulcie didn't want to ask how her friend
had found out this particular tidbit. It sounded too close to what
she herself had done. Besides, Trista was still talking. 'I mean,
deep stuff – family background, where she'd lived. It was like
he'd made Melinda his pet project.'

'Maybe the dean found out?' That could explain the student's
appearance at the police station. 'Maybe he got jealous?'

'And killed Melinda?' Trista greeted someone, and Dulcie
heard a door opening. 'It's possible. He was definitely into her.
But Dulcie, I'd take a serious look – a serious and careful look
– at your handsome undergrad. I'm thinking Andrew was a
stalker.'

FORTY-EIGHT

'**D**ulcie, you can't.' Suze was adamant. 'You cannot question Andrew Geisner. It would be more than inappropriate. It would . . . well, let's just say, it could make things worse.'

Dulcie had called her old friend as soon as she'd gotten off the phone. Suze and her boss had already warned her about continuing her own investigation when they'd dropped her off the night before. 'Highly inadvisable,' had been the phrase Elizabeth Ventner had used. But Dulcie couldn't help but feel that now she had new information, a certain amount of poking about would be justified.

'No.' Suze knew her well enough to anticipate the arguments Dulcie had begun to frame. 'Under no circumstances. The cops called you in for questioning. You're a person of interest. They might charge you yet. Please, Dulcie, stay out of it.'

Dulcie had been suitably scared by the time they had rung off. However, she had not promised anything beyond the vague idea of 'being sensible'. By now, she was definitely late, however, so when the phone rang again, she resisted. A glance down as she ran up the Emerson stairs showed her the caller was Lucy, and she switched the phone off as she made her way down the hall.

Thinking of her mother, Dulcie said a silent prayer of thanks to the goddess as she entered her section. Upperclassmen, a mix of sophomores and juniors, this small group was usually perfectly capable of entertaining itself for a few minutes. As she took her accustomed seat at the head of the table, she wondered if in fact her presence was necessary. The three women and two men were already deep in conversation about that week's reading: biographical material on the Victorian novelists.

'I don't see the point of Strachey,' Tom, a lit major, was saying. 'All we're getting is second-hand gossip.'

'Don't be such a prig, Tom.' Jules liked to bait the self-important young man. 'Strachey's a stylist. Reading him we get the essence of the era, boiled down to a few well-placed anecdotes.'

'That's the problem,' Tom fired back, flipping his long golden hair off his shoulders. 'Nothing in Strachey is boiled down. Ever. And with the reading I've got for the Victorian Novel? I cannot help but remember how many of these guys were paid by the word.'

Dulcie couldn't help smiling. She'd been doing this long enough that she could have anticipated this particular discussion. Part of the problem was timing. For some reason, she always landed the Tuesday section. Because the lecture was held on Wednesday, the day before tended to be tense, as the students hurried to catch up. Part of the problem was, she admitted, with Professor Baer. A throwback to the old school, Baer recited his lectures like they had been written in stone, pronouncing each syllable as if it contained some great weight. Add in a reading list that hadn't changed in at least half a century, and the result was deadly. Required, essentially, for any student who cared about nineteenth-century fiction. But dull as a bag of rocks.

Since they couldn't complain about Baer, not in public anyway, they took it out on the section: particularly on the seemingly non-essential assignments. Every year, the students questioned the supplemental material. Every year, they missed one of the biggest reasons for it being assigned. As she pulled her notebook from her bag, Dulcie silently thanked Trista. It was her friend, a Victorian specialist, who had given her the key to teaching this course.

'What about context?' She kept her voice soft. It was bad enough that the professor held forth in stentorian tones. In her section, she preferred to keep things conversational. 'Isn't that important?'

Her simple question shut the discussion down immediately. 'Context?' Tom finally fired back, his voice rising half an octave on the second syllable. 'You mean, like, about the author?'

'Exactly.' Dulcie recognized her student's sarcasm, but chose to ignore it. Academic fads came and went, and once again it had become fashionable for students to pretend that literature existed in a vacuum. The easiest way to break these undergrads of such a sophomoric idea was to be straight with them. 'Context. It's not a dirty word.'

The looks on the faces that all now turned toward her showed her they believed otherwise, so she continued.

'Jules has a valid point.' She smiled and looked around, making eye contact with each of her students. There was no point in antagonizing them. 'Strachey is a stylist, and in his writing we can see how many of the later Victorian stylings made their way into non-fiction. We can use these as a basis of comparison with the fiction of the authors he's discussing. But the content of what he writes is important as well.'

Ignoring the stagey gasps, she continued.

'Books, as much as we may not like to admit it, are written by people. People have lives, and these lives influence what they write.' She was reciting, just as much as old man Baer did, though she hoped with more feeling. She'd given this particular talk every semester for the past three years. 'Where they're from, what their background is. Did they have spouses, children, or other dependants? These all help us evaluate what we read.'

She saw one of her students about to interrupt, so she raised her hand to stop him. 'Yes, Charles Dickens wasn't much of a family man. But isn't that interesting in light of, say, Tiny Tim and *Bleak House*?' She named several other examples, before bringing them around to her conclusion. 'These works have to stand on their own. The author's biography is not an apology or an excuse. But for a serious scholar, context – and that includes biography – can only add to understanding. It's another tool, another weapon –' she paused for a moment – 'for your arsenal.'

With that, she stopped and looked around. Although her smile was now firmly back in place, inwardly she groaned. It was that word – 'weapon' – that had tripped her up. She'd given this little talk so often, and it was a good one. Watching the faces around the table, she could see that, once again, they were beginning to reconsider, to admit the possibility that more knowledge just might be a good thing. It was the beginning of a bigger lesson, a stealth lesson that Dulcie always tried to sneak into her sections. Basically, it was the beginning of shaking these young scholars out of their preconceptions.

'If you can forget about what you think ought to matter,' she added her customary postscript, 'then you open yourselves up to really see, to really read. And that's a discipline that will serve you not only in academia but throughout life.'

It worked. Already they were reconsidering. She saw Jules whispering something to the girl to her right. Tom was actually paging through the reading, his usual affected moue softening as he read. They were good students, Dulcie knew. They just needed a push.

What she needed was something else again. All the while that she was speaking, Dulcie couldn't help but think about her dream. This latest iteration seemed to make things clear: Yes, her author had written a new novel, in which a grisly murder played a role. But also she had – Dulcie didn't want to use the word 'participated,' not even to herself – at least been a witness to a similar act. And for some reason that Dulcie could not yet discern, she had felt the need to change details of the scene. She shook her head. The evidence was piling up; her author had somehow been involved with the gruesome death of that handsome young man.

'Ms Schwartz?' At least, this wasn't her imagination: her class really was more engaged now, and she spent the next fifty minutes answering questions and guiding them toward finding their own avenues of research. Her own questions remained unanswered, however, as the church bells – quite loud up here on the second floor – announced the end of the hour.

'See you next week,' she said as cheerfully as she could. Thoughts about her author had led her back to her own predicament. Next week, she could be arrested. Or expelled. As she stood, several of her students looked up, as if to approach her. But while normally Dulcie would welcome that, today she had too much on her mind. At the very least, she wanted to get back to the Mildon, to see if Thomas Griddlehaus had shown up.

Ducking her head down, she moved toward the door before any of them could stop her. Next week, goddess willing, she'd take their questions.

For once, she was grateful for the section's room assignment. Emerson Hall was made up primarily of classrooms. In the ten minutes following the hour, its hallways and staircases were jammed, and Dulcie was able to lose herself in the crush of bodies. If only the buzz of conversation could drown out her thoughts.

'Oh, hi, Ms Schwartz.' Dulcie saw a broad chest in a blue sweater before her. Looking up, she saw the chiseled face of Andrew Geisner. Thalia, by his side, turned and saw her.

'Oh, hello.' Dulcie managed a smile. 'Am I in your way?'

'What? No, I walked into you.' He smiled a big sunny smile, and Dulcie found herself floundering. He seemed so friendly. Could there be any real harm in asking him a few questions?

'Actually, I'm glad we ran into each other.' The three exited the main doors, and Dulcie turned with them toward Widener. 'I was hoping I could ask you about something.'

'Me?' Andrew looked puzzled, and warning bells went off in Dulcie's head. Thalia, meanwhile, was staring daggers.

'Oh, just some things I was wondering about.' Dulcie smiled at Thalia. There had to be some way to let the girl know she wasn't going to break her confidence. 'Some things I heard from the dean's office.'

Thalia didn't appear any more relaxed, but Andrew was waiting, so Dulcie continued. 'I gather you were doing some background checks on visiting scholars?' Neither student responded. 'You were looking into Melinda Sloane Harquist?'

'Yeah, I was.' He glanced around, suddenly uneasy. 'I shouldn't really talk about it, though. It was all kind of confidential.'

'I gather it got a bit personal.' Dulcie didn't know what exactly she was fishing for, but his discomfort hinted that she was on the right track.

'I was only doing what the dean asked.' He looked distinctly uncomfortable now, and Thalia was pulling on his arm.

'He must have been sizing her up for a position.' She waited, but he only shrugged. 'Pulling up family records? Where she'd lived? What she'd done?' Dulcie was on the right track. She knew it. 'Sounds a bit like stalking to me.'

'It's not what you think,' Thalia burst out. 'You make it sound like it was romantic, but it isn't. It wasn't. You don't understand.' Dulcie looked over at the younger woman, her dark eyes bright with fury. 'You've got it all wrong.'

With that, she pulled her friend's arm so hard the sweater nearly came off, and they hurried away. Dulcie made a move to follow, though whether she'd apologize to the young girl for disillusioning her about her handsome friend or confront him about his actions, she didn't know. All she could think of was Suze's warning. She'd stepped right into something, and she was still no closer to getting any answers.

FORTY-NINE

S uze had been right. Dulcie kicked herself mentally as the young couple walked off. She should never have accosted Andrew, never have asked him about his research. Maybe he'd had his reasons, much as she had. As she watched them go, she bit her lip, sending up a silent prayer to all of Lucy's various deities that her thoughtless actions would have no major consequences. If Andrew felt persecuted, or Thalia betrayed, they could make Dulcie's situation a lot worse.

'I've been such a fool.' She was outside now, standing by the base of the stairs.

'Not a fool.' A soft, calm voice spoke, apparently right by her ear. *'Headstrong, perhaps.'*

'I don't know, Mr Grey.' Dulcie found herself staring at a fat grey squirrel. The comparison would have been anathema to the living cat. Dulcie could remember how her pet would lash his tail and chatter whenever the furry rodents ran by. Now, however, it didn't seem that odd. 'I was acting on emotion, rather than what I knew to be right.'

'Your heart is your best guide, Dulcie. Never forget that.'

'If I listened to my heart . . .' Dulcie didn't know how explain. Chris, her thesis. It was all so jumbled up.

'Unjumble it, then.' The answer was so direct, so straightforward, it startled Dulcie.

'You're right, Mr Grey.' She pulled out her phone to call Chris, and then stopped. It was only a little after eleven. He'd been up all night. As her phone powered on, she saw a text – from Chris.

Need 2 talk. 2night pls?

Suddenly, the day lost its warmth. Surely, this wasn't what Mr Grey had meant. But as she looked around, she realized even the squirrel was gone. How was she supposed to untangle things now? Unless, the sinking feeling made her limbs feel like lead, 'unjumbling' was a synonym for disengaging.

OK, she typed back, and then turned the phone off. Maybe she couldn't salvage her romance. But there were other parts of her life that she could deal with, or she wasn't Dulcie Schwartz.

On her way to the library, she made a plan. First stop, of course, would be the Mildon. If Griddlehaus were there, she would insist on seeing what else he had found. That fragment had been golden, and if he had more, she wanted to read it for herself. If he wasn't there, well, she had other friends in the library. She'd inquire about the chief clerk, and then find out if anyone else could give her access. Until anyone said otherwise, she was a scholar at the university. She had the right to library access – to the folder in the Mildon that bore her name. Her buddy Mona would know whom to contact. Maybe Mona herself could get the keys, and they could have a congenial time of it, rooting through the collection.

With a new determination, Dulcie strode through the entrance hall, barely giving the guard time to check her bag. As soon as the elevator appeared, she pressed the button for the door to close, ignoring the frantic wave of an older man still at the guard's desk. As soon as it had descended to the right floor – Lower Level C – she was out, almost knocking over a frail-looking clerk, carrying an arm-load of bound volumes to a cart.

And, yes! The Mildon was open! The security gate that had covered the entrance had been rolled up, leaving only the gleaming white counter between Dulcie and the riches within. The only problem was, there was nobody to sign her in.

'Hello?' she called softly, leaning over the counter. The reading area, off to her left, was lit up but empty. To the right, where the actual collection was stored, was quiet.

'Hello?' A little louder this time, but still she got no response. 'Hello?'

Something was definitely odd, and so Dulcie reached over the counter to where the release button was located and pressed it. The catch on the counter gave way, and she raised it, entering the restricted collection.

For a moment, the audacity of that act stunned her: Dulcie Schwartz, alone inside the Mildon. The whole scenario was so absurd, she couldn't believe it. And yet, if nobody was going to stop her . . . She turned to the right. There, on rows of metal shelves, stood volumes she had only begun to explore. In locked cabinets, large, flat display boxes held fragments of paper, the stained and damaged pages that had already proven so useful. Papyrus and vellum had their own cases, controlled for humidity and temperature. It was like a fairyland, Dulcie thought. A candy store for book lovers. As if in a dream, she proceeded.

And turned the corner right into Thomas Griddlehaus.

'Oh!' He looked up. She'd startled him, she could see that. 'Oh,' he said again.

'Mr Griddlehaus!' She waited for him to respond, to greet her, but he continued to stand there. 'I didn't know if you were here,' she said finally.

He looked at her without speaking. His eyes, unnaturally large behind his big glasses, blinked once.

'I mean, you weren't earlier.' Dulcie was suddenly aware of having broken the protocol. She'd let herself in; she'd also, she realized belatedly, started toward the collection without donning the white cotton gloves that were required before handling any of the Mildon material.

'I was. Here, that is.' She had definitely overstepped. 'At nine forty-five and . . .' The reality of the situation came to her. 'I was worried about you.'

'Oh, well.' He turned away, apparently flustered. 'No need. There was a meeting. I mean, I meant to post that opening would be delayed. Though I'm sure I was here on time.' He turned to face her, those big eyes blinking wildly. 'Perhaps you were mistaken? About the time, that is?'

'I don't think so.' Dulcie watched as the clerk scurried away again. This time, she went after him. He'd gone into the stacks and as she watched, he took two volumes from a cart and started walking along the stacks. One he re-shelved, and immediately removed again. The other he stared at, as if he had never seen it before. Something was wrong, and Dulcie knew she was to blame.

'Mr Griddlehaus, I know I shouldn't be here. The gate was up, and all the lights were on, so I . . . came in.' It sounded lame, and she knew it. It was, however, the truth. 'I'm sorry.' Nothing. 'Is there something the matter, Mr Griddlehaus?'

'Nothing is the matter.' He walked away, still holding the book, and Dulcie could hear him muttering. *Trust your heart*, Mr Grey had said, and suddenly the implications of her own actions hit her. She'd been rude on the elevator, worse in the hallway. And now she'd barged in on what she knew the little clerk considered his private domain.

'I was wrong to come in here,' she started. 'And I am truly sorry about yesterday,' Dulcie spoke softly, but she was sure her voice carried through the open metal shelving. 'I know you would never do anything malicious.'

The answering sigh was so deep and so heavy, she worried for a moment that the little man had expired. But as she ducked around the stack, she saw him still standing, although he was now leaning forward, his forehead pressed against the metal shelving.

'Mr Griddlehaus?'

He looked up, clearly weighing something in his mind. 'I am sorry, Ms Schwartz. I did hear you. I was simply . . . simply . . .'

Hiding. She didn't need him to say it. In fact, courtesy seemed the better part of valor. 'It's OK, Mr Griddlehaus. I haven't been the best company recently. It's only that you said you'd found something else? Something you put in my folder?'

He blinked at her, looking for all the world as if he were scared.

'Mr Griddlehaus?'

'I'm sorry.' He collapsed into the chair next to her. 'I just don't know what I should do. They brought the material back this morning. I was told that, finally, I could file everything, after they questioned me . . .'

He broke off, blinking again, and she thought she saw tears welling up in his eyes. She thought of the manuscript page, the one he had sneaked into her folder. 'Oh, Mr Griddlehaus. I'm sorry! I never wanted to get you into any trouble.'

This was why he'd been late, and this was what he hadn't wanted to mention. What perhaps he had been *warned* not to mention. Dulcie knew the dean was going to be looking into her research. She hadn't realized he or his staff would be interrogating – no, intimidating – her friends and colleagues, including the quiet clerk.

'I should go.' Sometimes, she realized, her heart really did know what to do. 'I can't subject you to any more of this.'

'No, please.' He reached up for her. The soft glove made his touch feel like that of a small animal. 'You see, I haven't told you the entire story.'

She paused and waited, and after about five seconds he nodded, sharply, as if he'd come to a decision. 'Indeed, you have a right to know about it.' He turned and faced her. 'It all began last week, when I got that letter, the one from the dean. That was the last time you and I spoke at length.' He looked to her for confirmation, and she nodded. 'What you didn't know was that Ms Sloane Harquist came in early the next day, and she brought something with her.'

'Actually, I knew she'd visited—' Dulcie started, but the little clerk raised his hand for silence.

'Please, let me get this out.' He licked his lips as if they were dry. 'She asked for my help, and gave me a copy of some pages. They were, I realized, a chapter of her thesis. Or, at least, the rough start of a chapter. She said she only needed to confirm some things, to "fill in some blanks".

'Now, I like to think I've been of some little help to you, Ms Schwartz.' He stopped her before she could protest. 'We have shared some experiences and, I believe, we share a certain world-view that makes encouraging your work enjoyable for me, as well. But this is not usually a service we here at the Mildon provide. We are a research facility, a resource for trained and able scholars. Not a . . . a . . .' He sputtered a bit, and Dulcie decided to help him.

'It is asking a lot, but surely, she just needed your help verifying a quote or some such?'

He shook his head. 'I don't know what to tell you. I came as close as ever I have come to disobeying a direct request from a dean of the college. Because, you see, Ms Schwartz, I read the chapter. And I was . . . flabbergasted.' He blinked again and turned away. She could see him swallow, and then he turned back. 'Ms Schwartz, I have to say, I have never seen such a blatant case of academic balderdash in my life.'

FIFTY

D ulcie was speechless. 'I never . . . I never meant to . . .'
Plagiarize. She couldn't even say the word. 'If I did it,
it was unintentional, entirely, on my part.'

The little man beside her jumped up. 'Oh, no! Not *you,* Ms
Schwartz! I didn't mean you! I meant *her* – that Sloane Harquist
woman.'

She was hearing him, but none of this was sinking in.

'You hadn't seen her writing.' He was shaking his head in
disbelief. Clearly, he didn't know all she was accused of. 'Her
so-called research. I tell you, Ms Schwartz, I don't understand
it. There was nothing there. It was all speculation and assumption. Lots of fancy words and not much else.'

As he was talking, Dulcie thought about the pages she had read.
She'd found them pompous, but that was it. The idea that it had
sounded like someone trying to bluff had occurred to her, but she'd
never allowed herself to believe that could really be true.

Griddlehaus was still talking. 'She was publishing, when
frankly, you already have so much more. And for her to be getting
all this attention, this special treatment? To be completely honest,
it reeks of favoritism.'

'No, it doesn't.' The shock had worn off, but Dulcie was still
a little stunned. 'She did have one bit of real research. She had
an excerpt from the rough draft, the one that I found the day
before . . . the day before it all happened.' She shrugged. 'Who
knows what else she had? The bottom line is, she got on with
her life. With the business of establishing herself as an academic.
She wrote, and I didn't,' she said glumly. 'It's my own fault.'

'But you have so much more – more in your notes – than she
ever did.' He was searching her face now. 'And you've published
that one paper. This Ms Sloane Harquist, nobody had even heard
of her until she showed up. It's almost like she read your paper
and zeroed in on you.'

'Maybe she did.' Dulcie shrugged. 'Maybe I could have been

real competition for her. Without her entire manuscript to read, we'll never know.'

'Harrumph.' Mr Griddlehaus adjusted his glasses. 'I don't think she was up to snuff.'

'Well, thank you,' said Dulcie, hoping to put an end to it. The topic was just too painful. 'May I ask about that page?'

He started, as if he'd forgotten, and retreated down the hall. When he returned, he was carrying five archival boxes, all marked PHILA, 1803–10, which he placed on a shelf. As she watched, he set one on the table before her and, as was his usual procedure, opened the lid. On top, Dulcie saw a page she had examined before.

'Mr Griddlehaus?' She knew he had shown this material to the dean. He'd told her.

'They were insisting on the entirety of the sequestered material, you see.' With both hands, he carefully lifted out one page, and then another, laying them on the table to be read in the standard Mildon procedure. While Dulcie had advanced to being allowed to lift pages out by herself, she didn't question his actions. She had already overstepped, and it was time to let the clerk re-establish the rules.

'They seemed interested in tracking down certain quotes,' Griddlehaus continued. 'Certain pages that you had already seen.' He was staring at her now. 'The pages Ms Sloane Harquist had requested.'

She nodded. 'Yes, that would make sense.' Even if Melinda wasn't trying to fill in the blanks of her own research, these would be the pages the dean would want for his investigation of Dulcie.

'And so we removed those pages, for the dean to examine. Five at a time, as is our policy here at the Mildon. Just as we did for Ms Sloane Harquist.'

He was looking at her with intensity, as if willing her to understand something. 'It's not like we've made any secret of the policy,' he said. 'It is founded in library science. The sheer weight of these papers would be enough to contribute to their deterioration, even with the protective coverings, were they to be piled carelessly.'

He looked down at the pages. 'The policy is clearly posted.'

Her gaze followed his to the documents before her, and then back up to him. And slowly, it began to dawn on her. 'They thought this was it.' Her voice was barely a whisper, as if someone might overhear. 'The one box I had already seen. They didn't look any further.'

Griddlehaus leaned over and picked up one page, then another, and in reverse order, replaced them in their box. 'And neither did she,' was all he said.

'Mr Griddlehaus,' said Dulcie, her voice taking on strength as she made the formal request. 'May I see the contents of the next box, please?'

'Why, of course, Ms Schwartz,' he replied with the beginnings of a smile. 'By the way, I replaced the manuscript page that I had – ahem – temporarily misfiled,' he said, as he laid out the next set of pages. 'It is now back in its proper place. I'm sure you'll want to read it for yourself.'

There it was, the first page of the second box. Adjusting the magnifying glass, she began to read. *Much like her terror, like the screams frozen in her throat, life's elixir had begun to solidify and darken, staining the red-gold hair a dull brown, its very essence transform'd before her eyes, which too began to dim . . .*

It was the passage Griddlehaus had copied out for her. Only there was more.

Those red-gold locks, besmirch'd by life's gore, she now addressed. "The Sire of my troubles, and also of my deepest joy," proclaim'd she, though would ne'er again respond.

Would have been better for this woman to stand alone, for to be friendless is to know that which is true for our Sex. 'Tis better far.

The next line was unreadable, and so she jumped ahead.

'Twas not yet break of day as she descended the stairs to stir the fire in this, her most homely abode. Indeed, the glowing embers on the library hearth warmed her as no bonfire in a greater hall could. Red and golden, so like the . . . The next bit was obscured, and Dulcie skipped ahead. *E'en the shadows playing on the wall, lighting the golden bindings of the books and warming to more human tomes the marble bust upon the mantle, made for better company than she had fled.*

Yet whilst she was thus occupied, the malignant storm outside did seem to encroach, throwing open the door to let in a blast so cold as to take her very breath away. In great dismay and wary of her charge, she turned to find standing before her,

Esteban, wild with the night. In his fury, the Young Lord appeared a very Devil. The stormy ride had disheveled his—

The next bit was blotted out. Dulcie thought she read 'red' or 'raven,' but, impatient, she moved on. The next line was half obscured, but clearly a dramatic confrontation was taking place.

"What would you have of me?" His voice like thunder threaten'd rather than promised, and his outstretched hand – that very hand which had so recently caressed her – trembled with the desire to grab her, to pull her away. "You have had your will of me, as I of you, and yet now, when the matter is of the most grievous import, you repel me."

It was her, she was sure of it. The phrasing, the detail. Even the description of the marble bust on the carpet. Even the dead man now had a name, Esteban the Young Lord. She didn't need to read more, to continue on to the phrase that Mr Griddlehaus had copied down for proof. This was the book she'd been dreaming of, the one her author had written here, in America. The lost masterpiece.

'This is wonderful,' she said in hushed tones. 'Thank you.' She looked up at the clerk, who blushed and turned away.

'You're welcome,' he said so softly she barely heard. 'I thought this might be what you've been looking for. You've been working so hard, Ms Schwartz, and it just did not seem fair. Besides,' he stood up straighter now, 'they never asked.'

'So, the dean never saw these pages. Nor . . . Melinda?' A tickle of a thought was forming in Dulcie's head. Just a smidgen, but enough to give her hope.

'Nobody has, as far as I can tell,' said the clerk. 'Not since these came in and were sorted – let's see.' He fumbled with a ledger. 'They were part of a bequest from a Philadelphia alumnus in 1943.' He replaced the ledger. 'I just don't understand why the police were bothering with any of this. From what I read, that girl didn't have the slightest clue.'

'The *police*?' Dulcie turned to the clerk, alarmed.

'Why, yes. Who else did you think would be in here, after the fact, looking at documents and asking questions about your work habits?'

Dulcie knew her mouth was hanging open and that no words were coming out. It was all she could do to shut it and to shake her head in disbelief. The idea taking shape in her mind was as crazed and convoluted as anything in a Gothic novel. What was stranger still was that she was beginning to think it just might be true.

FIFTY-ONE

C louds were gathering overhead as Dulcie stepped out of Widener, and she looked up at the darkening sky in dismay. September was too late for a thunderstorm, wasn't it? She had, of course, not taken an umbrella.

The weather, for the moment, pushed other thoughts aside, and it was with a bit of effort that Dulcie made herself focus again. Out here under this looming sky, the idea she had formed inside the shelter of the Mildon seemed less substantial. A ghost, almost, born of wishful thinking and fatigue. Standing on the Widener stairs, looking up at a particularly grim cloud, she wanted to ignore it. It was too great a reach – farther, it seemed, than that steel-grey cloud – and it relied too much on her own confusing dreams. Nobody would believe her; none of it would hold together. But something about what she'd read and what she'd just heard – specifically, that the police had been talking to Thomas Griddlehaus and not the dean's hand-picked investigators – made her not quite able to let go. It was far-fetched, to say the least. But it still might be true.

The question was what to do about it. Maybe it was the threatening sky, but the idea of running off to confront anyone was suddenly more imposing, and Dulcie wondered if breaking for lunch would make it easier. Lala's, after all, was barely a block away, and if there was going to be a storm, she could wait it out there. Besides, most demons were better faced over a three-bean burger with special sauce. She took out her phone. Maybe she could even get some company, somebody she could bounce her ideas off of.

For a moment, she almost turned it off again. Who would that be? She and Chris already had a date 'to talk' later. Since she couldn't see any good coming out of that, she most definitely didn't want to move that conversation up. Lloyd was, well, Lloyd was in too deep – one way or another. Until she could find out how those pages had gotten into her desk, she knew she should stay clear of Lloyd. She'd just spoken to Trista, and Suze had already given her enough of her time.

As she stood there, Dulcie realized she had a voicemail. With some trepidation, she clicked on to it and held the phone up to her ear.

'. . . that same vision again.' It was Lucy. Dulcie's mother never could get the hang of waiting till the beep. 'Your grandmother. You don't remember, but she had that lovely red-gold hair.' Dulcie sighed. She'd never met any of her grandparents, thanks in part to Lucy and her father's travels. 'She's saying something about blood, or maybe it's the blood. Be careful, Dulcie. Especially around knives – Mars is in your house, you know, and you know what that means.'

With a sigh, Dulcie turned the phone off. As Lucy's daughter, she should know what that meant, she was sure. She had no doubt she could call her mother back and ask her, and be told that Mars controlled the warlike aspects of her nature and after another twenty minutes of mumbo jumbo, she'd be told to look both ways before crossing the street. If history had taught her anything, Mars wouldn't even have been warning her to take an umbrella.

Lucy meant well, Dulcie knew that, and she loved her only child. But Lucy lived in a world of signs and portents, the kind of world where weather – Dulcie cocked an eye to the clouds – was more than meteorology. Dulcie, on the other hand, had made the conscious choice to live in the world of facts. If anything, she thought with a smile, Lucy's call had been a warning. It meant she'd been silly. Rather than try to piece together some strange conspiracy out of some story fragments and an odd dream – or worry overmuch about rain – she should focus on what she knew how to do: research.

Martin Thorpe might not be a white knight, but he would be interested in her latest discovery. What she'd found was new, and that would reflect well on both of them. The only question was, before or after lunch?

She walked to the gate and looked across the street. The window of Lala's was full of diners, the counter seats apparently full. That didn't mean anything, of course. She could wait, or hope for a table inside the small café. Or, she realized, she could simply get the inevitable over with. With that in mind, she dialed her thesis adviser.

'Mr Thorpe? This is Dulcie Schwartz.' She had turned away from the street, sheltering in the relative quiet by the wall. The call had gone to her adviser's voicemail, and for a moment she pondered what to say. 'I think I've found something that may be useful. New material.' That sounded too vague. 'A handwritten first draft, Mr Thorpe. In the Mildon.'

As soon as she hung up, she kicked herself. Griddlehaus had told her more than he should have, and now she was going to let people know. Maybe she should warn him?

Dulcie half heard a low rumble, and for a moment she thought Mr Grey was once again with her. But when she neither heard or felt any kind of follow up, she decided her stomach, excited by thoughts of Lala's, had growled. Well, first things first. She'd set things right with Griddlehaus – and then get some lunch. Dulcie turned back into the Yard. She'd run out so precipitously, she knew he'd raise an eyebrow at her return. Still, that was better than risking him being taken by surprise the next time the police came by.

The police. She stopped in her tracks. That had been what had set her off before. No, she shook her head. She wasn't Lucy. She would go by the facts, by the evidence. By—

'Dulcie!'

At the sound of the voice, she turned. Rafe Hutchins was walking quickly up the path. 'I'm glad I caught you.'

She waited. He was smiling, apparently unaware of her suspicions.

'You see, I just ran into Andrew Geisner, and I wanted to explain.'

'Oh?' Dulcie tried to make her voice as frosty as possible. The result just sounded like she had a frog in her throat. 'Do tell.'

He looked at her, puzzled, and for a moment she was afraid he was going to ask after her health. Instead, he opted to continue. 'He says you didn't understand. That he was working for the dean.'

'He told me.' Her voice was back to normal, but she wasn't buying it.

'No, but he really was.' The senior tutor looked amused. 'He wasn't supposed to tell anyone, but I don't see the harm in it, now. Melinda – Ms Sloane Harquist – was a special project of Dean Haitner's. He green-lighted all sorts of access for her. I mean, more than you're aware of. More, to be honest, than I was comfortable with. That's what Darlene and I were – ah – discussing on Saturday, outside Dardley. I'd thought Darlene was jealous and was doing it on her own, but she wasn't. Andrew explained it all. They really were on assignment for the dean. He said he had to be sure of her.'

'Sure about what?' Dulcie could feel the hairs on her forearms stand up. 'What do you mean by that, Rafe?'

'Background. Education. You know, her whole pedigree.' He seemed unaware of the effect his words were having on her. 'That's why he needed to examine all the other work on the subject, I guess. He's a big one for protecting his legacy.'

'Rafe, you're a genius.' A flash, like lightning, seemed to go off. 'I think you just saved my life.'

FIFTY-TWO

L eaving the stunned senior tutor on the path, Dulcie started running. Her thoughts raced alongside, piecing together everything she'd heard. A lot of it didn't make sense, but of one thing she was sure: she needed to talk with Dean Haitner, the one person who might have the answers.

She was breathless by the time she mounted the stairs to University Hall. Panting when she knocked on the dean's door, the heavy, humid air only making her sweat more. It was probably her red face, she realized, that caused Dean Haitner to look at her with such alarm when she pushed the door open to find him at his desk.

'Ms Schwartz.' His eyebrows almost made it up to his unnaturally dark hairline. 'What a surprise.'

'I'm sorry to barge in without an appointment, Dean. But—' She didn't get a chance to finish. Outside, a peal of thunder cracked the air like gunfire, and an answering growl caused her to turn. Behind her, beside the opened door, stood Detective

Rogovoy, clearing his throat. Next to him stood Trista, who stared at Dulcie with an intensity that made her wish she really did have the familial psychic ability. 'Tris, what is it?'

Her friend opened her mouth, only to be cut off by another loud crack and bang. The room was growing dark, and the click of Dean Haitner turning on his desktop lamp brought all their attention back to the front of the room.

'Thank you for dropping by, Ms Schwartz.' The lamp, with its low green shade, cast stark shadows on the dean's face. 'I was just about to send Andrew out to look for you.' He gestured, and the tall student stepped out of the doorway beside the desk, accompanied by a uniformed Cambridge cop. 'He had another errand to complete first.'

From the movement behind her, Dulcie guessed that neither Rogovoy nor Trista had known that the undergrad or the cop were there, just inside the open doorway. Another low rumble, and Dulcie found herself wondering just what sort of scene she had stepped into.

'These two came to see me,' the dean continued, the lamplight playing up the crags and crannies in his no-longer-young face. 'They had quite a story to tell.'

Dulcie turned back to her friend, but Trista was staring straight ahead – at Andrew. 'Trista, it's not what you think,' she said. 'It's not Andrew.'

'And you would know, Ms Schwartz, because . . .?' The dean left the question open, turning to smile at the cop. Outside, the wind had picked up, whistling through some slight opening in the oversized windows.

It was the smile that did it. 'For the same reason you would, Dean Haitner.' Dulcie swallowed the lump in her throat, determined to get this out. 'I was doing research, and I found out something today.' She paused. No matter what, she couldn't get Thomas Griddlehaus in trouble.

'Melinda Sloane Harquist's thesis was a sham.' There, she'd said it. 'She had no original research, and was trying to piggyback on what I had already found. I'm not sure how she knew what I had uncovered. I've only published one paper thus far . . .' She paused, caught up suddenly in an image of her computer screen, awake and moving. Of Esmé, agitated, batting at the mouse pad.

'Ms Schwartz?' Rogovoy had moved up to stand beside her. 'Are you all right?'

'Yes, I'm sorry. As I was saying, there are some things that I don't fully understand yet. But I do know that I was the one who had been doing the research. I was the one who had made the breakthroughs. But Melinda Sloane Harquist was being promoted as the next great scholar of the Gothic novel. She was getting extensive support, including unprecedented – and, may I say, unwarranted – access to the university resources, all the while I was being shut out and shunted into some kind of outsider status.'

'And you have proof of this?' The dean's voice was quiet, barely audible above the wind.

'No, not really.' She couldn't betray Griddlehaus. She didn't know if he still had his copy of the chapter. 'But it fits with the pages . . . the pages . . .' Another loud crack, this time followed by a flash of lightning, saved her. 'The page that was found in my desk.'

'The page that you stole from her, without shame.' The dean stood, and a flash of lightning cast his shadow across the desk. 'And that page is evidence, just as it may be evidence of your involvement in the more heinous crime, which was why I alerted the Cambridge Police to the evidence in the Mildon.'

'No!' Dulcie was sick of being interrupted. Outside the rain had begun in earnest, pelting the window. She raised her voice to be heard. 'That's not true! Melinda was stealing from *me*. She was copying *my* research.'

She turned toward her friends. In the darkened room she couldn't make out their faces. 'That's why she needed special access. Somehow, she knew about everything I had found, and she wanted to be able to refer to the same primary sources. Only she hadn't had time to retype her manuscript and write them in. She quoted what I had before she ever had a chance to see the manuscript I got it from.'

'That's some story, Ms Schwartz.' The dean's voice was still soft, yet somehow he could be heard over the storm. 'If anyone believes it.'

'They will when they see the original material,' Dulcie was shouting. 'Melinda quoted only the one passage I had typed into my computer – and nothing from the rest of the very same page. You know the truth. You gave her access . . .' Esmé. The laptop. The missing excerpt, corrupted, somehow, within her computer.

Another piece fell into place. 'You gave her access. I don't know how exactly, but somehow you helped her to hack into my computer.'

'I gave her access, of course. But to purely legal sources.' The dean turned to the uniformed cop. 'She was brilliant, and she would have done us proud. If you –' he turned back to Dulcie – 'hadn't killed her.'

'Me? No—' But the cop was already moving toward her.

'Ms Schwartz, I'm afraid you'll have to come with me.' She looked from him to Rogovoy, who stood still as stone.

'You see, Ms Schwartz, you just confessed to knowledge of the missing manuscript.' The dean waited while the cop came up beside her. 'And it's quite clear from what you've been saying, here in front of witnesses, that you believed yourself to be her rival, unfairly bested in some kind of paranoid fantasy. Which sadly explains your motivation—'

'No!' Trista jumped forward, throwing her arms around her friend. 'It's not her you want,' she yelled and pointed to the stunned undergrad who was still standing beside the desk. 'It's Andrew! Andrew Geisner! He was stalking her.'

'No,' said Dulcie, everything suddenly becoming clear. 'It's the dean. He was helping her cheat, though maybe he didn't realize it at first. Though why he would want to kill her, to kill his own daughter, I'll never understand.'

FIFTY-THREE

All hell broke loose. 'She's a crazy woman!' The dean was on his feet yelling. 'Take her out of here!'

'What?' Even Trista looked confused. 'Dulcie, what are you saying?'

The city cop, meanwhile, had his hand on Dulcie's shoulder and with steady pressure was moving her away, toward the door. Outside, through the rain-streaked windows, Dulcie saw the flashing light of a cruiser. She wouldn't have a chance to call Suze this time.

'Wait just a minute here.' It was Detective Rogovoy who restored order, stepping in front of them both, crossing his arms over his not inconsiderable chest. 'I want to hear what the girl has to say.'

'We know she's your favorite,' the dean said, accenting that last word in a particularly distasteful way. 'That doesn't mean she—'

'Officer?' Ignoring the dean, Rogovoy turned to his colleague. 'I think you'll agree we're in no great rush.' As if to underline his point, another wave of wind and rain rattled the windows. 'Spare me a minute here.'

The city cop must have nodded, because Dulcie saw Rogovoy relax a bit. His hand remained heavy on her shoulder, however, and she realized this was the time to talk.

'I didn't read Melinda's manuscript,' she said. 'Yes, I saw it in the suite library. Last Saturday, the day . . . the day . . . Anyway, I saw it, before it disappeared. But then two pages showed up, both from my desk. At first, I thought they were student papers. They were full of hyperbole, overwrought writing and such. Only there was one quote – one quote that she kept going back to. And it was the same quote I had found, in a handwritten manuscript.

'Still, I didn't get it. I thought, gee, she must have gotten there before me. Then I went back to the Mildon.' She was talking to Rogovoy now. He probably didn't understand the vagaries of research, but he nodded for her to continue. 'Melinda Sloane Harquist had dropped by, for an hour before a lunch date. A lunch date with her father.' Dulcie stared at the dean. 'And she had gone right to the material I'd been working on.'

'Of course she did.' The dean's voice was dismissive. 'Despite your psychotic imaginings about her identity, you knew she was writing about the same subject you are. No wonder you attacked her . . .'

'No, she was checking on something. Checking on a quote.' She paused. 'A quote that she already had typed into her manuscript, but that she couldn't have seen before.'

'That's nonsense. As crazy as your claim—'

Rogovoy raised one large hand and the dean shut up.

'A quote from a handwritten draft. A quote from a manuscript that only exists in our library, and that she could only have known about if someone had hacked into my laptop for her.'

Dulcie paused, partly to catch her breath and partly to consider how to continue. Dreams didn't fit into this, nor did fiction. She had to be logical and clear, entirely in the here and now. 'And the other side of it was how much the dean was involved. We found out Dean Haitner had Melinda thoroughly investigated. Not just her academic history, but also her family, her background. Everything.' In the corner of the room, Andrew nodded. 'We all thought he was – ah – interested in her romantically. But he has a sweetheart, an adjunct professor of semiotics over at BU.' Now it was Trista who was nodding, disbelief on her face. 'We all thought that, because we all know his reputation as a ladies' man.'

The dean reared back and opened his mouth to respond. Rogovoy's paw came up again, silencing him.

'But the one thing he cares more about than the ladies is his reputation.' Dulcie looked around, as both Trista and Andrew nodded. 'His legacy. Melinda Sloane Harquist was his hope for the future. That's when I realized—'

'Dulcie!' She turned around. Everyone did. Standing in the main doorway stood Chris, soaking wet. 'What are you doing here?' he asked as he dripped on the rug.

'Chris?' Dulcie took a step toward him, but the hand on her shoulder restrained her. She turned. 'Does anyone have a towel?'

Andrew ducked back into the passage and came back seconds later with a small hand towel.

'I'm here to see the dean,' said Chris, drying his face. He looked around for a place to put the towel and, as he handed it back to Andrew, saw the puddle collecting at his feet. 'Oh, I'm sorry.'

'Chris, what are *you* doing here? You didn't know I was . . .' She paused. Had her boyfriend come to rescue her? Or was he that desperate to break things off that he'd tracked her down to University Hall?

'I'm sorry, Dulcie. I wanted to talk it over with you, I really did. But I just couldn't live with it any longer.' He had a desperate look, pale and drawn. The drop of water collecting on his nose didn't help. 'I simply can't do it.'

It was the latter. Dulcie felt herself swaying. Here, in front of all these people, this was the final straw. She closed her eyes, hoping for the dizziness to pass and waiting for the awful words. What she heard next made her jerk them open. Chris had turned from her to the man behind the desk.

'Dean Haitner, I can't take that job,' Chris said. 'I'm sorry. I really appreciate the offer, and I know I said I'd give anything to get off the overnight shift. But, really, this has been Darlene's job, and she needs it too. You should keep her. I can train her to do anything she doesn't know yet. But, please, give her the job back. I couldn't live with myself otherwise.'

'Wait – job?' Dulcie shook her head to clear it. 'This was about a job?'

Chris nodded, his dark hair still plastered against his forehead. 'The dean set up a special project, and hired Darlene to do it. Data mining, surveillance – lots of fun programming. And I guess Darlene was having some problems, so he sought me out. I am her adviser, after all. And, Dulcie, I know how hard it's been with me working nights. I know we never see each other. I just couldn't take her job, though. She's living on grants and fellowships, too, and I'm supposed to be her adviser, not her competition.'

'Oh, Chris.' This time the cop let her go, and she embraced her sodden beau.

'But Dulcie.' Chris looked around as if seeing everyone else in the room for the first time. 'What are you doing here? What's going on?'

'We've been sorting through some issues,' said Rogovoy, with a look at the city cop. 'As always, your girlfriend has brought some interesting insights to the conversation.'

'Dulcie?' Chris stepped back and looked at her, then looked over at Rogovoy. 'If she's in any trouble, I demand to hear about it.'

The burly detective shook his head. 'This is for us to worry about, Mr Sorenson. That said, if you could tell us a bit more about this data mining you were asked to do for the dean?'

'You should really talk to Darlene about that. I'd given her a few pointers, but that was it. Then again, the dean would be able to tell you more. Dean Haitner?'

They turned. The dean was standing by the side door, where

Andrew had been only minutes before. His face was ghastly white against the unnatural black of his hair, his eyes wide. Without a word, he faced them – and then turned and ran.

'Damn,' said Rogovoy, and motioned the young cop to go ahead. Following him to the doorway, the detective turned. 'Hey, kid,' he addressed Andrew. 'What's back here?'

'Private bathroom. Storage closets.' Rogovoy visibly relaxed. 'Of course, at the end, it does open up again on to the main stairwell. I think there's a fire door.'

With a muttered curse, Rogovoy peered into the dim hallway. As he leaned in, a loud cry from outside made everyone turn. Dulcie joined the others at the window. Dean Haitner, flat on his back, lay on the pavement at the base of the stone steps. Leaning forward to catch his breath stood the young cop. Neither of them looked happy; the dean was holding his knee. Only Dulcie noticed a small movement, a few feet away on the wet grass. A squirrel, grey and so large as to be almost cat-sized, sat up on his haunches and watched the proceedings. As he turned to look up at the office window, Dulcie was almost sure he winked. Then he bounded toward the nearest elm, scurried up, and was gone.

FIFTY-FOUR

Dulcie was a little disappointed that she could not follow suit. However, Rogovoy himself escorted her down to the Cambridge Police Headquarters, and had no objection when she called Suze on the way. Chris had insisted on coming along, too, despite Dulcie's stated objections.

'You're soaked, Chris,' she'd said. 'I'll be fine. You should really go home and change.'

'Come on, kid.' Rogovoy had held the door for him, as they both ignored her. Once they'd gotten to the station, Dulcie laid out her theory for the record, which took the form of Rogovoy and the young Cambridge police officer. Chris then tried to explain about computer access, about how his student had been told she was

'testing security', as she breached Dulcie's private files. Rogovoy
didn't look like he got it, entirely, but he let them talk, until Dulcie,
finally, asked if it might be possible to break for lunch.

'I don't even know if I can think straight.' Dulcie didn't feel
like she was exaggerating. From the look Rogovoy gave them
both, neither did he.

But something must have clicked, and by the time they had
finished with their sandwiches – Rogovoy had sent the young
cop to the deli next door – the paperwork was nearly done.
Somehow, between Rogovoy and the uniform, whose name was
James, Dulcie was free to leave.

'We have copies of all that Mildon stuff, which supports your
testimony,' said James. 'But you know the routine: we may need
to speak with you again, and we would appreciate it if you did
not leave town without checking with us first.'

'I've got it, Officer . . . James.' She paused, not sure what to
say. 'And thanks.'

Esmé greeted them both as soon as they were in the door, letting
loose with a chorus of chirps and mews that soon had Dulcie
laughing.

'What is it, kitty?' She scooped up the purring cat. 'You'd
think she knew what had happened today.' Chris only smiled.
'What?' she asked the cat. 'Were you and he trading notes?'

Esmé didn't respond, but Chris did, taking the two of them
into his arms. Before long, the young cat had wriggled free,
determined to follow her own plans for the afternoon and leaving
the young couple to their own pursuits.

By the time they'd had dinner, Dulcie opening up the last of
the dumplings for Esmé to lick at, Dulcie was ready to call it a
day. Trista had been calling, however, and she and Jerry came
over soon after. Curled on the couch, Dulcie declined the offer
of a beer, and listened as her friends tried to piece it all together.

'I get it,' said Trista. 'Andrew wasn't stalking her. He was on
assignment for the dean. But what happened? What went wrong?'

'He was in too deep,' Dulcie said. She'd had a lot of time to
think this through, and the knowledge brought her no joy. 'I don't
know if she really was his daughter or not, but he wanted to
believe it. He wanted to believe he had a brilliant scholar for a

child. He gave her access, he broke the rules for her, but I don't think he realized just how little she had – and how much she was planning to steal from me. At some point, he must have confronted her, but by then it was too late. He had no choice. If he didn't play along, she could blackmail him. Maybe he found out she was playing him, that she wasn't the result of one of his old affairs. We'll have to hear what Andrew says. All I know is he wanted to maintain his legacy, and he realized that she was not going to do it for him.'

She looked at her friends. 'I still like to think it was an accident. He shoved her against the bookcase, maybe, and the statue fell.' She remembered seeing the dean, flustered, as he hurried across the courtyard. 'But he left her there. He left her alone to die.'

The friends sat in silence for a moment, even Esmé seemingly considering the import of what Dulcie had just said. Then Chris got up to get another beer, and handed Dulcie a diet Coke. Taking a deep swig, she continued.

'Once he realized what he'd done, he realized he had to destroy the manuscript, too,' she said. 'I think that's why he went back to the suite library. Only, when he saw me there, he realized that he could use her perfidy to shield himself. Instead of revealing how she had begun to plagiarize my work, the pages could be used to make me out as the plagiarist.'

'So what happened to the manuscript?' Trista didn't like ambiguous endings.

Dulcie shook her head. 'I don't know.'

'And how did those pages get in your desk, anyway?' Again, she had no answer. Besides, there was another question on her mind. One concerning a red-haired man and a woman. A woman who might have had reason to commit murder.

FIFTY-FIVE

The next day, the abrupt resignation of Dean Haitner was the talk of the university. Or so Dulcie thought when, grateful that her last section was over, she could retreat to her office.

Lloyd looked up as she walked in. 'Dulcie! Are you OK?'

'Yeah, why?'

'You look a little tired, that's all. Working late?'

Dulcie smiled. Count on Lloyd to be the sole scholar not to have heard the latest scandal. Unless, of course, he was part of it.

'Lloyd,' she turned to her balding friend, 'I didn't want to ask you the other day. But has anyone been in here? Has anyone searched my desk?'

'Well, yes.' He nodded. 'The cops came. That's why I called you.' He swallowed. 'Tried to, that is. They told me I wasn't allowed to.'

'No, I mean before then.' He looked puzzled, so she tried again. 'Has anyone at all been here besides our students or Raleigh?'

'Only Dean Haitner.' The way Lloyd said his name, Dulcie knew he hadn't heard the news. 'He was here early on Monday. Only, he didn't come for you so I didn't say anything. He came to ask me about the new security procedures.'

'What?' This was unexpected.

'You know, the new card reader, the swipe machine? I guess someone had passed my complaints along to him,' said Lloyd. 'He came here, to our office, and he sent me out to try it, a couple of times, to make sure it worked.'

'The card reader?' Dulcie knew she was repeating what he'd said. She couldn't help it.

'Yeah, it just wasn't working right. I thought it was pretty impressive that the dean came himself to check it out. Why, Dulcie? What's up?'

'Nothing, Lloyd.' She smiled at her friend. Her good and honest friend. 'I'm just glad you're so conscious of our security.'

FIFTY-SIX

September wound to a close and as the first semester headed into midterms, Dulcie was still spending too many nights alone. If anything, Chris was working more overnights than before, but Dulcie couldn't blame him. His junior, Darlene, had only been reprimanded for her work, breaking into Dulcie's system; nobody could actually blame her for following direct orders from the dean. However, she'd been so shaken up by the experience that she was taking the rest of the semester off. From what Chris told Dulcie, she was earning so much in the corporate sector, he doubted she'd come back. Academia, they both knew, wasn't for everyone.

That left Chris and Jerry, therefore, to fill the overnight shifts. And while Trista dragged Dulcie out as often as she could – Dulcie still had no idea how her friend functioned on so little sleep – most nights found Dulcie in the apartment, with Esmé, poring over her notes. Subsequent days in the Mildon had unearthed a trove of compelling scenes, all written in the elegant, if nearly illegible slanted handwriting. The connection between her author and the red-haired – or was it dark? – man still puzzled her. There was something her author was hiding. Something she did not dare write about, except obliquely, and Dulcie was on its trail.

When she wasn't working, Dulcie was puzzling over the mysteries left behind by Melinda Sloane Harquist. The dean, it turned out, hadn't been Melinda's father. She had used him, he had confessed finally, leading him to believe that there was a link, and laughed when he had uncovered the truth. That was what had pushed him over the edge. Not the heartbreak, which he had assumed she would share. But the scorn. It was the kind of story that made Dulcie grateful for her own family, as wacky and disconnected as it might be.

Esmé seemed to think this solved everything, although she didn't bother explaining herself to Dulcie. Beyond a certain feline look of satisfaction at how everything had played out, the little cat still didn't speak much. If anything, she seemed to imply, it was Dulcie's fault if there were any breakdowns in communication.

'*I was sitting on her computer,*' Dulcie heard quite clearly late one night. She'd been half asleep, lying in bed, but she could see Esmé on the window sill, silhouetted in the moonlight. '*What more did she want me to do?*'

Dulcie had strained to hear the reply, knowing it had to come from her senior pet. All she'd heard, though, was a rustling of the curtains as Esmé jumped down, heading for the kitchen. As

September ended, the nights were getting frosty, and Dulcie got
up to close the window, then followed after her pet in time to
hear one final snippet.

'*I'm the cat of the household now. That's my job.*'

'*I know, little one.*' This time, the silhouette in the window
was larger; the luxuriant whiskers outlined in the bright light.
'*And that's why I chose you both.*'

Dulcie paused, waiting. At her feet, she saw the tuxedo cat
pause as well, looking up first at the moonlit window and then
back to Dulcie.

'*You* chose *us? I thought . . .*' Dulcie had rarely heard Esmé
sound unsure before, but she resisted the urge to comfort the
young cat with a cuddle. '*Surely, from the fur . . . from the
whiskers. Aren't we . . .?*'

'*We are family, little one. All of us are family here.*' As Dulcie
watched the window, she felt the soft, warm pressure of Esmé
leaning against her bare shin. '*Haven't the last few weeks taught
you anything about the ties that bring us together, little one?*'

Dulcie froze. Was Mr Grey talking to Esmé – or to her? She
thought of her author, of a red-haired man. Of what mattered
most.

'*What matter flesh or blood, fur or whiskers?*' the voice said.
'*What are these compared to the bonds that hold us? For we are
bound to each other, little ones, each in our roles. Bound by
love.*'

Dulcie felt, rather than heard, the purr that filled the kitchen.
Standing in the moonlight, she lifted the little cat and buried her
face in the soft, dark fur.

That's how Chris found them, curled in bed, when Mr Grey
welcomed him home later that night, asleep together as the bright
moon set.